# Among Friends

# Among Friends

HAL EBBOTT

RIVERHEAD BOOKS
NEW YORK
2025

RIVERHEAD BOOKS
An imprint of Penguin Random House LLC
1745 Broadway, New York, NY 10019

BOOK DESIGN BY MEIGHAN CAVANAUGH

ISBN 9780593854198

Printed in the United States of America

The real hell of life is that everyone has
their reasons.

JEAN RENOIR

I

In the distance, boys sweep across sharp, neatly cut grass. The ball predicts their turns; sweat spreads like moss on their shirts. Eventually they will stop and come up the hill, their smiles brilliant, exhausted. One pushes another. The group receives him, this act of love.

It's he Amos studies, the boy pushed, whose brown eyes accept the campus like something owned, whose legs toss his feet forward in loping, comfortable steps. He hasn't spoken much, but his silence doesn't diminish him. His presence seems, to the rest, so inevitable it needn't be noted.

As they ate, bent like soldiers over their trays, someone had thrown him an apple. Ford, they called out. The boy plucked it from the air, took a clean, violent bite, and, with a pat, set it down. Others laughed. The meat glistened like bone.

On the field he'd moved with the lazy grace of a prodigy,

natural and untended. Amos was better, and at the time had been glad. But walking beside him now, he feels ashamed of his effort. The summer hours spent sweating grow needful and unsightly.

Around them, the college lies stilled by August sun. Empty paths vein its lawns. Only athletes have returned; they move in small clusters, their voices distant and soft.

"This is me," the boy says.

The rest nod and walk on. Then Amos remembers it's his dorm as well. He turns, jogging back.

"You live here?" the boy asks.

"Aye." Amos squints like an old man surveying his farm. "Ever since this morning."

The boy laughs gently. He offers a warm hand, tanned as a glove.

"Emerson."

"Not Ford?"

"Either is fine."

"Amos."

"So you're the guy who brought lamps."

"We're roommates?"

The boy gestures with his arm.

"Aye," he says. "Ever since this morning."

# 1

They had left on schedule and were making good time. The sky, taut as a sheet, stretched overhead. The roads were clear, the light a cool, cathedral blue. Amos didn't drive much, but he liked it: the way the car enclosed them within tasteful curves, how it leapt forward under his foot.

The land dashed by—trees, trees, an interruption of rock. He watched a barn approach and snap past. Faded shingles, stacks of wood on the porch. It was early October. The summer had been defeated, the chill of winter wasn't yet at the eves. Things seemed amenable, open. There were still good days left.

Claire sighed and shut her book. Amos turned, touching her knee. She smiled wordlessly and lay her head against the window. From the back, Anna watched.

"If it rains," she said, "can we see a movie?"

She could tell her father had been trying to think of something to say.

"Is it supposed to?" he asked.

Claire looked up. "How unprepared will you be if it does?"

Her chiding wasn't without affection. She did rather enjoy the loose calm with which it would dawn on him that he'd neglected to pack something important. And yet there were also times when carelessness left him wrongly dressed that she felt a startling anger. Then she wanted almost to slap him, as if he were a child, a drunk who refused to stop talking. He seemed, in some crucial sense, an unserious person.

Amos waved this away.

"Is it?"

Anna shrugged.

"Regardless," Claire said. "No hard candy. Doctor's orders."

Amos snorted.

"What?" Anna asked.

"Your dad had a toothache and thought he was dying."

Amos let this pass without comment. He looked at Anna in the mirror. She looked back. He screwed up his face and frowned, as though someone had asked for the music to be turned down. Claire's gaze alighted like heat on his cheek.

"It won't rain," he said. "Not on his birthday. Emerson would never allow it."


THAT MORNING, Amos had sat on the edge of the chair while an assistant went in search of the dentist. Blood in the sink had brought him, a small swell at the back of his jaw.

Swell—that's how he'd described it over the phone. Like a little hill. What had he not wanted to say? Lump, of course. Because everyone knew what came next when you found a lump, and spitting blood was a sure sign that someone in the movie was going to die.

Claire had assured him it was nothing.

"I'm a doctor," she said.

"Who's also my wife," he replied. "I need an impartial opinion."

"The more reason to trust me. Shouldn't I be biased in favor of alarm?"

At the time it had seemed like a fair point, but as Amos listened to the chair squeak beneath him, he realized how quiet the room was, how empty. Yes, he thought, she should've been.

"Amos," Dr. Phillips said, coming through the door. He gestured toward the counter. "Floss?"

Amos shook his head. "Better you know the real me."

"Right," the man said flatly. "Let's have a look."

Amos sat back. It was an odd joke, he allowed. Was it funny? Yes, sort of, not terribly, but enough. Funny enough for a dentist's office certainly. What did he expect? Were people making better jokes than this? To whom was he explaining himself? Why not simply say nothing at all?

Here his mind went, scurrying in search of thoughts and tasks, observations and quips. It groped like the hungry, desperate fingers of a boy fumbling with the clasp of a dress. He knew what he was doing—smiling, laughing, offering up wry asides. Look at me, the show was meant to say, how easy, how casual. It was all hope, fearful and empty.

After a moment, the man withdrew and swiveled away.

"You've got nothing to worry about."

Amos felt newly aware of wanting his expression to appear calm, but in spite of himself he shuddered with adrenaline and relief.

"Nothing?" he asked.

"Never had your wisdom teeth out, I see," the man said, tossing his gloves into a bin by the door.

"No," he replied, "my mother . . ."

But Amos had stopped listening, even to his own words. The room seemed suddenly bright, almost friendly. It became routine once again.

He was no longer needed. He would go back to work. He would call Emerson. He would tell him that everything was fine and would be OK.

ANNA INSPECTED A small mole on her knee, then sat back. To her right was the sketchbook she'd lately taken to carrying, its pages thick and expensive and mostly empty. She touched the cover. She wasn't ashamed of it yet. She still believed it might play a role in who she'd become.

Trees poured along the sides of the road. The car seemed to swim through them. At some point, the city had dropped away. Now there was land—green, sprawling, delicious as sips. The thought of blunt streets became harder; the click of pigeons faded, was gone.

Anna opened the window.

Claire looked up from her book. "Must you?"

"But it smells so good."

Her mother said nothing. After a moment Anna shut it again. The rumple of wind continued outside the glass.

"How long were you scared?" she asked.

"What?" Claire replied.

"Not you. Dad. About your tooth."

"Oh, muskrat. I wasn't scared. I just—"

A flash of his father's gangrenous leg.

"I just wanted to be sure."

She seemed unconvinced and Amos imagined going on, adding to what she already knew—that her grandfather had died before she was born—details about the way he'd looked, lying there in the living room, his bones run through with tumors, his calf like a squash left to rot in the sun. Maybe he'd continue, describing how they'd stood around the cheapest pine casket, a casket which wouldn't have moved him one way or another had his mother not screamed that of course there was no money for that, of course he'd not taken care of one goddamn thing.

It could be quick. With the right details Amos might manage a picture that captured some truth. My dad: a man of tragic, annihilating neglect; twice divorced, smoking and drinking and eating himself to death. He was sixty-two at the end. His sallow eyes like embers left to burn out overnight; in his closet, a box of unopened bills. And me? A small laugh. I turned twenty that spring. When we threw out his bed, the mattress was full of ants.

He could picture Anna's face as he laid all this out. Earnest, a little confused. He could picture Claire's, too, its quizzical bemusement inflected with irritation. She had heard it before—not in decades, not since the days when, propped on elbows, they'd dumped their histories into the tangle of sheets. But that was so long ago; there was no need for it now. Why, her expression would say, was he telling her this?

It was a question to which Amos had no answer. He just felt it sometimes: that a thing must be shared with their daughter. And when he did, it came strong as the need to confess.

But then again, it was such a lovely afternoon. They were quiet and together and on their way to celebrate his best friend. And though there was an occasion, it could just as easily have been a weekend of no consequence. Because this was the world he had fashioned, the one he had gone out and made. So what was to be gained by exhuming some piece of fetid past? Nothing. Very little at most. He set it aside, smiling instead—to himself, to the trees, to the cool, composed car.

Amos felt Claire looking at him.

"It's good we're going," she said. "He pretends he doesn't care. But . . ."

He grinned and nodded. A proper party would follow next week, something befitting the idea of fifty-two. Friends, colleagues, their legs sheathed in practical pants; oysters, pickled onions by the bar. It didn't matter. Sunday was the day itself, whatever might be remembered would happen then. Noisemakers, hats, a candle stuck through the crown of a soft-boiled egg.

From the back seat, Anna yawned. Claire stretched her arms forward and drummed on the dash. The silence of families is never really complete. The roots speak, the breath.

Each in their own way will think of this drive. They will marvel at its ordinariness, they will search it for signs. Was it already broken? Was it already lost? They will wonder. They will have no idea.

Claire turned to him.

"Thanks for manning the ship."

He put a hand on her leg and she shifted in order to pin it between her knees. The car flew on. Amos felt himself move with it—this smooth, edgeless life.

## 2

Emerson had kissed his wife when he came in, which was the right thing to do. Even though she'd been sitting at the kitchen table, empty bowl before her, with the spaceless look in her eyes that made him think he could slap her and she might not even notice. She started at the sound of his voice. His lips grazed her hair.

"Making headway on the human condition?"

Retsy gave him a look—the kind he respected and, in a way, loved. One of idle disdain. He didn't think she held him entirely in contempt, but that she could express the moments she did with such a lack of restraint appealed to him on a primitive, sexual level. So he kissed her again, this time with feeling, and told her about the crash.

Upstairs, he stripped off his sweater and pants, the belt buckle sounding faintly against the floor. There was no need for the change of clothes: though he had come from the city, he'd not worn a suit to the office and what he was about to put on would hardly be different from what he'd removed. Still, after an ordeal like that, he wanted something new.

Emerson preferred to receive visitors having spent at least a day or two in the house. Being there beforehand ensured that when he opened the door, clapped them on the shoulder, and lifted their children, it was clear that he belonged in some essential way, that they were his guests, that long after they'd gone he would stay. Perhaps, then, the unnecessary change in attire was an attempt to achieve some version of this effect.

He dressed as one would expect. He entered clothes like opinions, with the graceful assurance of someone who has not questioned their choices. Legs, arms. The small leaping of muscles, the suggestion of strength. Any broader and his mouth might have been too large. Instead, his smile held like an embrace. Dazzling teeth, lips like folds of rich fabric, a smile in which one wants to believe. It was the kind that can only belong to a man: it had no sense of history; it seemed unaware of the world.

He was not smiling now, however. He was pulling on his slacks and wishing Amos were already there so he could figure out how he felt about what had happened. Which was that he'd hit a woman with his car. True, she hadn't died, and the consensus was that she'd be fine—but still, it was something, wasn't it? Plus, the details which emerged after had raised big-feeling questions, questions he didn't want to think through on his own.

Retsy had said the right things, the ones to be expected, but there was a limit to how far she could go. When it came to thinking, she was like someone who tidied but never cleaned. He laughed to himself. That was a clever way to put it. A little mean, yes, but so the truth tended to go. He could even imagine it slipping out one day as something he actually said.

Anyway, Amos. The thought of his friend made Emerson pause and look toward the barn. His mood brightened. His chest lifted with a pleasant, deliberate breath. Something about his friend seemed to promise a purging. Time spent with Amos was like taking a damp cloth to dusty windows: in its wake, the world of nuance sprang forth. He should tell him, Emerson thought. Why not say it exactly like that?

Oh, but Amos already knew. Decades now, their friendship. Since college, since the first day of college. They confided in one another, they hugged. Not like men, but like friends. Real, loving hugs, clutches without irony. People envied them; they measured their own lives against what they had. He's my Amos, one might say. It wasn't true, of course. But Emerson allowed them their hope.

THROUGH THE WALL he heard Sophie call to Retsy. He smiled at the tone. They weren't fighting, but it had an edge. Sophie was newly sixteen, and the word itself—*Mom*—had become a soiled rag, one she uttered as if holding at arm's length.

She's awful to me, Retsy had complained recently. Oh, stop, he said, patting her knee. Amos says Anna's the same with Claire. Then he kept reading—a history of great battles. Turning the page, Emerson wondered whether, had circumstance demanded, he might've been shown to possess a similar genius.

Sophie was going downstairs. A quick, sock-footed patter described her descent. He could picture the way she'd trace the railing with the tips of her fingers. He pulled at his cuffs and inspected his palms, brushing them clean of nothing. He had not once looked in the mirror. He was vain, of course, but it was a powerful kind. He did not stop to wonder. He did not need to be reminded.

He would go down and make sure they weren't at each other's throats. Or, if they were, he'd break it up and lighten the mood. He was still strong enough to heave Sophie over his shoulder. She claimed to hate it, but he wasn't sure. Besides, it was his birthday, he loved her and it was fun.

## 3

Their car plunged through the woods, borne along by the road. The yellow paint had begun to crack, but the pavement was smooth; it unfurled itself across the land. On either side, the earth sprawled in the languid stupor of a storm which has passed. Overfull, bleary and content.

Occasionally the trees dropped away. Then the great river emerged. Slick, gray, it shimmered like the scales of a fish. A town approached. A town of sheds where vegetables were stacked—nearby, prices scrawled in chalk, a cup left for money that no one guards.

The road ran on, dipped, then climbed a bluff. There, a sharp bend—the one directions warn newcomers about, otherwise the driveway is easily missed. The ground creaked under the tires, roots jostled the bags in the trunk. Hearing them, the neighbor's dog came bounding out. He followed alongside, barking, wagging his tail. Birds fled the bushes and freckled the sky.

"I feel relaxed already," said Claire.

"Good," Anna said. "I like you better that way."

Amos clicked his tongue.

"Ladies, your destination is on our right."

The house sat waiting—like a verdict, like the last line in a book. Gray stones climbed to the eaves. The door was green, the windows had many panes. Toward the edge of the wood was a barn, both sides drawn open so that a square of forest shown through. The grass in the yard had been allowed to grow long. A ball, thrown for the dog, disappeared in the tangle. He rooted around, turned, rooted some more.

Inside, the smell of years. Certain rooms felt as if they were underground. The dark air was cool, almost damp. In others the light poured in, washing the walls and warming the latches. A grandfather clock sat by the base of the stairs. A contented breeze came through the window, a breeze like the chatter of friends. There was a certainty in everything. The days lush, smooth as pebbles.

EMERSON ACCEPTED THE WINE as Claire embraced him. He handed it to Retsy who made an expression, as though asking whether it should be served with dinner. Claire shook her head.

Everything—the light, the hour—was familiar. Five. Five thirty. The hour of excitement and calm confidence, when the things that will happen have not yet begun. The sound of glasses taken down from the shelf, of bodies arriving, coming in from the dusk.

Sophie looked at Anna and shrugged with a familiar confusion, as though confirming a happy bafflement at having once again found themselves in this position. Wordlessly, they climbed the stairs. Amos was the last to enter.

"Hi, hi," he said. He turned to the dog. "Hi."

Retsy held him by the shoulder as she kissed his cheek.

"Oh, I'm sorry—you hurt your mouth?"

"No, not really." Amos felt Claire's presence beside him. "It's nothing."

"Well, that's good," Retsy replied.

Claire pinched the back of his leg.

"But thank you for treading with caution," she added.

"Speaking of which," Retsy began.

"Wait till we're sitting," Emerson said.

He was standing behind her and for a moment Retsy seemed extraordinarily small—like a doll, a thing he had made.

"OK," he added, as though they could get down to business. He clutched Claire's shoulder with the roughness of cousins, then turned to Amos.

"Easy drive?"

"Oh," Retsy cried in a small, useless voice. A moment later, the floor glistened. The pieces were everywhere, the label was torn. She had bent and was leaning toward one.

"Stop," Emerson said. He swept her aside like a curtain. "You'll cut yourself."

Retsy stumbled slightly, then stood. She offered Claire a wide, unconvincing smile.

"I thought it would be nice, starting things with a splash. Besides," she added, "he's always telling me to make my presence felt."

"Am I?" Emerson said. His broad back was filling his shirt.

"I'm sorry, though," she went on. "It did look good. And your shoes . . ."

"That's why we only gift white," Claire grinned pleasantly. The way he'd moved Retsy was too much, even a little bit cruel; and yet, she allowed, also somehow appealing, correct, a way of punishing and protecting at the same time.

Amos returned, his hands full of tea towels.

"A lot less dry than advertised," he observed.

They looked at him. Emerson was smiling as he shook his head.

Watching them both—one gathering shards in quick, confident reaches, the other swabbing damp spots—the arrangement struck Claire as fitting somehow; and, having thought it, she found this to be an idea with some edge. Then it was gone and she was laughing a little. What her husband had said was funny, after all, so why shouldn't she?

"You know what I want for my birthday?" Emerson stood. He was brushing his hands on his pants. "A dustpan. Maybe even a broom."

Before she disappeared, Retsy gestured toward their bags.

"Come, come. You know the deal."

When she was gone, Emerson touched his tongue to the spot between two knuckles where a run of blood had appeared.

"Hey, Tooth Fairy," he said. He reached toward Amos and stroked his cheek. "Fuck you for getting us worried."

# 4

Amos stood watching as Emerson prepared their drinks. His back was turned. Music was playing. Strings, a woman's voice. He held a bottle up, showing the label.

"Great," Amos said.

"Ice?"

"No."

"Water?"

"No. Yes. Just a little."

Emerson had done this when they were students, too. These gestures, these questions. Amos remembered feeling that he'd been witnessing a kind of straddling—that of a boy, filling his father's tumblers with his father's liquor, somewhere between playing the thing and having fully become it. Now, here they were: this was the room his friend had always been meant to inhabit. Scalloped frames on the walls, the furniture dark, smooth as pews.

"What's this?" Amos asked.

He was talking about a canvas that stood wrapped against the desk.

Emerson shrugged.

Amos smiled. "Long week?"

"Not really."

They both laughed.

"Hey." Emerson held out a glass.

Amos took it and sat.

"God, it's good to be here." He let out a little breath after he swallowed. "Any news since Paula?"

Emerson made a noise of mild entertainment. They'd already spoken at lunch, when he called to relate, a little sheepishly, how he'd asked his assistant to rewrite a check for the woman who cleaned, his own handwriting having proven too illegible for the bank to accept. Amos had mocked him—as Emerson expected, as, in a sense, he had wanted. Because to be ridiculed by his friend was a benediction of sorts: it allowed him to go forward absolved.

"Actually, some."

"Oh?"

"Not really, but I got in an accident on my way up."

His reluctance surprised him. Emerson had thought he wanted to discuss it, but the idea of doing so now made him tired. The truth was that Amos's mind could demand a certain rigor toward which it was possible to feel not only annoyance but exhaustion and boredom. Sometimes things were just things. It wasn't all so symbolic. You really could do stuff without needing to worry what it implied about who you might be.

Take the time he'd brought Amos to the firm's Christmas party. They were young still, twenty-six or -seven, and, having recently discovered that he really was good at the job, Emerson had been excited, hopeful even, that a partner might say something in front of them both about what a lawyer he made. Instead, however, they'd talked mostly to another associate whom Amos had insisted on needling for his suggestion that the homeless's poor English was the cause of their plight.

The point wasn't whether Amos had been right, or if the man deserved contempt. He was a placeholder, a cutout, someone in the shape of a person who was to be allowed his comments without challenge. Not because anyone agreed, but because what he said didn't matter. Plus, one day he might be of use; there could come a time when something was needed that he'd give or do. And when it arrived, the rules—the way things were done—would reveal their patient logic. The cost was so small: just let some things go.

"I'm fine," Emerson said, looking around as though in search of another topic.

"Well, good. What happened?"

He sighed. "It's . . . I don't know. I'm not in the mood."

A faint confusion played on Amos's face.

"You think this could be a symptom of something internal?"

Emerson patted his sides.

"Ask your wife."

Amos smiled. The drink had made its way into his chest. He stretched out his legs.

"How's . . . what is it, Shields?"

"We'll settle."

"Oh, good. You seemed worried before."

"Did I?" Emerson was inspecting a thread on the arm of his sweater. "What news from the couch?"

"Parents, et cetera. An affair, or several."

Emerson nodded. "All else aside, I do admire the energy those must demand." He paused. "How often do people actually take your advice?"

Amos touched his chin. "How often do people take yours?"

Emerson frowned to acknowledge the suitable retort.

"Not often enough to rid themselves of the need to come back."

"I suppose we're both counting on that."

They each smiled. Amos lifted his glass. It had passed, whatever that was.

"I read a good line the other day," he went on. "'We look at the world once, in childhood. The rest is memory.'"

Emerson shrugged. "I don't buy it."

"OK."

"Where?"

"A poem."

Emerson's eyes were still cast toward his sleeve, but on his face a slight smile emerged. A vindicated smile, Amos thought, meant to impugn his life.

"I mean, sure." Emerson lifted the toe of one shoe and squinted at it. "But who cares?"

"I don't think it's supposed to change how you live," Amos said. "It's just interesting."

He stood, a little current of anger running through him,

and went to the wall inlaid with shelves. He leaned forward, inspecting their titles.

"Reading anything good?"

This question always felt like a bit of a dare. Predictably, Amos thought, Emerson preferred historical tomes, accounts of war and theories of civilization. It wasn't that Amos couldn't see their appeal: he was fascinated by the way speeches or storms or the collapse of a bridge might ripple across history. But why they appealed to Emerson was less clear, and though Amos could hardly have defended such a claim, there seemed something bankrupt, almost sinister about his taste. After all, wasn't it rather inhuman— parceling time into periods during which this or that method of farming was used? Didn't it do more to obscure than reveal the essence of how people were?

But then again, wasn't this the same person who'd expressed surprise when Amos mentioned his trip to the dentist, saying he thought things were fine; and who, after Amos explained that, no, it was just Claire who felt certain, said, "She's the worst" in a way that made Amos think he might cry. Because it was something only he could say—he who'd known Claire longer than Amos, who had introduced them, no less, and who, being bound up in her history and her family and the idea of what she was, had the power to reach out and give Amos permission. Which was something. Which, when you thought about it, was really quite something. So who cared what kind of books he liked to read?

"Know it?" Emerson asked. He'd lifted one from his desk.

Amos squinted.

"I don't think so. How many people died?"

"The perfect amount."

Amos laughed, then sat again. He watched his friend. Emerson's face wore its age lightly, like dust. Amos could look across now and see the same restrained grin that greeted him late one night as he returned to their first apartment; he could remember—it took no trouble at all—how Emerson perched cross-legged atop the checked tablecloth beside a small plate of *palmiers*. They were both twenty-three. Their spoons did not match. Where had this come from, and why. Emerson dismissed these questions with a lazy gesture. "I knocked on a few doors," he'd said. "What else is a father to do while he waits for his son to get home?"

Amos leaned forward. The ice on the sideboard was melting, the tacks in the sofa were catching the light. Affection and concern—these were what he felt, were all he ever wanted to feel.

"A car accident," he marveled, releasing a breath. "Jesus. Shouldn't Claire at least touch your ribs?"

Emerson gave him a chastening look. "You of all people . . ."

He finished his drink with a single, handsome swallow.

"OK," he said. "I need to get started, assuming you want to eat."

Amos sat for a minute after he'd gone. He could picture him at work. The large knife flashing, the dish towel over one shoulder; his face growing serious for moments, then calm, impassive. He'd handle herbs gently, the garlic exploding under the heel of his palm.

# 5

They were standing in the kitchen, the women. Not uncomfortably, but not without a sense of what brought them together. Copper pots hung overhead. Along the shelves were spices, tea, jars with dates written on tape. A basin sink, porcelain, deep enough to wash fruit. The floor was made of wide boards painted white. Through socks, one could still feel their grain.

Retsy nodded toward the library. "He's been waiting all week."

"And it's been at least lunch since they spoke," Claire replied.

Retsy laughed. Her dark hair was drawn up, her neck bare. She was smiling in the broad, dissolute way that could make her legs not feel like the achievement they were. She stroked the back of one hand. That her fingers were wider at the knuckles made her feel safe.

"Are you hungry?" she asked. "We have cheese. And I think melon, too."

"What about a Pernod?"

"That sounds much better," she agreed.

Claire didn't intimidate her, but people in medicine had a certain way about them—capable, inured, they seemed always to be waiting for the point. It was why, in anticipation of visits like these, Retsy often found herself grateful to come upon some worthwhile anecdote. Like what the clerk in the bookstore had said. Would Claire already know that the same doctor—he was a charlatan, really—had been responsible for the death of Beethoven *and* Handel? Perhaps, but that was less important. What mattered was that it was precisely the right kind of fact. Or, Retsy thought now, she could tell her about firing Raymond. He'd overseen the set crew for a theater on whose board she sat, and Claire enjoyed knowing the forms failure could take. Plus, Retsy didn't mind the thought of her realizing there was a part of the world in which people looked to her, where they said, Retsina, can you take care of this?

And yet, as the two stood, she found that having dropped the wine made such a thing impossible to say. I know I seem clumsy, but last week I took away a man's job. It would appear like the fumbling rejoinder it was: flimsy, irrelevant, protesting too much and so on.

Retsy knew she was being foolish. This was the worst part of herself. But still: she faltered. She set her chin in her palm.

"Do you think he'd forgive me if I hung streamers?" she said finally.

"Now?" Claire crossed her legs. Her expression was flat and a touch withholding. "Or on Sunday?"

"I suppose I could wait," Retsy allowed.

"That way you'd have the element of surprise."

"A thing he famously loves."

They smiled at each other. Yes, this man. They both knew him; about him they could speak. The girls entered. Sophie lifted herself onto the counter and began peeling an orange.

Machinations aside, it was a comfort to Retsy, having them there. She loved Claire, and Anna of course—not only as people but for what they seemed to mean. Because they existed, she made sense. They affirmed her bracelets, the shirts in her drawers.

"How's school?" she asked.

"I'm bad at math," Anna said.

"Good. That's the least important one."

"Everyone acts like the opposite."

"Precisely."

Anna smiled. More with her eyes than her mouth. It was grateful, but also restrained. She opened a cupboard, then shut it again.

Watching this, Claire felt an angry little tremor. Her mind filled with an image, some years from now, of Anna in an apartment. Wearing only a shirt and slim briefs, she sat at a table. Her skin clung to the wood of the chair, the windows were thrown open to the city's thick heat. There was a man, too. On his plate lay slices of fruit. Claire didn't know who he was and could not see his face. But he was real. Or would be. That was the point.

"Hungry?" she asked. Her tone was sharp, intentional.

Anna looked back at the cabinet and shrugged. She turned to Retsy.

"You look pretty," she said.

Sophie laughed—a small, surprised noise to declare the novelty of this.

Retsy touched Anna's shoulder. "Well, thank you." A glance toward her own daughter. "It's nice to feel seen."

Sophie sighed and dropped to the floor.

"We're going upstairs."

As Claire watched them leave, she had the strange impulse to reach out and yank Anna by the hair or the hem of her shirt. Because "You look pretty" wasn't something her daughter said—or, if it was, it never sounded like that. Claire knew she hadn't been trying to imply her own mother wasn't: it was less catty, but more daring—an attempt to claim a peer's kind of space, a way of saying, I'm one of you now.

And, partly, it was true. Recently Anna had changed, beyond the obvious bodily stuff. How she looked at things had become possessive, almost sexual; she moved with the arrogance of an appraiser, one who thinks themself fit to decide something's worth. It could leave Claire feeling that she'd given her something important and now changed her mind. It was being misused. It must be taken back.

When they were gone, Retsy sat. Emerson had come in. He stood, trying to make sense of the room's atmosphere.

"God," Retsy sighed. "They're awful at this age."

Claire smiled appreciatively. "Hadn't we meant to make drinks?"

Emerson began washing his hands.

"Oh, please," he laughed, "you're both lucky. Boys would be even worse."

# 6

"My dad hit someone with his car," Sophie said from where she'd thrown herself across the bed.

Anna turned. "What?"

"Yeah," she said to the ceiling, "she was depressed or something. There was a letter in her pocket."

"Is she OK?"

"They said she'd live, but apparently it was bad."

"What was in the letter?"

"I'm not sure," Sophie replied. "My dad knows. It was to her husband, or her boyfriend." She paused. "I hope someday somebody loves me that much."

Anna let out a single shocked cackle.

"Don't you?" Sophie asked.

Anna shrugged.

"Any boys?"

"No one good."

"Me neither."

"Makes you wonder what class is even for," Anna said.

They both laughed. There'd been a point when this might've come with some prickly undercurrent. They attended different schools now, and for a time Anna seemed to believe that whatever discomfort Sophie might feel over not having been offered a place at hers would be alleviated by crudely deployed scorn. Of course, such methods achieved nothing and only reeked of the arrogance they professed to deny. But that was over, or seemed so. This, Sophie could tell, had been without pretense.

Anna lay next to her and looked up at the beams.

"Do you think they'll let us have wine?"

"Not if you ask like that," Sophie replied.

"Like what?"

"Like a child."

Anna allowed this to pass without comment. She rolled over and raised herself onto her elbows.

"Do you remember Crime Stoppers?"

Sophie smiled. It was a game they had played, weaving intricate plots for neighbors, bellhops, the woman seen trailed by two loping Great Danes. What do you think, they wondered. What were they plotting? Maybe a heist at the Frick or the bank on Third Ave. The mailman might be a guy gangsters call when they want someone dead.

"I probably still have our logs at home."

"Good," Anna said. "Though in fairness, we never did make any arrests."

Sophie wagged a finger.

"That's the power of deterrence."

Anna's real laugh, the one she gave now, was round and authentic; it could only be earned. Hearing it, Sophie felt a rush of happiness. She wasn't thinking too much, she was just talking; she was being the way she wanted to be.

It was a welcome departure from how she acted sometimes—which, to put it plainly, was like a bitch. And though Sophie would not have denied this, few things left her as confused as when people called her mean. On one hand, she felt glad. Even when it came from classmates she'd hurt—their faces cowed and skittish, their voices like bruised fruit—she couldn't help hearing it as a kind of compliment. Smart, powerful, clever, funny. Wasn't that what they meant? Wasn't that what they'd really said? But a part of her also felt misunderstood. It was as though she were sorry *and* that she'd been falsely accused.

Anna heightened all this. Fairly or not, Sophie felt goaded by her presence, at once glad for the nearness of someone who seemed so self-possessed and yet also enraged by what such a demeanor implied.

Take the afternoon they'd been walking near the reservoir and Sophie had spotted a man in the bushes. His hair hung in filthy coils. His eyes darted about with fearful aggression.

"Oh my god," she said. She grabbed Anna's arm. "Oh my god, he's taking a shit."

Anna frowned and wrinkled her nose.

"Some people are animals," Sophie went on, feeling a touch of shame at having tried to sound like her father.

Anna said nothing. After a moment, she let out a sigh.

"I bet he really didn't want to."

How typical, Sophie had thought. How like Anna that was—making one feel at ease and then, when it suited, drawing back, disclaiming everything in favor of her safe, superior perch. This was the reason Sophie poked at her friend. Just to keep things even, just to know that she could. Like what she'd said about the wine and Anna's having asked like a child. It was exactly the sort of swipe she might take and then quickly regret. On some level she knew meanness ate its way out from the inside, but the power to wound was better than nothing. At least Sophie had that. At least she could remind Anna she would always have that.

She tossed her a pillow.

"Do you think we'll be friends like them, in thirty years or whatever?"

"Why not?" Anna said.

Sophie shrugged to hide her disappointment. She'd hoped for more than an absence of doubt: she wanted Anna to want to be friends. It would mean something if she did—not so much to her but, she felt, *about* who she was.

"Is there any candy downstairs?" Anna asked, not noticing. "I'm craving a sweet."

"Candy?" Sophie scoffed. "Have you seen my mother?"

## 7

Having asked to help and been dismissed with a wave, Amos climbed the stairs. His thoughts returned to how the day had begun—rising early to shave before his appointment, the gray office with its smell of sterile rubber. And yet, it had been nothing. Nothing: the word itself like the whooshing relief of a long-held breath. What had the dentist said? Just a case of good news. Amos smiled. It was, he allowed, the faintest bit clever. He took the steps two at a time. He was going in search of his wife.

"What a look," Claire said.

Amos set his drink on the dresser. Her eyes followed him in the mirror as he approached.

She stood over her suitcase. He held her shoulders and watched as she lifted her neat, precise things. Linens, wools,

slacks of deep blue. The sight made him feel safe in a sprawling, impenetrable way.

Downstairs, Emerson called to Retsy, asking her to taste
the broth. Ten more minutes, she said, maybe fifteen. Amos
let his lip curl into the hint of a smile. He traced Claire's necklace, sliding his finger under her shirt like the edge of a letter.

"Don't be absurd."

"But that's my way."

He was behind her now, speaking into her hair. Her body
softened. Barely, but still. He felt it: this thing his hands had
done.

"Stop."

"Stop what?"

She said nothing.

"Claire, when I woke up I thought I might be dying."

"Oh, please." She turned toward him. "Save that for something worthwhile."

Amos gave her a look, then returned his expression to its
sultry pout. "Why should I stop?"

"Because I can't take you seriously when you look like
that."

Whether she'd meant it to, this wounded him. He withdrew and sat on the bed.

Once, when they were first dating, Claire remarked casu-
ally that there'd been a time in college when she threw up
her meals. Amos had winced and placed a hand on her arm.
To this she gave a look of pitying annoyance, as though his
were the concern of a nurse who, for want of purpose, re-
fuses to accept that something is only a scratch. It made him

feel inept, then angry in a new, masculine way. He'd tried to play a role, and she hadn't let him.

That returned now, the feeling of being denied. It wasn't her he was owed, but the ability to want anything at all.

Claire sensed the change and laid a hand on his chest.

"OK," she said. "Later."

"What if I drop dead?" he replied as though reminding her of the obvious risk.

"A deal's a deal," she said, turning away and reaching for the clasp of her dress. "I'll fuck your corpse."

Amos lingered after she'd gone. They weren't one of those couples for whom that had grown calloused and dry; from the start, theirs had been the right kind of heat. Neither too tender nor too intense, the core burnt like dense logs. He could, if he wanted, run his hand along certain scenes. He could close his eyes and be there.

THEY'RE TWENTY-FIVE AND in the bathroom. The shower is running but hasn't grown hot. It's morning. Ten, eleven, perhaps. Claire in a shirt, nothing more. How had Emerson put it when he told Amos there was a friend he should meet? She's very composed. And that was true. Mostly, at least. But here she is now, wearing only this thing, seeming all the more naked for it.

The night before they'd met Emerson at dinner. He wants to admire his handiwork, Claire said as she pulled on her stockings. Amos laughed. Six months, she added. Six months and so far so very, very good. Time to meet our maker, Amos said. She smiled and hugged him, showing her teeth.

She slid her cold hands under his shirt and along his bare back.

The bathtub stands several inches from the wall. The soap-scummed curtain runs its curled edge. They climb in—gently, careful not to slip. Claire bends. He enters her and she jerks slightly, filling like the end of a hose. Then he begins to move in calm, powerful strokes. Like someone pulling up an anchor, a bucket from the base of the well. He is taking something, he is conveying a message.

Yes, she says. Then, quieter, please.

Outside, along the river, her parents move with the traffic. A lunch has been arranged. They're driving in from Connecticut because she has a boy she would like them to meet. Amos pictures her father—this businessman, this professor—guiding his car down the wide road. The gleaming city rises beside them, bleached by the cold. The Hudson blinds; his wife watches the buildings go by. As they check into the hotel, a man receives their bags. His skin is ocher. On his lip, a small scar. Why, Amos wonders, is he imagining this?

From Claire's throat, sounds tumble. Her small moans are events. They land at her feet and rush into the drain.

Later, everyone will meet in the lobby, shaking hands while guessing and intuition begin their slow work. But right now it's as though Amos can draw their whole life together—and take it. Not to live for himself, but to keep on the shelf. Like sea glass, like a trinket bought on a trip.

Claire coughs. She's laughing at water she's swallowed. So is he. His belly shakes. The ends of her hair are wet and stick to her back. Stop, he says, stop. I won't last. She turns and he comes. It's her eyes that do it. Brown like the chest at the foot of one's bed. Oh, well, she says, standing. He kisses her as streams run down their cheeks.

He has discovered a part of her, he has claimed it. It's only an hour or two until John says he has a firm grip, until he makes Laura laugh. And Claire—Claire who will stroke his knee while her mother apologizes for such an outburst— he will live with her forever, he decides. If he can. If she will have him.

8

They were talking. It was dinner, it was after dinner, it was the long, easy hours when the meal is done. On the table were plates, the hard rinds of cheese. They spread their stories like cards. Broad, familiar smiles. Hands, teeth.

Amos was speaking. He stretched toward his glass without sitting up. "This week I was in line for the bathroom at a café."

"Hellish," Emerson interrupted.

"And the man behind me reached to pound on the door."

Retsy folded her napkin as she listened. The girls, too, were still there; they had not left.

"Then he just stepped back like nothing happened, like it was some great favor and he was too gracious to want credit."

Emerson laughed. "Wasn't it?"

Amos continued. "So of course when this woman finally

came out—this old lady with a cart and bags full of bags—she shook her head and gave *me* a terrible look."

"I don't think this sort of thing only happens to you," Retsy said. "But only you think to tell people."

Amos laughed. "Are you bored?"

"I didn't mean it like that."

"I'm enthralled," Claire said, running her fingers through his hair. "And this is my second time."

"I'm sure he loves his children," Retsy offered.

"Perhaps," Emerson grinned, "but just think how they were toilet-trained."

At this Anna laughed sharply. The others had, too, but hers was the loudest and for that she felt a twinge of regret. To have been so taken by such a joke seemed to betray some lingering childishness. She glanced at Sophie who lifted her eyes toward the ceiling in order to ask whether they should leave. Anna shrugged, glad not to have her fears confirmed.

"The real problem with waiting for bathrooms," said Claire, "is the longer someone takes the more you need to go, but the more afraid you are of what'll be inside."

"Paradoxes all around," Emerson said, waving his hands. "The only solution is everything you want, all the time, exactly when you want it."

"That actually sounds much worse," said Amos.

"Wait," Claire said. She sat up. "Why are we talking about this? What about your accident?"

Amos nodded, surprised it hadn't been he who noticed.

"OK, OK," Emerson said. He lay his knife alongside his

fork. His eyes swept over the table. His face was full, immaculate; it gleamed like a showroom.

"I was coming through Cold Spring—you know where the light is?"

"At the gas station?"

"No, before that."

"At the hill?"

He nodded. "And on my way in, maybe halfway down—where those big trees are—a woman jumped from behind one. Right out in front of the car."

"Jesus," Claire said, in a tone Retsy felt some amount too performed.

"It's crazy," he said, "I almost think I was looking at the spot where she was. That's the only way I could've stopped."

"So what happened?"

Amos turned. It was Anna who'd asked.

"I really stood on the brake—like actually stood," Emerson said. "Enough to knock my head on the roof of the car." He touched his hair. "But she hit the headlight, right on the corner, and kind of . . ."

Sophie groaned. "Just say it, Daddy."

Emerson winced, pursing his lips. "It was bad."

This seemed calculated to Amos, designed to make a show of tasteful restraint while still indulging them all in crude violence.

"What did it . . . ," Anna started before stopping. "What did it—look like?"

"Not great," Emerson said.

Despite his suspicions, Amos gave him an appreciative nod.

"Will she die?" Sophie asked.

Claire watched closely, trying to decide what the girl hoped the answer would be.

"No, thank god."

Retsy put a hand on Emerson's arm. "Because of you," she said. She nodded her chin as though urging him forward to accept an award. "Because you stopped in time."

"Is that true?" Claire asked.

He shrugged. "So say the police. But who knows?"

Amos took a sip in order to disguise his contempt for this pretense of humility.

"So it wasn't an accident?" said Claire.

"No. Definitely not. She had a letter in her pocket. A suicide note, more or less."

"Are we sure . . . ," Amos began.

Claire dismissed this with a wave, as if to suggest that it was fine or already too late. "You never know with people," she said. "You just never know."

"Well," Emerson said. He raised his eyebrows. "The thing about a letter is that sometimes you do."

"You read it?"

"No, but the cops—the police gave me the gist."

"That seems unethical," Amos said.

Retsy nodded. "Actually, yeah."

Emerson shrugged at Claire who returned the gesture. They were like children who'd found a wallet and decided against trying to find its owner.

"And?" she said.

"And apparently she'd been having an affair with someone, some guy at the high school."

"A student?"

"No, a teacher. Anyway, I guess he'd broken things off, and," Emerson paused, gathering himself, "this is the most remarkable part. From what they told me, he and I have the same car. She'd been waiting for him to come by, she wanted *him* to be the one who ran her over."

"What?" Anna said. She was holding her napkin between her hands.

"Yeah. It wasn't random, it was just a mistake."

"Wow." Claire coughed. "I mean, thank god you were paying attention."

Everyone nodded. Even Amos found himself unable to withstand this twist.

"That's truly extraordinary," he said, feeling guilty for his cynicism. His friend, his best and oldest friend, had been in a car crash, had very nearly killed someone, had—imagine: a jerk of the wheel, an oncoming truck—come close to death himself. Yet here Amos was, parsing his tones and his motives, piecing together some imagined crime.

"People are so crazy," Retsy said.

"But why would she choose a way like that?" Anna asked.

"Because, darling," Retsy replied, "she believed in her cause."

"That's not funny," said Claire.

Retsy smoothed her lips. "Who knows why someone acts how they do?"

"Maybe it was revenge," Sophie said.

"Maybe she was a manic-depressive," Anna tried, prompting her father to wonder when she'd become fluent in this term.

"Well," Emerson turned to Amos, "what do the books say?"

He looked at him. They all did. An air of expectation. Now was the time when he'd put a stop to their amateur fun.

Amos smiled—thin and tolerant.

"My only guess . . . ," he began massaging his palm with one thumb, "is that she was having an extremely hard time."

Emerson sighed. "Fine."

Their attentions scattered again. The silverware shone. Slivers of light in the curls of their plates, the air smelling faintly of wine. Retsy chewed the last bit of meat. After she swallowed, she spoke.

"The problem is people don't talk to each other enough. No one says what they're feeling."

"You do," Sophie said.

Claire laughed. "And aren't you lucky." She reached to tousle her hair. "Aren't you lucky to have such a wonderful mother?"

Sophie ducked with playful, not unloving disdain. She turned to her father. "I'm just glad you're OK."

"Me too, baby," Emerson said. "I mean really, what are the odds? Same color, same everything."

"It's just a wonder you were paying attention," Retsy repeated. "The way most people drive."

Amos continued to listen, but their voices and movements, the sound of their coffee spoons, had become clouded, remote. They'd not sensed him leave, but he had, gone to the part of his mind he went in order to feel disgust. Because what they were talking about was the unutterable sadness of a woman who stepped into traffic, who, for a moment at least, had thought she wanted to die. And yet none seemed able to grasp anything but the absurdity, the dumb luck. Can you believe it? The same model, the very same color.

He wasn't thinking of his own mother, though he could have been. Nor had any one patient come to mind. It was her, it was all of them: it was their chewed nails and savage unhappiness and how quickly, in the dull mind of another, it might be reduced.

Amos grew angry, then sad and tired—tired of being angry and sad. He felt a hand on his shoulder. Claire's. Without turning she'd placed it there as she spoke. The legible edge of their words began to return. They carried him back. He was one of them. Guilty, safe. And he was glad. He was ashamed to be glad, but he was.

Amos shifted forward and set his chin on his fist. "How are you feeling?" he asked. "How are you doing?"

Emerson turned. "Shaken, obviously. I mean just imagine, finding out you drive the same car as a teacher."

"Oh my god," Claire said through a disbelieving laugh.

"Dad," said Sophie.

Emerson showed his palms. "Sorry, sorry."

Amos, too, was laughing. A silent, airless cough. He shook his head. Emerson smiled with the coy arrogance of a man who has accepted his nature.

"I hate you," Amos mouthed.

Leaning forward, Emerson took hold of his hand. It was sarcastic. It was sincere. "That's why I trust your opinion."

"You know," Claire said, "it's a triumph of my marriage that I don't envy what the two of you have."

"Our marriage."

"I don't know," she replied, turning and stroking Amos's hair. "Sometimes I think each person has their own." She smiled to show she was not entirely serious.

"Well, I'm glad," Emerson said. "There's nothing worse than jealousy. That's why I spend so much time with all of you."

Amos felt easy and loose. Rather than feigning insult, he took up the thread.

"I think when most people talk about friends what they mean is someone they haven't fallen out with; they don't mean a person who's actually in their lives."

"That's sad," Retsy said.

"A lot of friendships—especially when you're young—are like scaffolding. You're searching, you know, you're figuring things out. Which is fine. No one wants to be lonely."

"It's bad out there, folks," Emerson said in a weatherman's voice.

"I don't mean it to sound like that. But I do think it's true—that you're leaning on each other, you both are. It's not bad. It's just a particular thing at a particular time."

As he said this Amos felt himself grow sad in a profound, disarming way. In order to stop speaking he smiled and refilled his glass.

Emerson turned to Claire. "Speaking of friends, do you have any idea how long *we've* known each other?"

"Too long."

"Longer than that, fifty-two and a half years."

"Are we really out of things to talk about?"

"It's remarkable is all."

"I suppose."

"Oh, it is."

Amos recognized the pitch of their voices. They had left, they were in the garden of their history. Since nursery school, since the playground, since the womb, Emerson sometimes said, meaning how their mothers had walked the halls of the Metropolitan, chuckling at the hope that it was "doing something" to bring unborn children to this place of great art.

"Can we be excused?" Anna asked.

"You're still here?" Amos replied.

"She adores you, you know," Retsy said when they were gone.

"It's mutual," he allowed. "Mostly."

Claire looked at Retsy. "Do we need to be up for anything tomorrow?" Then, before she could answer, turned back to Emerson. "Am I the same?"

"As when?"

"As always."

It was only after asking that Claire realized she would care what he said.

Emerson paused. "You're . . . ," he drew the word out, "less violent."

She laughed.

"Go on," Amos said.

"Oh, yes," he continued, "you should've seen the number she did on Michael Roman."

Claire was stunned. She felt almost confronted. This ancient memory, lying at her feet like a photograph tumbled from the pages of a book.

They were five, maybe six. Gathered in a circle, the teacher counting them off into groups. Claire had determined the right place to stand to be among those in charge of puppets: she was the best at them and so it made sense. Then, to her left, Michael Roman started to shift. He raised his hand. She could tell he'd changed his mind, that he wanted to play outside instead. Which would ruin her plan. Would ruin everything. And after she'd taken such pains, done the numbers, stepped nimbly into place to receive what she wanted, what she now deserved.

Claire felt a coiled, startling anger. Powerful, already tensed. She tried to tell him *no* with her eyes. She felt her face quiver with meaning he was meant to receive. But of course he didn't notice. His round, stupid cheek was turned toward the teacher, his feet were bent inward, a doltish arm flung over his head. Then came a wail. His—she'd hit him. When? It seemed only seconds ago. The room was quiet. The others watched, their eyes blinking, hungry. On her shoulder, Claire felt the teacher's hand. She turned to follow while inside her, hate for the boy, the dumb, idiot boy, continued to shriek like a kettle left on the flame.

Claire looked up from her plate. "You remember that?"

"Of course." Emerson's eyes were excited.

"Remember what?" Amos asked.

"Your wife has a mean right hook. She knocked a boy's teeth out and then made him eat them."

"Oh, please," Claire laughed.

Outwardly she'd regained herself, but her mind continued to hum. There had been a best way. The way was hers. Rage happened when such a thing went ignored. How strange to discover a memory like this could remain so raw, to realize she still believed she was right.

"Fine. But you hit him pretty hard."

"Not *that* hard."

"It's fifty years later and I'm still talking about it."

"Well," she laughed lightly. "I suppose the idea was to make an impression."

"I think it sounds modern," Retsy said. She smiled and yawned.

"Why did you?" Amos asked.

Emerson held up a hand. "The work is the work," he said solemnly. "Beyond that, the artist need not explain."

The evening had passed. At once, they all felt it. They were comfortable, tired, weary only from things they had chosen to do. Retsy reached for a cookie, broke it over her plate, and set the halves down. She would not touch it again. Everyone knew. They understood her. She was forgiven— out of love, out of pity, out of the kernels of hatred that must always also exist.

Amos put a hand on Claire's back. She smiled and nodded.

"Yeah," Emerson said. "Me too."

"This was good," said Amos. "This is the best."

Retsy began stacking plates.

"No, no," she clucked as they tried to join. "Go on, get lost."

# 9

"Hey."

Amos could tell from the sound of her voice that Claire was lying on her back, and that she was upset. Then came a rustle as she turned toward him.

"You said something the other night which bothered me."

The precision with which she delivered such lines had long struck him as both girlish and adult, as though she were a child who'd been sent back to the playground to stand up for herself. The sentiment was real, but at the same time seemed to lack a certain feeling. Perhaps, Amos thought, it had something to do with her being a doctor and the way such work forced extreme things together. People needed to be cut open, lunch ordered.

"I'm sorry," he said. "When?"

"At dinner on Wednesday."

He thought for a moment.

"About Anna's dessert," Claire continued.

The scene returned to him. So, what do you think? Anna had asked, having just served her lemon tart; and Claire, seeming lost in thought, summoned a benign smile. It's wonderful, sweetie, she said. One of the best I've ever had. At this Amos had banged a playful fist on the table. What? he cried. Not *the* best? Let's hear the competitors. I want a full list.

Amos raised himself onto an elbow.

"You mean the thing about what could be better?"

"Do you know why?" she asked.

He admired this tactic as much as he resented it.

"Because I'm taking her side?" he offered, knowing this wasn't entirely wrong but reluctant to spell out the truth.

"It feels competitive," she said, "like a wedge."

"It's not," he replied. Which it wasn't, exactly. What it was was something he wanted to say to his daughter, something he needed to be sure that she knew.

Anna cooked oddly and with an obsession for certain dishes. Dumplings, scones, *galette des rois*. It thrilled him to watch her knowing hands, the crease between her eyes. Claire enjoyed it, too, though in the manner of a parent who is simply glad to see their child occupied with something so utterly unproblematic; by Amos's excitement she seemed almost confused. Occasionally he'd fumble for words about the marvel of Anna's inner life and its unbridgeable distance from who they both were. Yes, Claire would say, it's cool, I agree. But she didn't seem to understand what it meant, what it was he was trying to express.

Claire's love felt natural, inevitable. Anna was their daughter; of course she loved her. But it struck Amos as the nondescript love one feels for a roof in a rainstorm: it hardly matters whether the beams are made of this or that wood. He, on the other hand, felt swallowed by his. He felt that Anna could be no other person, even, sometimes, that he might not have been able to love another child. He didn't mean this. Not really. But it was a way of conveying what he wished to say.

Which was what? He wasn't quite sure. To explain, he had only fragments and glimpses, the snatches of understanding one feels in a church. Like the line from the story she'd written when she was eight: "The man climbed out of bed like an old spider." Or how she'd laughed watching him mop up detergent, saying, when he got angry, I'm sorry, but it's funny that soap is so hard to clean.

So when Claire had given barely a thought to what she made, Amos felt the incredulous anger reserved for those who would squander something infinitely precious. He wanted to bury a knife in her lazy reply—so that his daughter could see, so she knew that one of them cared.

Claire sighed. A moment passed. The bed lay in shadows, their limbs seemed stiff and arranged.

"But do you see how it looks that way?" she asked. "Like you're winking at her. Like you want me to be the butt of a joke."

"I do," he said. "I'm sorry."

"Thank you."

Amos touched her wrist.

"Why didn't you say something then?"

It was a sincere question, and he asked it with a blush of melancholy.

"I was tired."

"That makes me sad."

"I'm not trying to make you sad."

"I didn't say you were."

"It's not like it's been on my mind ever since, I'm just saying it bothered me."

This last bit, about Amos's fear of learning that days had gone by when he'd thought things were fine only to learn something had been amiss, was well known to them both.

"OK," he said, the word stale in his mouth. "I'm sorry."

"Thank you," Claire said.

"This feels like an old conversation," he ventured. "Like one we've been having for years."

Claire sighed. "I guess that's what I meant by fucking your corpse."

Amos laughed loudly and felt himself reach for her.

"Only you get turned on by jokes," she said, rolling away.

"Just the good ones," he replied. "Otherwise think of the hassle."

CLAIRE KNEW WELL ENOUGH why she'd brought this up. Though it was true that she hadn't been brooding, a little rupture of jealousy over dinner had dislodged it from the artery wall.

It happened after they'd finished—the plates pushed back, the wine beginning to dry—when Anna said something to which Amos made a gesture as though her words were dust he'd caught with his finger, inspected, and brushed onto the floor. In response, her daughter waggled her head back and forth in a facetious display of cartoonish offense. It lasted only an instant; perhaps no one had noticed but she. Which was worse, of course. That it wasn't for show. That it was just this little fond thing done without thought at all.

Yes, it was easy for Amos lately. Easy, it seemed, to say the right thing. Or not to say something when it turned out that nothing should've been said. But that wasn't the whole story; in fact, it didn't even come close. Because Claire knew the parts of her ears Anna never cleaned well and the way she spread mustard to the edge of her bread; knew, too, how her fingers had felt when she'd pried them from the side of the pool—because she needed to learn, needed to discover that she really could float. And all that was something. All that was more than just something, it was what went inside a mother and made her so full—of love and, yes, because of that, anger—that sometimes she thought she might burst. So fuck Amos and whatever he'd been up to with his little dig. She would allow him his triumphs because in the long run they would fall away.

As for their conversation just now, Claire could sense him withholding, though what it was she couldn't quite glean. Which was OK. A little annoying, perhaps, but in the grand scheme OK. Because in marrying a man whose mind she respected she'd been prepared to make certain concessions, and this—the canny, askance part of him—was bound up in why he'd been the one with whom she chose to build her life.

To the question of when she'd first known she loved him, Claire had no idea. At some point she understood that what she felt for Amos was strong—stronger than anything she'd felt prior, strong enough that it would need dealing with. By which she didn't mean fixed or undone, rather that it must be confronted. Plenty of things could be managed by simply allowing time to run its course, but not this, she could tell.

For all her composure, Claire wasn't immune to the joy of discovery and, truly, she *had* been caught by surprise. By this boy who not only knew the right way to hold her arched back, but who spoke in easy, pretensionless metaphor, observing once that a man at a party looked like a dog being brushed: a little confused, but resigned to this agreed-upon human experience. Amos wasn't just clever, he was good and kind. He forgave her her thoughts because sometimes his were the same.

What, then, was the problem? There wasn't one, really. Problem was such a serious word. They were what, twenty-five? Introduced by Emerson Ford. That helped, of course, his coming from an old friend, a family known so well to her own. And by way of good, sturdy schools—names familiar to her parents, names promising a certain shape to their days. Needless to say, she didn't care about such things, but that didn't make them not real. And it was just—how to put it?— a matter of fit. Like matching paint colors or choosing the right rug for a room. Things wore over time, it was important to consider how they would age.

And while all people had stories, there was an intensity to Amos's childhood that set him apart. Not just its poverty, but the whole thing. What he described was harsh, real in some way that felt distinct from others she knew. Listening to him recount it, she couldn't help but think of her parents and the bland sea of faces forming the tides of her life. The Porters, the Elroys, Edward and Lydia French. All these names. They didn't matter but they would be everywhere; it was among them he would have to live. And would he be happy? Would she? Or was the idea of them just a nice thought, a wonderful plan that has taken everything into account except for the wind?

Then came the night at her parents' when Graham Dunn, that old, tired friend of her father's, hectored them both with his pretensions about the wrong metaphor being worse than a lie before pointing across the room toward his wife and saying ruefully, "You know what it's like, being married to her?"

"Choose wisely," Amos had said, taking a deadpan sip from his glass.

In a flash, Claire had seen it: not just his intelligence and his wit, but an ease, an intuition, a sense for where and how much to push. He understood who Graham was, he saw his place in things, and because of all that, could assert himself— not too much, but still. It was the sort of thing that could never be taught, only learned. I see you, his joke said. I see this room and these people and I know how things are. I can lay my ear alongside it, tell you precisely what moves and how. Claire knew then she could marry him. She decided she would.

So while there was clearly more to the thing with the tart, it was born from a part of Amos she needed, loved, and for which she was happy to pay. And beyond that, when it came to whatever he hadn't quite said, Claire felt most of all that she simply didn't care.

She turned toward her husband. He was already asleep. His lips parted slightly. He seemed held, calmed by the great stillness of the house. He lay on his back, one arm thrown over his face. She lifted her knees. It was how she liked to drift off. By the time she awoke things would've changed: they would face elsewhere; their limbs would be bent in new ways. But for now she felt the heat of her breath gather in the crook of his neck. She set her chin on his shoulder. As though she were about to whisper something. As though she had a secret to tell.

## 10

Emerson lay, staring into the dark. Retsy was asleep beside him and he noted, not for the first time, that despite all the alluding to her anxiety, she seemed to have no trouble drifting peacefully off. He, on the other hand, was prone to spend an hour watching his mind move from one thing to the next. Now, for instance, his thoughts lingered on the way Amos had asked for dessert.

"I don't suppose," he'd begun, eyes darting from face to face, "you've got anything sweet to munch on?"

Of course they did. And Retsy had stood as she said as much, thanked him for reminding her, and gone to get the tin.

He'd said some version of this hundreds of times. Always with the same boyish grin, the same simpering, conspiratorial hope. And for reasons he couldn't quite place, it annoyed Emerson. In fact, if he were being honest, it made him mad.

To call it childish seemed ridiculous: he knew it was meant to be silly. Not a joke, exactly, but comic, a funny way for a grown man to behave. Still, childish was the word. Because even though Amos was acting in part, Emerson knew this disguised a certain helpless compulsion. He had a sweet tooth, and without something to mark the end of a meal was apt to squirm in his seat.

Emerson understood where this came from. He'd listened over the years as Amos unspooled what it was like in his mother's house, how hard it still was to quiet her voice in his head. There were the big things, of course, but even something as small as dessert could be cause for anxious misgiving. What else was to be expected of a child made to sit for hours until he confessed to eating chocolates? Once Amos had gone so far as to say that, thanks to her, he wasn't sure he'd ever fully enjoyed a meal. That was almost certainly overstating the point, but Emerson had nodded, knowing it was meant to convey something true.

Still, it grated. Had he been less composed, what might he have yelled? For god's sake, ask like a fucking man. Or don't ask at all. Have a glass of wine. Have anything else. Just don't act like a kid. Just shut the fuck up.

Because here was the thing: Emerson had stories, too. His life hadn't just been one way. Take the bath, for example, the night with his dad in the bath.

Charles had knelt by the side of the tub, sleeves rolled to his elbows.

"Here," he said, opening the shampoo. Emerson lowered his chin to accept it. While his father's hands moved in new, unsettling circles over his scalp, he thought of his mother's and their familiar habits.

"Hold still," Charles snapped. "And don't open your eyes."

Emerson nodded, lips sealed against the bubbles that clung to his face. Suddenly everything—the way the bathroom had vanished, the stiff thickness of his father's touch—seemed wrong and bad. He wanted it to stop. Or to bring the room back. What would happen? What's the worst that could happen? Gently, he fluttered his lashes. To check. To know if he could.

The burning came quick and total. He cried out, sucking lather into his throat. Plunging beneath the surface, Emerson writhed, hacking and spitting as he ground his small fists into his eyes. Finally he grew still. He could feel Charles looking at him.

"I told you not to do that," he said with the calm, confused detachment of a mechanic speaking to someone for whom he has no respect.

"I know," Emerson said. He continued to massage the swollen skin. "But I wanted to see."

A short silence followed, then a peal of round, billowing laughter. In his father's face was a cruel satiation, as though he'd been pleasantly surprised by an entertaining twist to a task he assumed would be plodding and dull.

"To see, eh?" Charles was standing now. He began to fasten his cuffs. "And how did that work out?"

Emerson looked down at the wrinkled tips of his fingers.

His father paused to regard himself in the mirror.

"Well," he said. "I suppose I'll let myself out."

Emerson sometimes felt badly remembering this as though it were important at all. How could he not, when hearing about the muffler and the mold, or the straitjacket, or the wires Amos's mother had run from her mattress out the window and into the ground? Against that, the pain of some soap in the eye and an unfeeling father could barely be tallied. Still, he resented this, too. The way there were always more stories, how they gathered like snow at the windows, blacking everything out, implying he didn't count.

So yeah, he said to himself, shut the fuck up and forget about dessert.

It was a strange hallmark of friendship that you could have such thoughts—violent, profane—and then move instantly on. He forgave his friend his thinly veiled wants. He was so glad to see him, to know he slept under their roof. So often life seemed a storm of years, at once crashing against him and then, just as quickly, swirling for an instant before being swept into the drain. But Amos had lasted. If Emerson's life were a town, he was the church to which an old woman might point, declaring proudly that it had survived the war.

Now his attention turned to the following morning and how he hoped they'd play tennis. He would ask while they sat with their coffees. Amos was always the first to awake.

A sound interrupted his thoughts. Retsy had rolled over. He smiled pleasantly, as though at a neighbor. A bad dream, she explained.

"Sorry," he said.

She shook her head.

"I don't mind."

He'd not been expecting her touch, but it didn't surprise him either. After all, Amos and Claire were there and the presence of company made the two of them real in a way they otherwise weren't.

In the beginning, they'd fucked like men fight. Rough, a little ungainly, their kisses taken rather than given. Often it was after a party, each of them motivated by something unpleasant the other had said. Then they lay spent, the blanket at their feet, flats of light on their heaving chests.

It could still be like that sometimes, and he enjoyed when it was. But it could also be gentle, too, something one wouldn't have been wrong to call loving. There was a kind of experience in it, the understanding of soldiers, passengers from a crew rescued at sea.

Now, she put her hand—her warm, quizzical hand—on his hip.

"Oh," he said simply, and began to sit up.

"No."

She rose, her limbs seeming to form as they emerged. She turned his head to one side; he let it fall like a doll's. She began to move. Slowly at first, then more assured. As they went, he found himself thinking that it was good. It had caught him off guard—her desire, her conviction, her lack of annoyance at having woken—and it made him feel like he really did like her, like he was glad they lived in the same house. It sounded silly, he knew, to put it that way. But you had to say things plainly sometimes to get at the feeling. Otherwise, it all got abstracted and dull.

Then, suddenly, Retsy stopped. She sat back; light from the window shaded her throat. A small breath left her lips, as though she'd settled some private debate. He raised himself partly.

"Don't be upset," she said. Her hand was on his shoulder. It was clear they would not start again. "I'm just a little bored."

Emerson smiled. It was all he could think to do. He tumbled backward and flung an arm over his head. A cool, eerie void invaded his chest. Retsy had gone; from the bathroom came the sound of the sink. He felt aware of the house—of its rooms and their thick, imperturbable walls. He wondered what he might say when she came back. He thought to himself, I'm going to die.

11

Saturday. The first movements were small. A leg, a fist, plunged into the light. Overnight, a calm had descended. The floorboards were cool; the drapes gathered like pleats of snow. Downstairs, the kitchen sat quiet. In the sink, only a pan left to soak.

Outside, sun flooded the trees. It spilled onto the grass, the walls of the barn. A deer looked up, blinked, and ran off. Their breathing had become familiar, their movements. The brown court seemed almost gold in the dazzling October light. Across it moved flashes of color. Racquet, wrist; a moment later, the ball.

They'd worn sweatshirts at first, Amos's borrowed from the bin in the hall, but now they were warm and both lay abandoned, left to hang like moss from the bench. In the hair by the edge of Emerson's ear, a breeze touched the first cool drops of sweat.

"Nice," he called over his shoulder; then, to himself, "Come on."

They could both feel the morning—its newness, its shape. They were inside their lives. If, someday, someone asked whether they'd missed it all as it went by, neither would be lying when they said no.

"Thirty fifteen?"

Emerson shook his head at first, then nodded, lowering himself to receive the serve.

What was the difference between them? Two or three inches at most. And except when they played, he rarely felt it. Now, though, Emerson did notice that Amos seemed a bit small. Perhaps it was because of the distance—the clay and the paint and the net. It left him far enough away to seem, for a moment, like just some other man.

Already, the sun felt higher. The grass had begun to dry, the barn was lit up like a flare. Points passed, the first set. Amos had won. Not easily, but without having spent all that much. They met at the bench to trade sips of water.

Emerson handed the bottle back and sat, picking at his laces. From the moment he woke up he'd known he wanted to talk about what Retsy said.

He wasn't sure how he meant to put it, and he knew it might not make any sense. But that phrase—I'm just a little bored—had lodged itself in him. Like the knock one fears, or a bill coming due, it was the feeling that something was waiting, the knowledge that someday no one would need him, or think about him, or even care who he was.

Emerson shifted his foot. He wanted to say something like, I was scared. But besides feeling bad to admit, it was made even worse by the thing that had done it—that his wife was bored of his dick.

He stood, trying to summon his courage.

"Retsy . . . ," he began, before looking out toward the barn and scratching the back of his head. "She kind of threw me last night."

"Oh?"

Amos was bouncing his racquet against the heel of his palm.

"Yeah."

A pause.

"How?"

Emerson felt glad: that little bit was enough.

"It's dumb."

"I doubt it."

He accepted a ball. The muscles in his forearm jumped as he squeezed.

"Well, we were fucking—"

That word was a mistake. Its aspirations were transparent and graceless; it felt, for a moment, more pitiable than the story itself.

"Seems good so far," Amos said in a mocking, jocular tone.

"Stay tuned."

He tossed the ball in the air and swatted it across the court.

"In the middle she stopped—and said she was bored."

Amos's laugh was quick and sharp.

"Sorry. I'm not—that's not at you." His voice changed. "I

just mean, yeah, that's bad. That's one of those things you don't say."

The anger Emerson had been ready to feel gave way to relief.

"Right?"

"Yeah. Just say you're not in the mood. Or you're tired. Or that you have to shit . . ."

Emerson laughed—a little too loudly, he felt. It was greedy and needful; it confessed his hope.

Amos kept on.

"What did you say?"

"Nothing."

"Yeah. I guess that makes sense."

"What should I have?"

Amos furrowed his brow.

"Fuck you?"

Emerson laughed.

"Or, Fuck you. Don't be mean for no reason?"

"Next time."

Amos was inspecting the hem of his shorts. "It reminds me of my mom, in a way."

"Yeah?"

"Not—well, somewhat. Just that sort of egregious—like when she got out after being committed."

Emerson nodded. He remembered the winter: a few years after college Amos had come back from Thanksgiving and described her wandering from room to room in a nightgown, stopping occasionally to weep quietly or scream about how no one had started a fire. Sometime later, she'd grown er-

ratic enough to spend several weeks in a sanatorium, the kind
that stripped people of belts and shoelaces and only allowed
pens under close supervision. But he didn't see how these
were related, and the turn left him teetering on the edge of
upset.

"And she called," Amos said. "To tell me she'd thought
about killing herself, and to ask how I would've felt if she
had." He closed his eyes and gave his head a small, incredulous shake. Then he laughed softly, the sound seeming to imply being in spite of itself.

Emerson made the right face, the one he did every time
Amos brought this up. He pursed his lips and shook his head,
an understated disapproval whose restraint was meant to be
somber and self-evident.

"I remember," he said after a moment. "But I'm not sure
I get . . ."

Amos paused briefly, as though trying to recall why he'd
opened a drawer.

"I just mean it's one of those things everyone knows you
don't say."

In another mood, Emerson might have appreciated the
idea that these things really were of a kind. But that wasn't
how he felt. Instead, for a second, he saw his hands on either
side of Amos's face, his strong fingers buried in Amos's hair.
Fuck you, he'd be saying as he shook him back and forth like
a rattle. Fucking fuck *you*.

For what? For that little laugh. That little laugh meant to
have it both ways. First it said, Can you believe that? Hard
to think of a worse mother! And then, But don't worry! I
know it's amazing, but I'm OK! It was gluttonous and ob-

scene, like someone who makes a show of how they're injured or ill, then insists they can manage on their own.

And anyway, so what? Parents did things. They tried their best, or didn't; they failed, or never hoped to succeed. His own father had died alone in the hospital. Not because they wouldn't visit, but because he'd checked in under a false name so that no one would be able to find him. As to the obvious question: who could say? Maybe because he was proud. Or afraid. Or too proud to admit being afraid. Or perhaps he was just sick of them. Maybe he wanted to settle the tab on his own. And yeah, that was hard. But Emerson didn't bring it up every ten fucking minutes.

OK, yes, neither did Amos. But still, that wasn't the point. The point was that they'd been talking about him and he wished they still were. Because it was a small, cruel thing of Retsy to do. Or maybe it wasn't that small. He didn't know. He needed his friend to help him sort everything out. Which was why he was mad. He'd been brave, after all; it took courage to say when your feelings were hurt. But instead of helping, Amos muddled everything up. It was like Emerson had shown him a cut and all he'd done was point to a much bigger scar.

He sighed.

"Yeah," he said simply. "It's one of those things."

He looked at his friend. Behind him, the trees moved slightly; wind kicked leaves across the court's burnt, earth-colored clay. Amos was stretching his arms over his head. At his waist, a seam of skin showed like a weakness.

"Ready?" Amos asked.

Emerson nodded but didn't move. It was rare, knowing

you had the right words. But these felt good, they were measured out for precisely what he hoped to achieve.

"It's been a while now," he said, "have you made up your mind?"

"What?"

On Amos's face was the faintest breath of confusion, the weightless moment before it dawns on someone that things aren't going the way they usually do.

"Since your mom said that. It's been, what? Thirty years?"

"Something like that." Amos was picking the handle of his racquet. He didn't look up.

"So, how would you have felt? If she'd done it."

Now Amos turned. His eyes were cool and liquid. He seemed suddenly to have grasped that their conversation had changed.

"Are you really asking?"

Emerson shrugged. He didn't know what he was trying to do. He just knew that he felt angry, and anger gave you a certain vantage on the world. It made things seem big and clear. It was why, in the midst of a fight, you could shout things that were obviously false and still believe with your whole heart they were true. So what was he seeing? Something about Amos. Or the two of them together. Their friendship, perhaps. His thoughts came in quick, slippery bursts. They appeared like glints on a river, there and then gone. He didn't know. He didn't know what to do.

"I would've felt fucking great," Amos said.

"OK," Emerson retreated. "Sorry."

"I would've drawn a picture, or maybe knit a scarf. I

would've called you and said, Get to Delmonico's, because dinner's on me!"

"I get it."

"You get what?"

They stood there like children, or lovers, unsure how to feel.

"Never mind," Emerson said. "Sorry. I just . . ." He shrugged. "What's that line about the woman who's blind on one side?"

"Don't be a prick. Don't act like you weren't just being a prick."

"I'm sorry."

"OK."

"But what is it?"

"What?"

"The joke."

Amos watched him. He seemed to be deciding what he would do. "You're an idiot," he chuckled finally.

"I know. So just tell me."

"It's the thing you're not supposed to say, to someone with a glass eye."

"Right."

"That must be hard."

Emerson laughed—quiet at first, then fully. He was happy again. He'd confirmed something important. Amos didn't have the stamina; more than anything, he wanted to get along.

"You ready?" Amos asked.

"Enough."

"Enough to what?"

"Enough not to be worried."

Amos dismissed this with a wave and went to retrieve the ball.

Emerson walked to the baseline. He smiled. He picked at the edge of his sock. He'd forgotten about what Retsy said. Or set it aside. He flung a few strands of hair away from his face with a snap of his neck. He was like a reptile, born already with the memory, the knowledge of violence.

## 12

From where she stood, Claire could see them both, the girls and the men. One window looked onto the court, and she watched as first Emerson then Amos won a point. She sensed they were trying. Between serves, their mouths moved briefly. The score, nothing else. Sophie and Anna were framed in the other. They sat at the table with the wrought iron chairs. Behind them, the lawn ran toward the woods.

It was after Claire had made her attempt that Anna said the annoying thing. The upsetting one. Or irksome—yes, irksome was the word. They'd been standing by the base of the stairs while Anna held the banister with a trailing hand—implying, it seemed, that she was being waylaid. No matter, Claire thought. She'd already planned her comment out. Because it wasn't just Amos who loved their daughter.

These were tough years, of course, but if you kept trying girls always came back.

"I saw a good one this week," she began.

"A what?" Anna asked.

Retsy had padded quietly by then, saying nothing as she passed.

"A good sign." Claire smiled. "A good bad one."

It was a thing of theirs: the sharing of strange and wrong-headed phrases, quotation marks that rendered something obscure and abstruse. Like the deli instructing customers to Please "Seat" Yourself, the store promising all items were One Dollar or More.

Anna smiled patiently. She touched a pinkie to her eye.

"Don't Enter When Locked," Claire said, spreading her hands apart.

Her daughter waited a moment, then let out a small, placating noise.

"Good one." She offered a lazy salute. "I promise to comply."

"I thought so," Claire said, wrinkling her nose to hide her spurned hurt.

She turned from the window now and surveyed the room. Why did certain things bother her? Why did she let them get under her skin? Yes, Anna's refusal to play along had been willful and ungrateful and, in its way, a little bit mean, but that wasn't even the thing she found herself fixated on. It was what Anna said next, after Claire had set aside her bruised feelings and asked what she was going to do with the day. At this, Anna cocked her head toward the ceiling.

"Paint," she said simply, before sauntering off. Her voice deft and efficient, its tone a judgment already rendered.

For someone who prided herself on a composed and orderly mind, Claire was unmoored by the ability of this girl, her daughter, to rattle the shelves and throw things into disarray. Worse still was the fact that the moments upsetting her most were often the ones, like this, she felt least able to describe. Had she been speaking to a jury she might fumble her way through hunches and intimations, ending pathetically with a plea that they simply must trust her—that she knew, she just *knew*.

And what did she know? What was it she'd be claiming to see? The arrogant sweep of youthful conviction, scorn for adulthood's concessions, the importance of art, or something like that. Perhaps. Anna did seem to regard being a doctor with a certain disinterested contempt, the kind Claire reserved for accountants and electricians, people whose work, necessary though it might be, was tepid and rote and unthinkably plain. But if what her daughter had meant to express were really this trite, why did it rankle so? Was it, as Amos might say, a projection? Maybe, but only in part. There was something real there. Claire was sure. She could tell.

Beneath all this was the embarrassing fact that it was a child she accused, a girl barely more than sixteen. Then again, Claire thought, children were capable of plenty, adolescents even more so. They straddled the line, wielding adult powers and feigning ignorance when called to account.

She sighed and traced her cheekbones, set about tidying

the room. Straightforward movements settled her mind.
They helped her remember that there was no need for such
angst. What Anna thought didn't matter. She was young,
prone lately to rudeness, and more to the point, had no clue
what she was talking about.

THE SUN FOUND THE BALL: green on blue on white on
blue. It rose before dropping away. Below, behind, Emerson's racquet came up to meet it. The strings, his wrist. They
moved in a quick, crushing flash before it was gone.

Amos stepped forward. He was good now. Light on his
toes. So much better than before. His return came like a
joke—deft and cutting. Only an inch, maybe less, between
the felt and the net's rounded edge.

As he lunged, Emerson's shoe slid in the clay. Barely. A
fraction of a fraction. His ankle bent. There was a pop, the
sort of thing one feels as a sound. It traveled his leg, through
his chest, and left his throat as pain, as knowing. He half
heard it—strange, almost foreign, like one's shout in a
dream.

Amos, too, made a noise. A small laugh. Emerson limped
toward him as the ball bounced away. He felt something inside him. A curdling spasm amid shards of thought. I own
this house, it's all mine. So get out. And just stop. Stop asking without asking. You know what I mean—that you are,
that you do. And everything's hard. For you—we get it—
everything's hard for you.

He didn't so much think it as feel it. Or think it and feel

it. All at once. Like the last flush of blood from a heart which has stopped. Now he was smiling again.

"Ice, you asshole," he said, chuckling a little. His cruel eyes were hidden behind sunglasses. Only his clean smile. "Get me some ice."

NEARBY BUT OUT OF SIGHT, Anna was bent over a page. Her expression earnest, intent. Already she'd rendered a sandy flesh-colored limb that curled like a wave at one end. Around this, she began leaving quick dashes of green. It was nothing special, but she felt happy. Without looking, she bounced her brush in the glass of muddied water.

At sixteen, she'd begun to regard newfound hobbies with skepticism; in certain moods her bedroom could seem like a monument to past versions of herself—the one that carved soapstone, the one intent on mastering the art of Japanese tea—whose hypotheses had been roundly disproved. There was an embarrassing quality to the way they impugned any present conviction. Wouldn't this, too, pass into irrelevance? How could she be sure?

Yes, she allowed, perhaps the brushes would come to sit stiffly alongside dimpled trays of dried pigment. But so what? For now she believed in this idea of herself. And wasn't it enough for something just to be what she wanted to do?

These were Anna's favorite moments: when she knew with total, unblinking clarity what it was that she craved. For a mind given to buzzing, anxious distraction, a clear sense of desire was like the edge of a pool, a fixed point off which she could push.

"What *is* that?" Sophie asked. She'd come out a moment before. Her eyes still soft and bored with sleep.

"My ankle and my toes."

"You mean your foot?"

Anna said nothing.

"What's all the green?"

"Grass."

"You're weird." Sophie retreated toward the house. "I'm making more coffee," she announced.

Without answering, Anna continued to work. Even though she didn't care what Sophie thought, she'd been wondering the same thing herself. Why this? Why that day when she'd cut her foot?

It was years ago now, but still clear. This house, this very lawn. Rain arrived like breath on the back of her neck. Surprising, intimate. It tickled; she was screeching, dashing, to the thicket of trees at the edge of the lawn. Reaching it, a sharp pain. She stumbled—forest floor rushed to meet her; needles' scent filled her nose. Kneeling, she brushed herself off. Ah, there, the culprit: a spade plunged in the dirt. Blood crept from the gash in her foot. It hurt, but not so much that she was upset, not so much that she even cared.

Anna rinsed the brush and looked at the page. Poor toes, she thought, they had no idea. They were just there like always, lined up with the others—pressing and lifting, pressing and lifting—going where they'd been told to go. Maybe that's why she wanted to paint them, to capture the moment before the moment, when they were feeling good and free and—oh, never mind, she had no need for an answer. That she'd chosen to was more than enough.

She looked up. A sound—high-pitched and clipped—had startled her. It came from the courts. Her father, perhaps, making a joke or doing a voice. Now there was a stray mark on the ankle. She narrowed her eyes with displeasure at where it had already dried.

## 13

H alfway to the house, Emerson had stopped.
"Actually . . . ," he said.

It was such an old posture: one limping, an arm slung over the neck of another, who steadies and guides. It could belong to anyone—firefighters, children, strangers on the street, even two friends playing tennis in the midst of a decadent lawn; the sort Amos could find himself in and wonder, sincerely, whether he had ten times before or if this was really the first.

In that manner, they made their way back. The grass was dry, their racquets forgotten. Coming through the door, they were met by the noise of commotion and novelty. Here, let me. What happened? No, no, I'll get it. Emerson waved much of it off, saying only that he needed to sit, asking—shouting, for comic effect—Is there a doctor in the house?

It would've been impossible, at least briefly, for Amos not

to think of his father. After all, he'd died in much the same way. Not exactly, of course—consider the worn rug under his gurney, the stale light trickling through filthy blinds— but he, too, was a familiar man in a familiar space, tipped back with a look of confusion at his body's betrayal.

That was a summer in college. There was no money for care, no insurance. Deliverymen brought the hospital bed into the living room. It sat among the furniture as though at the center of a surgical stage. Sir, they said. Are you comfortable? His father's limpid eyes studied their movements as if for meaning. Dusk was falling when they left. He lasted three weeks—his leg spoiling, turning black, his lips dry. They found him in the morning; the straw had fallen out of his cup.

Afterward, Amos called Emerson. It didn't feel good to tell him so much as it felt good to have someone to tell. It made him feel like a normal person, one who confides in his friends when something sad happens, who says, Hey, this is what's going on. Which was unlike him. Because sharing could so quickly become a burden, Amos knew it was best to keep things buttoned up.

A couple weeks later they were on the phone again.

"If I drove down tomorrow, would you want to get lunch?" Emerson asked.

Amos laughed. He smiled. He didn't know why. He was standing in the kitchen. The driveway shimmered with rain.

"You don't need to drive all the way here just for lunch."

"That's not what I asked," Emerson said.

Amos blinked and looked up toward the ceiling. He pulled the words from the back of his throat.

"OK," he said. "Yeah. Lunch would be great."

The next day they carried their sandwiches to the edge of the river, and while Amos was working at the tape with his thumb, Emerson broke the silence to say, "You know, idiot, I would've come no matter what. You realize you're family, right?"

Amos squinted at the waxed paper and the spot of oil bleeding through. He wanted to believe. Even if it sounded a little bit trite. Even if it sounded like the thing someone knew they should say. Please just stop, he said to himself. Please just let something kind be.

He pulled at his lip and turned to meet Emerson's gaze.

"I'm not so good at asking for help."

Emerson snorted and looked out at the water.

"Tell me about him."

"Well," Amos said with a rueful chuckle, "there is one story I've been replaying."

"Perfect. Let's hear it."

So Amos described how he'd been standing outside school when his father arrived, having not only failed to fix the muffler, which roared so loudly that people nearby had to repeat what they were saying, but with it now dragging behind the car like a broken leg, shrieking against the pavement and sending up sparks as if it were the end of a fuse. And he'd explained the way it felt, not knowing what to do, because the longer he waited the more the shrieking and the sparks would go on, but to make them stop he'd have to get in that car, and be inside it while they drove off, imagining the family behind, waiting at their polite, disgusted distance.

"Fuck," Emerson said.

"Yeah."

"I mean, fuck, I'm sorry that's what you think about when you think about him."

Amos laughed quietly. "Yeah. Yeah."

"So then what?"

"I don't remember. I mean, I went home, obviously. And hated him. Or felt ashamed. Or maybe just sad."

"Why choose?"

Amos smiled. "Who says you can't have it all?"

Emerson nodded, his jaw working slowly.

"Good sandwich."

"Great sandwich."

"Well worth the trip."

CLAIRE WAS KNEELING. Her hair had fallen from behind her ears and covered her face. She held Emerson's heel with one hand and the ball of his foot in the other. Bars of light broke over the shelves, the spines of the books.

"Can you rotate?"

Emerson made a noise as he tried. He turned an eye toward Amos.

"Remember me as I was."

Amos ran a hand through his hair.

"This is more or less how I've always seen you."

Emerson smiled, then grimaced again.

The ottoman from another chair had been dragged over and somehow this transformed the room; now it felt like the setting of something, a kind of makeshift bunker in which decisions would be made. Emerson's outfit added to the effect. The white shorts and bare legs on the deep leather chair, the fact that he was still wearing one shoe.

"It's not broken," Claire announced.

"What if it is?"

"It's not."

"But—"

"Then it will heal."

She had set the ice against his skin. Droplets of water pooled along the edge of her ring. Amos watched her hands as they worked. There was, he admitted, something satisfying about the size of the ankle. How unlike an ankle it had become, now distended against unhappy skin.

"How long?" Emerson asked.

"A few months? If you don't act like a man."

He dismissed this with a look.

"Will it be the same?"

Claire was sitting on the ottoman now. She returned her hair to its place.

"We're a strange age," she said. "Things go both ways."

"How both?"

"Outcomes get more chaotic."

He let out a puff of pained air.

"Oh, stop," she said. She swept her free arm around the room. "If anyone will be fine . . ."

On their own, the words might have seemed dismissive. But that wasn't how they felt. Rather, they were a kind of reassurance, the reminder of an old faith. And with them it dawned on Amos what he was feeling: surprise. The energy in the room wasn't the way he'd have guessed, which would've been rambunctious, even sharp. It might've involved Claire saying, Don't be a ninny, or something about how she'd never seen a pimple so big.

But no. It was caring. And gentle. And it bothered him— in a way, it made him mad. Because how could he not compare this to her treatment of his tooth? Who wouldn't, standing there, think it was a little fucked up?

Emerson looked down at his legs.

"Can you . . ." He paused. "Take the other one off?"

His voice was reluctant, almost poignant—so much so that Amos thought it might have been played for laughs. But Claire simply nodded. She worked at the laces, rocking the shoe gently free. Emerson lifted his foot to let her strip off the sock. It came down slowly at first, then sprang away to reveal thin, boyish toes.

Amos sighed and uncrossed his arms. This seemed to remind Claire of his presence and she gestured in his direction. A kind of small reach, the way one might shush a child or grope for a wrench.

"Can you get us a towel?"

Emerson turned as she spoke. They looked at him together.

Us. That one word had sealed them up—in their history and their task and their knowledge. He felt the jealousy not of a spouse but a son, one who longs for the kindness a mother seems only to have for his father. Claire wasn't thinking when she spoke, and that made it worse: it hurt because she'd not meant it to.

They were waiting, their eyes. He nodded.

"Anything else?"

Emerson shrugged. "Seltzer? Maybe with lime?"

# 14

Amos could smell himself. And he liked it—particularly when, as now, he was about to shower. The thick, sour odor gave the impression that his body had been put to some use. Pulling off his shirt, he let out a satisfied noise of disgust.

Perhaps it was remarkable that he harbored no doubts. Not now, nor ever before. It's not like that with us, Emerson had assured him after his first date with Claire. And Amos could tell it was true. But that didn't mean they didn't have something. They did: it was what he'd just seen. Not quite tenderness—though perhaps also that—but a certain understanding. Of what, however, he couldn't say. And maybe that was the point. Whatever it was was beyond sex, or distinct from it, or, if sex were involved, it was only one of a hundred other things. But he didn't know. And they did. Which meant his whole life could be dismissed with a glance.

The water tumbled down in large strands, drumming against his back as he inspected the soaps. They were expensive, the names French. He filled his palm with the contents of one bottle. Overfilled, perhaps. It was, Amos allowed, an unnecessary, disloyal amount. The lather ran down his body in long tendrils. His skin grew slick, fragrant and pink. He worked slowly, with an air of detached focus. As though he were preparing himself for something, as though he were washing a corpse.

But so what? Who cared if his wife had been gentler with his friend? He tried to comfort himself with the affection brusqueness implies. Isn't it before those we love most that we feel able to be our least polished selves?

Working shampoo into his hair, Amos realized what he wanted. Or perhaps it would be truer to say what he wanted *back*. It was small—so small as to embarrass him—but it was true. What he felt lost was the thing Emerson had said when Amos called about the dentist, the bit about Claire being the worst. Now that kinship seemed tainted, corrupt in some way. Because *was* she the worst, as far as he knew? Or had Emerson's comment been more like one half of an adulterous couple assuring the cuckold that no, no, she's always late with me, too.

He shut his eyes and leaned into the steam.

Perhaps it wasn't so much a lack of fidelity on Claire's part as something in Emerson himself—a force, a core toward which things were drawn. Care, forgiveness, acts of grace. After all, hadn't Amos once tended to him exactly like this?

IT'S FOUR, maybe five in the morning, and Amos is standing outside the bathroom door. From its edge, light leaks into the hall. They're both twenty-three, the apartment is their first. In places the floorboards are warped like old glass.

Earlier that night they'd gone to a party where Emerson had gotten quite drunk. On the way home, he bounded atop a café table chained to some chairs and began dancing before it shuddered, snapped, and left him sprawled in a pile. It's nothing, he'd said, striding away, leaving Amos to follow.

Now it's much later. In the east, a first throb of blue. Amos knocks again.

"Are you taking a bath?"

Silence. What had begun as bemusement gives way to sharp dread.

"I'm coming in," he says as he opens the door.

Emerson turns and looks up. His eyes are wide, white as plates, like a child caught searching the shelves. After a moment, his gaze softens into confession.

He sits very still. His legs are drawn to his chest, his arms wrapped tightly around them as though they might otherwise flee. With a sigh he turns, showing his back. Amos sucks in his breath. The cut is raw and torn. At its center, something glints like a tooth.

It's obvious he will need stitches, but wounds must be cleaned, and for now that's all Amos can do. He sits on the edge of the tub. Water climbs his arm. The washcloth grows heavy and hot.

He puts a hand on Emerson's neck, which feels soft, almost delicate. It surprises him: the warmth makes it true. This grand body, this smooth skin, now red in the steam. Emerson bends his head toward his knees.

Around the edge of the gash, blood has dried in hard clumps, like rain frozen to the hood of a car. Amos dabs gently until they soften, tumbling in small rivers down his back. He feels Emerson's lungs work to conceal a pained breath.

What surprises him most is how little he fears there being confusion. He would have thought he'd need to say something—to make a joke, or use a particular tone. But no. It's as though he's washing his father, or a stranger, a vagrant in a camp. Someone he knows entirely and not at all.

"In the morning . . . ," he begins.

"I know," Emerson says.

Something in his voice makes Amos want to cry. It's not defiant or scared; he won't argue or hope. Because it's just true—there are limits, the world has its facts. He is, for a moment, soft and exposed. But not weak, no, something else. He seems—how to put it?—he seems suddenly real.


AMOS SHUT the shower off and stood dripping, his skin cool and alert. He began to dry himself slowly. A few wisps of hair hung from his chest and his shoulders; on his legs, a handful of spots whose presence he'd come to enjoy.

After Claire had dispatched him to get a towel—dispatched was precisely the word—he'd gone upstairs and stood in the laundry room. At first he cursed the manner in which they were folded: it was impossible to discern any-thing's size. But then, having quelled this bit of sulking, he took his time. His choice would be used to bind the ice to the foot, so it could be neither too small nor too big. And even after he'd found one that suited, he kept looking— for something softer, something that would feel nice as it was tied.

Because why wouldn't he be thorough? His friend was hurt and that's what you did.

Could Emerson act like a real piece of shit? Of course. Did it matter? Of course it did not. That had always been part of him; it was bound up in the charm, the boyish flaws that made his affection so straightforward and pure.

Amos stood in the mirror, puffed out his chest, and rolled his shoulders back in the way one was meant to stand. Ac-cording to experts. According to those whose only job was to decide how, absent all other factors, things ought to be. He relaxed and his stomach fell into place.

There, that felt better. Postures of rigid conviction didn't suit him. What he preferred was something softer and more considered. Because there could never be any forgetting how many vantages existed besides one's own. And people sur-prised. If he'd learned anything—from life, from work— it was that you never knew when the light might change, when someone might shift, and you'd discover the angle that opened everything up.

## 15

Emerson sat in the library. His legs were stretched before him, crossed at the ankle in order to pin the ice in place. The pose reflected his desire not to be hurt: if he sat in the usual, regular way, perhaps it might help things to become usual and regular again.

He was, he knew, terrible at injury. Bad at letting himself rest, unable not to constantly test the limits of what pain allowed. Even now he was thinking about lifting his leg to see whether he might rotate the foot without wincing. That was obviously foolish; it had only stopped swelling an hour before. But, craving progress, he was tempted. Most of all, however, he felt the hot, confined anger of a wasp. How, when the world seemed so intent on mocking his plight, could he feel anything else?

Just take the sun, for example. A few moments ago he'd thought what a shame it was to be inside on such a beautiful day. In response it had moved slightly and now reflected into his eyes in a manner he could do absolutely nothing about, except call, again, for help. Which, having done so not five minutes before, he wasn't going to. That time had been for coffee—coffee, he now realized, Retsy had set just out of reach.

Even the way Amos carried him made Emerson mad. He was grateful, yes, but upset that he had to be grateful. Likewise with Retsy's crying, Oh, sweetie, that doesn't look good. It wasn't just stupid, it was the hint of enjoyment he'd caught in her eye. In truth, only Claire's help had been tolerable. He couldn't say why, but it hadn't demeaned him. That wasn't to say he liked it, only that it chafed a little bit less.

Emerson looked at the coffee. He could get it, but it would involve thrusting his weight to one side, then lolling like some great ape in the other direction. How alone he suddenly felt. How jealous of everyone else and their unconstrained thoughts. They could, if they wanted, think about anything at all. He had only his leg. And the coffee, which he now wanted.

Gathering a bit of momentum, he rolled himself toward the side table. Not enough, it turned out. His hand swept uselessly short. Emerson sat back. Fuck me. Fucking fuck me.

How fitting that he should find himself here having already felt a bit shaky. I'm just a little bored, she had said. Just a little bit bored. It made grim, poetic sense that on the heels of that he should be confined to a chair, left to stare down at his worthless leg. Wasn't this just that kind of thing, too? The sort uncles and friends of one's parents were always talking about. The ones which never healed right, or acted up in this weather, or explained why they had to be careful when the snow got too wet. These inane tidbits came back to him like prophecy: they'd been describing his life.

Another, more undignified attempt was enough to get the mug, and despite his anger, Emerson allowed that the success came with some satisfaction.

"Fuck!" he cried out, having taken too confident a swallow. It was still hot enough to hurt, but more than pain what he felt was a searing impotence as it ran down his chin and into the threads of his shirt. He set it roughly on the arm of the chair, spilling more, which pooled in the dimples of leather.

"Shit," he hissed.

He shut his eyes and let out a slow, rasping groan. When he opened them, Anna was looking at him.

For a minute neither spoke.

"Come to bear witness?" he said.

"It sounded like you might need help."

He looked down at himself and the chair. Together they regarded the mug.

"Hold on."

"Will do," he said smartly.

She paused, smiling a little apology.

"It's really unfair. This weekend is supposed to be for you."

Emerson said nothing. He wanted neither to dignify the idea, nor admit he'd been bemoaning much the same thing. That was its own humiliation: to be, at fifty-two, unable not to think, On this of all days. Begrudging injury was reasonable enough; what he could not forgive was the need for a special occasion. Here he was in his broad leather chair; lining the wall were serious, informed books. And yet he could not help himself. It's my birthday, goddamn it. It's my fucking birthday.

He shuddered with contempt. The word itself was artless. Birthday. It sounded like a waxed paper plate. And that phrase—*my* birthday—was a crime, something between a curtsy and the needling moan of a child.

Or was he being too harsh? Claire had said it herself: this was a strange time of life. And it was true. On certain days, he could feel that he'd reached the summit. Clean air, meals, the age of attainment; seasons like runners on a chest of beautiful drawers. Still, falls came quickly. Not death itself, but the years when courage fails, when the most one can hope for is to be respected on account of elegant pants.

As it often did, the real indignity came from being forced to confront a desire Emerson would've preferred not to admit. He wanted to want without feeling bad. He wanted to be given without having to ask. Wasn't that what birthdays were for, anyway? Little reprieves from the requirement to pretend. A retilting of the axis so that it aligned only with you.

ANNA RETURNED WITH two washcloths, one damp with warm water.

"Here."

She wore a wheat-colored sweater whose sleeves she'd pushed up her arms. On her wrists, a few bracelets sounded as she gathered her hair. She was moving with a blunt efficiency he recognized as her mother's; the sweater, too, might even be Claire's. She was blotting his neck, the collar of his shirt. Little holds, little lifts away.

"Sorry," she said.

"Don't worry."

He could smell her now that she was near. It was soft, though not entirely sweet. Yesterday's soap, the last hint of sleep, plus something else—rich, a little bit acrid. It was underneath, pressing its way up and out; it was pungent and damp and made him think of the smudges under her arms.

The sun was marbling the rug at her feet. Her bare feet. He'd not noticed them before. When she leaned forward, tendons appeared like clotheslines beneath the skin.

"Thanks," he said. Though the silence was pleasant, something had compelled him to break it.

"It's fine," she said perfunctorily. "My dad always says he wants to live long enough that it evens out—who changed whose diaper more times."

Emerson chuckled.

"That's grim."

"Hopeful, too," Anna corrected.

He didn't like that—the speed of what she said or how it seemed to bat his words away.

"Where's Soph?"

Anna shrugged.

"It's nice," he said, "that you're close."

"Why wouldn't we be?"

"Plenty of reasons," he said curtly and in order to remind her of something.

She absorbed this without any outward appearance. Because she was standing above him, he couldn't see her face. But it was easy enough to imagine: the wry twist at the edge of her mouth, as though he were a boy who'd made a mess of his lunch, her gaze flattened in the way of women who wished to become immune and unaccusable, who had things to think about how incompetent you were.

Anna stepped back into view. She scratched at the side of her neck and looked away. It was, he realized, Amos's gesture, a thing he might do before delivering some sardonic barb.

"I just think it's funny," she said, "that you survived a car crash but got fucked up by my dad's slice."

Silence. A pause. Then a little laugh left him, the way it does when you're giving yourself time to hear. Now, though, he grasped the words and saw what they meant.

She hadn't been there. She could never have guessed what sort of shot he'd been chasing. No, she'd been told. The two of them—she and her father—had talked about it. Emerson stiffened slightly as Anna continued to swab.

Had she asked? Had Amos simply offered it up? Which would be worse? He imagined his friend recounting it all, every triumphant detail. And what made her so bold as to think she could say something like that? Like the word fuck, or that he'd been fucked up. Was it the fact that he was sitting here like this, the notion that she had any idea who he was?

He clicked his tongue like a playing card being set down.

"That's fine," he said. "That's plenty."

She stopped and folded the cloth into quarters.

It happened in an instant. Or didn't happen. Changed then

changed back. Like when someone leans against the light switch for a moment: had the room ever been dark? She was different, new; then the same once again. She flickered before him like an image in an old film. Who did? Amos's daughter. Claire's girl. But also—someone else. A person in her own right, a stranger one might see on the street.

He watched her with growing intensity, curious whether it would happen again.

"Sit," he said.

How long had she been here? Five minutes? Not even?

She complied absent-mindedly, touching one wrist with the opposite hand.

Had they laughed at him? He pictured them upstairs by the window, like conspirators, like lovers. Amos saying, You know how he can be. Anna smiling, thinking she did.

"You used to tell such good stories," Emerson murmured. "There was one, about an otter . . ."

Anna smiled.

"Who collects stones."

"Yes."

"That's true, you know. They have pockets—pouches."

He nodded. "It's hard being old."

The words surprised him. He'd barely been aware of having thought them and certainly never intended to speak them aloud. It was a mistake, more than she was meant to have.

Anna paused for a moment and he wondered, absurdly, whether she might say something that hurt his feelings.

"You seem like you have fun."

"Do I?"

"All of you."

"Maybe you're right," he allowed. "I mean, there must be some days."

"I hope so."

Suddenly he no longer felt sure to whom he was speaking. There was a certain dullness in her words he couldn't parse. Were they pliant or rigid? Which was she? He wanted to overcome them, to make her familiar again.

"Tell me one."

She sighed searchingly, then smiled at a thought.

"It's a little . . ."

She gestured vaguely.

"Tell me."

"Two friends were watching TV," she began. "A centipede and an ant . . ."

Emerson listened, or appeared to. But he was still there—up by the window, or wherever they'd been. Maybe Amos had demonstrated his grip, turning his wrist as he related the point.

"But they ran out of snacks, so the centipede offered to go get more from the store down the street."

And what had she done? Clapped her hands in one little victorious slap? Or perhaps she'd said something like, That's what you get when you mess with my dad.

"After he'd been gone a long time, the ant started getting impatient because the store wasn't very far and he knew it shouldn't be taking nearly this long . . ."

His gaze continued to accuse her, to examine. He was riffling through files, spilling them out to find where the secrets were kept.

"So finally," Anna threw up her hands, "the ant goes to

the front door to check whether he's even close and the centipede's still sitting on the stoop, tying his shoes."

Emerson smiled. Had he wanted, he could've laughed.

"That's good." He nodded. "That's—you've still got it."

She could go. He wanted her gone. This child, this nothing. He had some affection, some loyalties even, but she was—yes, this summed up how he felt now, seeing her there in her mother's clothes with the little rags in her lap—just another person.

So what if she was like a daughter? He had one, too, he knew how it was. And the thing no one seemed willing to understand or admit was that you could love your children; you *did* love your children; you would sacrifice for them, go without if need be—but that didn't mean you loved them more than your own life. It wasn't a question of wanting to or not, you just couldn't. Because even they didn't get all the way in. There was still part of you—unalterable, perhaps; inaccessible to be sure—that was the core, the dark knot, the place that would never care about anyone else.

He could see she understood she was meant to go, that she was no longer wanted, if she ever had been.

"Hey," he called as she went, "if you see Rets, tell her I could use a fresh shirt."

Anna nodded and he knew she would not wait to cross paths with his wife; she would go find her because that's what he had meant. Then he thought of Amos and wondered what he was doing. Eating something, perhaps. Something he'd felt free to take.

# 16

When Retsy had guests, moments like this—finding herself in the kitchen with only her husband—could feel like private summits; the sense was of having conspired to meet. Or so she preferred to imagine. It was a way of reminding them both of the teams.

Retsy liked Amos, loved him even, but on some level found him difficult to respect. She knew it was strange: he was funny and kind; he adored his daughter, cared for his wife, and his presence was among the few enduring sources of joy in her husband's life. Still, there it was—a misgiving, a scoff. She couldn't say what she believed he hadn't the will to do, but she sensed a weakness, something thin and concave.

It was true even when Amos mocked her, which he sometimes did. A few months before it had come up that, as a child, she'd memorized the length of every dog's tail. What! he'd cried. His eyes were curious, bright. Why on earth did you do that? Because I wanted one so badly, she said, but we needed to be sure it wouldn't knock over the art.

How he had laughed, not even trying to hide it. Incredible, he said. He touched himself all over, as though searching for a pen. Incredible. I want a thousand more details like that. I want a necklace of them. I want a giant bowlful—but high up, safe, where no pets can get.

Retsy had laughed along, too—wide, allowing. She didn't mind. She could be intimidated by Amos, but only amid the throes of a conversation whose thread she had lost. And even that didn't last. In the long run, she knew, those things hardly mattered. When the world ended, the poets and theorists would find their pretty ideas to be dust in the vault.

Retsy understood it was passé to revere strength of a certain kind. And she mostly agreed. But wasn't there something to be said for brutishness? Not cruelty, but force—the ability simply to *do*. What of moments like when her dad had crumpled in the dining room, clutching his knee as he moaned? Who but her brother was needed then? She thought of Philip, his blunt power. What use did anyone have for clever sophistications when what was required was someone who could, as he had, gather their father like an injured bird and carry him up the stairs in steps that did not falter?

She turned to face her husband. Emerson was finishing a glass of water. One sinuous wrist on the counter, a small impression at his elbow, like a cleft chin.

Muscle appeared at the sleeve of his shirt, the shirt she'd brought down. It was subtle, for the time being restrained.

"Good to see you standing," she said.

He nodded. "Though not bearing much weight."

"Give it time."

Too motherly, that.

She was drying her hands. "He's not above gloating, is he?"

Emerson let out a noise to indicate he understood.

"I know you hate to be hurt," she added.

He gave her a look. His feet were bare, the curve of the heels a bit pale.

"Unlike everyone else?"

"You know what I mean."

Emerson did, of course, and resented not only the way she knew this, but that she knew he understood. Far from enjoying the sense of being perceived, he felt a recriminating kind of anger—at himself for having revealed such information, at her for wanting it.

"What happened, exactly?"

"The court's loose," he said. "By the line."

"What?"

"It's too dry, it's chalky."

"You mean it's too wet?"

Retsy could feel things begin to unravel. Asking so many questions had been a mistake.

"No. What?"

"You slipped, you said. So I just assumed—"

"You're—" he began, then cut himself short. You're not listening was what he'd been starting to say. But that phrase, something about it, had stopped him. It felt more powerful than he understood.

"The clay?" Retsy asked. "You mean it's too soft? Is there a better kind? Or someone to call?"

Emerson shut his eyes and stroked the bridge of his nose.

"It would be easier to explain if you worried about anything besides staying thin."

Retsy said nothing. She touched one of her ears. That hadn't not hurt and she wanted him to know. Then, sensing movement, she looked to her right.

How timely and fortunate. This little witness. This excuse for something to say.

"Hello, dear," she called sweetly.

Emerson turned awkwardly to see Anna in the doorway, arms at her sides. He felt a rush of fuming chagrin and a crude, desperate smile forced itself across his face like a man wrenching open the blinds.

Seeming uncertain of what to do, Anna gave a quick, expressionless shrug. Then she was gone. Retsy, too. And he was left by himself, the floorboards cool under his soles.

WHAT WAS THAT, Emerson wondered. Her dumb little shrug. What on earth did that mean? That he was mad at a child for being inscrutable was only part of what made him feel absurd. What was he suggesting she owed him? Absolution? Clarity? Some assurance that she didn't think he was bad? Well, no, not quite—but then again, maybe? Because he wasn't all bad, wasn't even bad really. He was just flustered and upset, mad he'd been hurt and was being ignored. And who was she to judge? She who didn't know the first thing about marriage? Or adulthood. Or the way, as one crested fifty, a turned ankle could now smack of death.

His flailing rage found its way to her parents and their

high-minded ideas of how children should be left to themselves. He thought of his father explaining why the dog would
stay locked in the crate. If he shits, he sleeps in it, Charles
had said. That was neither good nor bad, but a straightforward causal event, the arrival of consequence for a choice he
had made.

Consequences, Emerson sniffed. What did she know of
those? The angrier he grew, the more he felt certain that he
saw who she was. He could imagine her in only a few years—
he'd dated such women—all whimsy and bohemian affect.
But beneath it, what? Nothing. Just flouncing disregard for
the proper order of things. She would use cigarettes like
props, find meaning in the lyrics of songs, and insist all the
while that hers was an original life. Meanwhile, in her wake
would be the boys she'd led on: some worthless, surely, but
others decent, respectable. She wouldn't care, not for them,
nor anyone else, as she careened through each day intent on
devouring the world.

With a start, he felt himself return to the room, as though
he'd looked up from furiously scratching an itch. The kitchen
stood in quiet judgment, waiting for him to do the obvious
thing. He let out a small, grudging sigh.

"Rets," he called. He paused and considered shouting
louder, but somehow the terms seemed already set: if she
heard and came, he would apologize; if not, it was fine.

Another minute went by.

Oh well, he thought, turning to the sink and refilling his
glass. Things happen, things heal.

# 17

As she went in search of Sophie, Anna tried to sort out how she felt. What, exactly, had she just seen? There'd been something brutal about it, illicit. And not only because it was private, but because it trafficked in things to which she'd not yet been given access. Or had she? That was the question. In seeing, had she stepped through the door? Was she one of them now? Initiated, entitled, wise to the meaning of glances. If so, it would explain her sense of invigorated new purpose.

It wasn't as though she'd never seen adults fight: her parents argued, even shouted sometimes. But that was different. What passed between Retsy and Emerson had been like a face drained of blood. The cold angles of their bodies, the way his words were intended only to hurt. These suggested something beyond an illness or wound. Are they not in love anymore, she wondered. But as soon as she thought it, the question seemed girlish and trite.

Despite the adrenaline, she also felt a certain sadness. To think of Retsy was to picture her playing Newmarket or drawing Anna close to get a stray lash. The same went for Emerson, too. He was the one whose shoulders she rode, who cut her bread as thick as she liked. They really were family: she couldn't remember a time without them, because, of course, there'd never been such a thing. It was in the best way that she took them for granted. They filled the rooms of her life with a familiar, comforting glow.

And yet, to know things was for them to change. That hadn't been Retsy playing along, or Emerson tossing someone on the couch. It was like discovering the butter knife is really a scalpel, grasping how deep the well goes. But seeing anew was its own kind of pleasure, even when it came at a cost. A life unfettered by truth was the life of a child, and it had been years since Anna felt herself one of those.

Despite all this thinking, she was careful to remember that nothing she'd seen was really that big a deal. She certainly didn't plan on telling Sophie. There was hardly anything to say.

So what *did* she want to do? Why had she gone in search of her friend? To check on her, Anna realized as she thumped down the stairs. Not in any particular sense, but to make sure she was all right, unchanged. And, yes, perhaps in addition to that she might also be after the straightforward pleasure of talking to someone who doesn't know what you do.

She found Sophie surrounded by a stack of old magazines—

brought, she explained, from the shelf in a bathroom. Outside, it was nearly dark: only blued bits of gray at the base of the trees. A fire was burning. One window had been left ajar. On the sill lay a beetle, its legs bent like broken matchsticks.

Anna knelt. The rug was soft and received her knees silently. The logs hissed. Slivers of paper lay everywhere.

"What are you doing?" she asked.

"Cutting out ads. Look." Sophie held up a page. "They're so weird and cool."

A man in a three-button suit floated through space. EVER FEEL A MILLION MILES FROM NOWHERE? it read.

"Why?"

"Just to have." She was trimming an edge with great focus. "Like a record, I guess."

Anna sat down and began thumbing through, the yellow corners cracking when turned. Despite herself, she allowed that they were rather interesting. In fact, Anna thought, this was precisely the sort of thing *she* might have done, the sort Sophie would've happily mocked.

"What are your parents like?" she asked as she inspected an image of a woman embracing a can opener, her eyes shut with bliss.

"What?"

"Together, I mean."

"What are you talking about?"

Sophie had closed the magazine and was looking at her.

"I don't know," Anna shrugged. "I'm just curious. I mean, you know people your whole life. But then, what if they're different when you're not around?"

"Did something happen?"

"No."

"Then what the fuck are you talking about?"

"It's just a question."

"Your questions are never just questions."

"What does that mean?"

"What are my parents *like*?"

"I only meant," she tried, "what do you think they're like as *people*, like before they had us, how do you think they were?"

For a moment, Sophie seemed to accept the premise.

"Cooler, probably. At least that's what my mom says."

Anna summoned a laugh she hoped would sound kindred and sisterly.

"Tell me about it."

"Seriously," Sophie said, "do you actually know something?"

"Why do you keep asking that?"

"Because you're talking to me like I'm a fucking idiot."

"You're not."

"I know that."

"Sorry."

"Listen," Sophie said, "if there's something, just tell me."

This she delivered in a familiar tone, one of staid reasonableness, which always left Anna feeling she were the child between them. All of a sudden she saw that what she'd been doing was wrong; it was hungry and small. Now she wanted to hug Sophie, to actually hug her. Not to say anything, but to wrap her arms tightly, to squeeze until they both laughed and agreed to go see whether Retsy would let them have a drink. She didn't, though. That would be dramatic and strange. But the thought was still nice.

"There isn't," she assured her. "I really just—look."

She pointed to a spread of a family unloading their bags from the trunk of a car. Above them letters were sprawled:

HAVE MORE FUN WITH THE TELEPHONE!

Sophie laughed.

"Why were people so dumb?"

# 18

It was interesting, Retsy thought to herself, that when it came to weekend dinners, there could be only one main event. Either it belonged to Friday and the glitter of its promise, or Saturday's ambling tranquility. As to the question of where tonight fell, it seemed clear that yesterday had been them at their best.

For one thing, the meat was too much. A good idea in theory, now the roast struck her as baroque—all the pomp of blood and slicing, how the pieces sprawled across each plate. For another, despite the upward turn of his mouth, she could tell her husband was still in a mood. Emerson was tipped back slightly. His lips were drawn in and he worked his jaw slowly, swallowing only when she could not imagine there was any food left. He lifted his chin as he listened to what Amos was saying.

"I could never," Amos declared. He was, for reasons Emerson failed to remember, talking about writing a novel in the first person.

"Nor, it would seem, from any other perspective," he replied, letting his chair drop.

"Do you want to write?" Sophie asked.

"No," Amos said. "I just mean, if I did, I could never be that close to only one character. I don't think I'm . . . ," he searched, "*brave* enough."

"Of all my patients," Claire said, "writers walk the most. Even more than mailmen."

Emerson refolded his napkin and laid it over his leg. He couldn't say why it occurred to him now, but despite not being prone to recurring dreams, he'd had the same one again last night.

In it he was cutting through the park on his way to work when he paused before a lawn where owners had gathered to unleash their dogs. Among the chaos sat a corgi, its hind legs splayed lamely in a small makeshift cart dragging pathetically across the grass. After a moment the dog stopped and began to bark—or rather, opened his mouth, tilted his head, and lurched slightly, as a barking dog might. But nothing came out. Not a sound, not even, from where Emerson stood, so much as a thin, empty gasp. He turned, searching for the owner. Someone should do something, he thought, someone should help. He began striding across the lawn, brown shoes flashing as they stepped nimbly around divots and piles of shit. Then he arrived and, with what felt less like shock than the quickening pulse of desire, watched his knee rise as he lifted one foot before bringing it down on the creature and its box. He could feel the way it shattered under his sole, the animal twisting, broken. People were running now; he heard shouts at his back. He didn't care. All that mattered was knowing what the dog meant. He crouched and leaned toward the crumpled lungs, so close he could feel their weak rasps. Then, just as it seemed ready to speak, Emerson awoke.

"You know what I mean?" Amos said. "There's something so true about the way we say someone 'throws' a tantrum. You really do hurl it. Like—there, take *that*."

Emerson nodded vaguely. Beside him, Sophie inspected a strand of her hair.

"And," Amos went on, "it also feels right that it's 'to be' upset. That's something internal; it's so much more *inside* you."

"Agreed," Emerson said, squinting into the distance as though trying to judge whether a frame was askew.

"How's it feeling?" Claire asked.

He looked up. "Not terminal."

"Well, everything is, if you wait long enough."

Emerson chuckled without opening his mouth.

"Mom," Anna said.

Claire smiled and shrugged.

Sophie turned to him. "Does that mean you'll stop being so sour?"

"I would hardly say . . . ," he began, before Retsy touched his arm.

He held up his hands. "OK, OK."

Anna watched this closely. She felt her eyes scanning for heat, meaning not apparent to everyone else.

"So no more yips?" Amos said.

"What's a yip?" Sophie asked.

"It's the noise someone makes when they don't want to admit they lost a point."

"Oh," Anna cried, "*that's* what that was? It made me ruin my painting."

Sophie laughed. "Sure. Right until then it was perfect."

"Like Amos's book," Retsy added cheerfully.

"My god," Amos said. He clutched Anna's head to his chest. "What have you done?"

Anna was laughing now. Claire, too. The noise swelled like champagne bubbles, abundant, spilling.

Retsy gave a small shake of her head. "People never believe me when I say I'm the tough one around here."

Sophie sat forward with an eager smile. "Maybe Dad's present to himself can be making sure everyone else is miserable, too."

As Claire laughed her eyes lingered on Emerson. He drank from his glass, his face smoothed by labored patience. All at once she saw him as the boy from her youth—tall, handsome, oaken skin and bright teeth, running across the dock to push someone in. Was there harshness in his hands? Was it more than a shove? No, right? It was just pushing; it was just boys knocking each other about. But then why, watching from shore, had she felt something else?

Now Claire began to pull back. She continued to laugh, but it was subdued. For reasons she couldn't express, she wanted space between herself and what was happening. She put her hand on Amos's thigh. He didn't notice.

"All right," Emerson said, like a teacher hoping to quiet the class. "It really does hurt, you know."

"Trust me, we know," Amos said. "We heard all about it."

"You're not . . . ," Emerson began, but stopped, feeling his voice fray. You're not listening to me was what he'd wanted to say.

Retsy stood. "Coffee?" She brushed the tablecloth by her place.

"I would," Anna said.

"Oh, would you?" Claire replied.

"Me too," said Sophie.

Anna turned to Emerson, a bit giddy, carried by the momentum of everyone's taunts. She lifted her chin, as though the comment were meant only for him. On her face, an uncle's flashing grin.

"Maybe try smaller sips this time?"

Retsy laughed, the quiet, approving murmur she reserved for remarks slightly too forward. After a moment, Amos did, too—his a little received smirk of comprehension, one that said, Right right, *that's* the joke.

Again, Emerson thought. They did it again. Why else would her father understand what she meant? Was nothing too small? Nothing not worth chuckling about. And how had she described it? He the soiled invalid? She the grudging, dutiful nurse?

He laid his knife alongside his fork, the white plate stained like clothes at the scene of a crime. He didn't want to be mad, but for Christ's sake, know when to leave it alone. He'd been a good sport, after all. He'd put up with their care and their looks and their nudging scorn. But goddamn it, enough; enough was fucking enough.

His smile turned; he felt it go sour on his face. His teeth

shone and he continued to laugh, but he was gone, his mind different now. He was aware of the room, the walls and the ceiling. His walls. His ceiling. Look at the wine that surrounded these people. Amos was pouring some now, calming his laughter to steady his hand. These takers. Everything on the table—the food, the dishes, the cloth spread beneath— was like evidence in a case. For what? For favors. So many and over so many years. In only an instant, he tallied them all. His vision filled with things he had given, moments of patience. He'd forgotten nothing. This dinner, that show. They tumbled like boxes from the back of a closet, overwhelming in their clutter and the need to be faced. He tried to speak, but the machinery of his anger ran on. Each noise was an offense, an unwanted clang of the bell.

"Are you sure?" someone asked.

Their voices returned. Slowly, from afar. Sophie was nodding.

"We had some for lunch," Anna said.

"Oh, to be young."

It was Claire who had spoken.

"Backgammon?" she added. Her question was meant for him.

Emerson thought for a moment.

"No," he said vaguely. "No, I'm all right."

# 19

Evening. A chill at the windows. Past the courts, the barn sat like a ship. The table was cleared. Only napkins and candles—short now, ribbed with wax, like the ruins of ancient columns.

They were scattered about the house, tossed like clothes by lovers moving to bed. Amos and Retsy stood in the kitchen, a half-moon of pie on the counter between them. Sophie had returned to the living room and her magazines. Claire, stretched on the couch in the library, opened a book. The air smelled of floorboards and spruce and, faintly, women's hair.

Later, Anna would wonder why then of all times she'd felt the need to do laundry. A stain, yes, though barely. More of a spot, a rusty scuff at the edge of one sleeve. From jam, maybe, or coffee, or a bit of wine by the sink. Regardless:

not urgent; not necessary; not even the kind of thing she was prone to caring about.

Had it been something else, then? Some slightly less innocent impulse. Perhaps, having glimpsed the inner life of adults, she'd hoped to steal another look. And if it was that, wouldn't it be fair to call it a very small gluttonous sin? Hardly grievous, but one with some cosmic weight. Or was it nothing? Absolutely nothing at all. Just a girl washing shirts. A girl who couldn't stop from doing the same thing every other girl did: to harbor some fear that it was partly her fault.

THERE WAS A RIGHT WAY to move in a laundry room. Careless, unthinking. Arm goes up, grabs for the box. Now that size scoop—OK, a little bit less. Shut the door, twist the dial—too far, back one—and you're done. Water trickles inside. The machine rumbles to work.

But when you don't know what's where and which the right setting is, the sense is of having intruded, of being somewhere you don't quite belong. And that was how Anna felt now, groping behind sheets and towels in search of detergent.

For some reason, she felt sure that calling for help wasn't an option. If she did, questions would invariably come. What? Why? Honey, we'll be home tomorrow. Just thinking of this made her tingle with embarrassed shame. Had she simply asked to begin with—said, Retsy, do you mind if I wash some shirts?—it would've been fine. A little odd, perhaps, but no more than that. The problem was that she'd made herself too familiar: if they learned what she was doing they'd picture her like an orphan, pawing through cupboards at night. They would perceive something strange and essential about her, even if she didn't know what.

No, she decided. She must find it herself.

She could get this way sometimes. Thinking and thinking, imagining too much. These were the moments when she felt most in need of her dad, as each new idea tendrilled and split, losing itself in a thicket of anxious confusion. She was like a toy too tightly wound, one arm twitching as it threatened to break. What she needed was her father to scoop her up and settle things down. He knew the places, the words.

Anna sighed. The small room smelled of soap. Hands on her knees, she stared at the crumple of shirts. Then, a noise down the hall. She turned, trying not to look like someone caught unaware.


EMERSON WAS IN a good mood as he entered the den. He felt expansive, generous; he found himself hoping someone would ask something of him so that he could give it. A pleasant appetite rose in his gut and he considered whether toast might be a good snack. Though still swollen, even his ankle seemed better. The awkwardness of his gait was now mostly put on.

"Alms for the poor," Amos said, watching him limp toward the deep leather chair. Emerson laughed—it really did strike him as funny—and he was glad to announce his return with this friendly noise.

They were all there, all besides Claire who'd fallen asleep while she read. And Anna, who might still be upstairs. Perhaps that was to be expected, a sign, if anything, of everyone's ease. Only the unfamiliar feel compelled to remain in one room.

Sophie sat by the fire, working a magazine against her scissors. Her back was turned toward him. She was placing the pictures into small piles according to principles he couldn't divine. He thought about asking what they were, and did she need help, whether she ought to call for Anna and see where she was. But he didn't. Strange as it might sound, this struck him as preposterously cruel. Anyway, there were other things on his mind.

It had already happened, but sitting here now it was almost as if he were watching, describing the scene. It was already done, but he still found himself wondering whether he would. He went into his head and set the reel to play again.

HERE HE COMES, up the stairs. Slow, halting steps. Not painful anymore, just delicate, tender. What must be made clear is that he has no plan, no intention; nothing more than dry eyes and the search for glasses set him down at the top of the steps. He arrives. He steadies himself, spots a light down the hall and goes toward it.

Then he sees her. Bent slightly as she peers at the dial. The air is cool and dark; his hands feel snug in their skin. Above her, towels are folded. Everything still, calmed by the neat rows of fabric. Her hair is pushed back behind one ear and it seems, in this moment, like a gesture of unthinkable confidence and undeserved ease. Something goes through him. It's excitement, anger; it's tension and nerves. He's almost aghast. Is she doing laundry? What gives her the right?

He understands now: to her, everything in life is like tissue paper that comes with a gift—for it she is glad but indifferent. It adds to the charm, makes a small noise when things are unwrapped, but quickly, of course, is forgotten. This is her power. It's what will draw men to her; it's the reason she will feel incurably alone. He wants to tell her; it's important she know. And yet, for reasons he cannot discern, feels unable, almost afraid.

The door shuts behind them. Anna turns. Her eyes climb his chest. Their whites gleam like china, each iris neat as a hole. It intoxicates him. It swims in his blood. The adrenaline of kisses and dances. The thing you imagine one feels before pulling the trigger or leaping in front of a train. Am I? Am I going to do it?

It's not the weight of a choice, though. It's like a test, an adventure. Can he—that's the question. Is it in him to do? He doesn't quite know. He thinks, but can't say for sure. What's about to take place is a discovery, but the thing they'll find out is for him to decide. He alone has the power to shape it.

For an instant, the room shimmers with heat. An electric fear pounds like rain against each inch of his skin.

It's not planned. No, he thinks again, not at all. He has only realized just now what it is that he's doing. It matters a great deal, this point. The thought of having designed things horrifies him; to have plotted would so clearly be wrong. But this, this feels different. He can't say quite why, but it's true. This feels—if he must confess it, then fine—this feels OK.

Strange rage, all at once. Her arm, her neck. He grabs them like hoses flailing in the yard. She makes a small noise. Fear has arrived. It's all fear now, fear and confusion. She looks up at him. Shh, he says. He hears himself say. The sound of his voice brings him back. He realizes he has no plan, no next. Which thrills him. Because in this tiny closet there are no limits: no plan is the same as all plans. His excitement is childish, almost giddy. But also this rage. He thrashes between them; his mind snaps like a flag in the wind. Another noise from deep in her throat. This mangled somehow, partway aborted. It's the sound of confusion that turns to knowing before it's all the way out. He shakes his head as if to someone nearby. To dismiss their questions, to allay their concerns.

She won't call for help. There's no need to cover her mouth. His hands are on her; her shirt is wrenched up. They talked. They talked about him. Words fly through his mind. So what. Years and years. They land like weak rain—faint, then dried out and gone. The corgi, too, flashes by. His foot, Anna's shrug. Anna's shrug again. Like a little loop, like a record that skips—shrug, shrugshrugshrug—until the noise blurs into a roar. How could you? Who, me? No. Maybe. Yes, but her, too. And him—the other him. Not just that, though. Something more. Something bigger and total. He needs the word, just the one word that's the name for it all. It feels close, slips away. His hands are moving, clutching, chasing it like a letter being blown down the street. Finally, the first thing between them. More sob than sound. "Stop," her voice pleads.

And he does. Just like that. As though never in his life has he been more composed. His hand slips out of her shorts; their waistband flees back to her skin. Outside, darkness drenches the lawn. Everything is quiet. The grass, the brittle night air.

"OK," he says.

It's as if she's asked him to pass her the bread, or he could please tell Sophie to give her a call. He's looking at her. She says nothing. Then he's struck by a thought.

"Here, wait."

He reaches over her shoulder and moves the dial a single, deafening click. She shudders at the sound. Or perhaps he imagines this. It's so hard to say. The water begins.

"It's just a small load, right? No extra rinse should be fine."

A LOG COUGHED in the fire. The rustle of pages, of socks on the rug. Emerson felt his eyes moving from one thing to the next. Books, frames, the bellows on its hook. How remarkable that such a thing could've happened and life had no choice but to simply proceed. It was all there: everything was perfectly fine.

Was it strange to say that he'd merely been trying to tell her something? It did feel odd, and more than a little bit rich. But even so, he couldn't quite shake the sense that he'd meant only to warn her, that things had simply gotten mixed up, muddled in what he had done. Oh well, he reminded himself, wasn't that the way of it? The world was complicated and everything was always being misunderstood. Frustrating, no doubt, but there was nothing to do but move on.

Amos stood and sighed. He stretched his arms overhead. "I'm beat."

He bent to give Retsy a kiss on the cheek. "Thanks for dinner."

"Of course," she smiled.

On his way to the door, he stopped and put a hand on Sophie's head.

"Night, bug," he said. She grinned up pleasantly.

"And you," Amos turned. "Come get birthday bagels with me tomorrow?"

Emerson cupped his chin in one palm and drummed his fingers against the side of his face. As he looked at him, Amos seemed to become not just one person, but a hundred, a thousand, refracted into all of his selves, every version he'd ever been at every moment the two of them had spent together. There was a manic, dashing energy to Emerson's mind, like a dog dodging someone who lunges to catch it. His thoughts moved in, then away. Toward a hot center he couldn't quite see and which he did not want to touch. How does regret come and at whose behest? Was it even regret that he felt? Yes, he had done this thing. But just look at them now, sitting here by the fire. Who could want more—than this room, than this life?

"Sounds great," he said, standing. A yawn parted his lips. "I should turn in, too."

Together they climbed the wincing stairs. Emerson went first. Amos followed, saying nothing, letting him take his time.

## 20

Claire had gone for a run, leaving Amos stretched alone in their bed. The light was muted, his skin a soft, ineffectual white. He pictured the day as it would roll forward: breakfast, coffee, bags in the car. Home—the city receives them; leaves have fallen on the stoop since they left. A light dinner. Bread, olives, cold meat, the last of an Alsace in the fridge.

It had been a mistake, bringing it up, especially in the manner he did. Things should stand on their own: how many times had he told his patients some version of this?

"It's not a big deal," he'd said, "but it made me kind of sad."

Claire had rolled over then and given him a confused, standoffish look.

"Because of how different it was," he paused, "from the way you were with my tooth."

"Jesus," she sighed.

That's when he'd invoked Anna's tart. His hope had been to give her a way into what he was feeling—the sense of sides, or insularity, or distance. But of course, to her, this had only revealed his true motivation. Because, as she put it, he wanted to even the score.

"Even the score?" he said.

"Yes." Claire was standing by that point. She dressed in quick, unthinking stabs. "Besides," she added. "He's actually hurt. You just wanted to be."

Amos pictured her running through the last of a dewy fog. The idea of her damp shirt and the rhythm of her meticulous breath left him with the impression that he might not know her at all. This happened sometimes, often after moments when they'd chafed against each other, and, strangely, it was in the wake of these that Amos experienced the most acute swells of gratitude for what comprised their marriage. It was like someone who's been in a bad mood and finally sees how silly they've been, struck down by a kind word from a stranger or the smell of croissants.

What he and Claire had was no longer delicate; it was durable now—years made it so. The foundation of days, of meals, of walks to the park, snow creaking underfoot. All that was like sediment forming a narrows: it could not be swept away. And yet, it wasn't so hard to remember when it *was* still fragile and new, when he'd felt like a boy gifted, inexplicably, with something precious, something he didn't trust himself to carry all the way home. Not without reason, either. Because hadn't he almost dropped it? Almost ruined everything before the two of them even had a real chance.

They'd been together a year, but he already knew how clear-eyed she was, how calm. She dismissed matters like a clerk; her reason cleaved things in two. And wouldn't she have—with him? It still being so fresh, wouldn't she have thought—correctly, perhaps—that surely there must be others as good without quite so many dents. There would've been no cruelty in it, hardly anything to say. Even he wouldn't have tried.

But no—it hadn't happened. And there was no question why, no doubt about whom he had to thank.

THEY'RE OUTSIDE NOW. It's June. Sixth Avenue is spilling cars. Emerson stands nearby. He'd walked off then turned back to face him. The sun is warm, the air soft. It feels wrong, though, like someone suggesting a plan, unaware what has happened and how things have changed.

"I don't get it."

"Neither do I," Amos says weakly.

"It's not a big deal, it's just weird. I guess . . ." He pauses. "Is it a big deal?"

"No," Amos says. "I don't know."

What I mean, the security guard had repeated, is that you're not leaving until someone you know comes to get you. Why, Amos asked, though he had no right to speak. The man looked down at him. So we're sure you won't come here again.

As he dialed the number, his body felt empty and light. He wondered whether this was what it was like to tell people you're dying, the way you alone lived in the instant before everyone knew. On the phone he'd explained only that Emerson needed to meet him. Then he covered the handset as he looked toward the guard who said quietly, Tell him to come to the back.

"Are you mad at me?"

"What?" Emerson says, then stops to consider the question. "I guess?" He scratches his cheek. "It just doesn't make sense. Toothpaste?"

Had Amos known how close they were until now? Is this a brother, he wonders. A father? Is this how that feels?

"I know."

"Can you at least try to explain?"

Amos sighs. He already has. Hundreds of times. To himself as he'd walked out the door and onto the street. What are you doing, he spat. You're twenty-seven years old. What the fuck are you doing?

He marveled at the stupidity of it. Gather all of his friends in a room and ask for only one word to describe him. What would they say? Rational, perhaps. Or practical. Something like levelheaded and sane. But here he was, the sensible one, stealing odds and ends from small stores. Why? Why on earth? It couldn't possibly just be about cost. It was, though. Not really, but sort of. It was about the way it felt to let even a little bit go. Because to save, or, rather, not to have spent, would mean he was—how to put it?—protected.

If he could just bottle it up, hand it over, and say, Here, try this, maybe Emerson might understand. Maybe anyone would. All those years. His mother's voice. The way she sat

at the table. These bills, she shrieked. When will they stop?
Or the rare night they went for pizza and he risked asking
for something to drink. Even when she said yes it came with
the stain of concern. Should I really have let him? If only he
just wouldn't press. But in his weakness, his wanting, he had.
So it arrived and he sipped slowly, telling himself it was
sweet and exciting and good. The silly, small soda. But of
course it was ruined. What had he done? How bad were
things really and what would this mean for tomorrow? He
was miles away from the taste in his mouth. Everything was
tainted; nothing was simply itself.

He understands now, standing there, how unnecessary it
was. All that worry, all the unceasing dread. No, they hadn't
had much. But not so little that every day should've been
bloated with fear. Plus, there were things that nothing excused. Like screaming at him for finishing butter too quickly,
or slamming the table when he asked if she'd filled out
scholarship forms. But knowledge like this came too late.
To be a child was to be porous; what few walls you had
could be blown down in a gust.

And that was just her. Think of his dad—muffler dragging as he drove home to his sad, dirty house. It was so perfect, so brilliantly structured. On one side, his mother and
her flailing, inarticulate fear. On the other, not so much a
parent but a pitiable friend. Kind but feckless, rotten teeth
and loose, unwashed pants. More than that, though, he was
the answer to the unspoken question. You want to know
what happens if you order too much, or things get too tight?
There, him. That's where you wind up. That's who you become when you don't keep track of it all.

What little wonder then that out in the world, in a sprawling city whose demands were unceasing, whose pleasures,
even the small ones, still added up, he'd found himself crip-
pled, brought to his knees by this thing it seemed everyone
had. So he went—not always, but enough, enough to feel
like he belonged. To dinner, to shows, to drinks after this
or that opening. It wasn't even close to too much. Had he had
the courage to hire an accountant, they would've said, Oh,
this is fine. But that wasn't the point. Growing up, things
were never explained. No one said, Here, this is what we
can do. It just lurked, wheezed in the dark. Not enough, the
voice rasped. Not ever enough.

So he took things, he stole them. Carried them home with
a face contorted to look at ease. It soothed him. It electrified.
It gave him somewhere private to go. If he found himself at
a meal at which more and more wine had been ordered, he
could loosen the noose by reminding himself there were ways
to manage. He tallied the items that, bit by bit, would balance
the ledger. Light bulbs, olive oil, laundry detergent. It was a
slow, patient strategy. But his was a life of endurance. He believed in small acts; he understood the truth of their sums.

Was he ashamed? Of course, all the time. But his father
was dead and his mother, like a stray thread on a sweater,
had been clipped from his life. Which meant he was out on
his own: he had only himself to let down and that, somehow, seemed the easiest.

Emerson has squatted. He picks up a pebble and tosses it
into the drain. Now he's looking at him, wanting something.
To understand, Amos realizes. To no longer feel so confused
by his friend.

"I'm really alone," Amos says. Every word is crucial and frail.

Emerson thinks for a moment. He threads his fingers and cups the top of his head.

"Do you have any idea how strong we all think you are?"

He kicks at the curb, seeming to speak to himself as much as to Amos, as though he is having this thought for the very first time.

"We don't stop to think. We don't even wonder if you're OK."

Amos looks up, then quickly away. Years later, he'll wonder if this was their best moment, the truest, most well-chosen thing Emerson could ever have said.

"I don't know if I am."

He'll hug him, he thinks. It will be desperate, like a child clutching the leg of someone they fear might leave. No, never mind. That won't make sense, it won't convey what he means. Nothing can. A sob rises in his throat. He catches it. Now his body is all gratitude, or relief, or arrival. He can't quite say what he feels. But it's clean. Not new, but washed. Like a rain which breaks the heat, in whose path humidity flees.

Only one question remains. And though he feels ashamed as he asks, Amos is certain he needs to know.

"Will you tell Claire?"

Emerson sighs and rubs the bridge of his nose. "Do you love her?"

"Yeah."

"Then no."

Amos seems to hear this vaguely, as though from a distance.

"She'd break up with me," he says, watching the light change and the traffic begin to move with greater speed.

"Probably. Maybe."

"Does she love me?"

Emerson nods. "Yeah." His hard, handsome chin. "Yeah, I think she does."

Standing there, Amos feels suddenly that they've reached an agreement. Is this the moment he'd decided to marry her? He commits to a certain life, he accepts its promises. He wants them. Just some comfort, some ease. He can change, he feels certain. He really can change. He just needs some space to stretch his arms out and breathe. And life with her can give him that. There won't be worry, not about this, anyway. Which is something, maybe more than enough. Just think what he could do with all that space. There will be so much more room—for love, for attention, for anything else.

He puts a hand on Emerson's shoulder. His friend brushes it off in order to give him a hug.

"Just be OK?" he says. "OK?"

"OK," Amos says. "I can do that."

THERE WAS A QUICK POUNDING at the door before it flew open. Emerson stood, fingers curled around the top of the frame, body bent like a bow.

"Bagels."

Amos pulled a pillow over his face.

"I changed my mind."

"Too late for that."

"Never."

"Come," Emerson said.

"No."

"Come on."

Amos lifted himself onto his elbows, squinted and sighed. "No."

"Come on," Emerson said again.

Amos stared back impassively.

After a moment, Emerson shrugged, grinned broadly, and leapt toward the bed, bouncing on his knees like a child. The frame shuddered and groaned.

"Come on," he said. "It's my day, you bastard. Don't be an asshole."

Amos was tossed about in tiny heartbeats of flight. He smiled. He had lost, he was glad to be beaten. It felt old and good, like drinking from a stream. This man, now fifty-two, still possessed of an unhateable joy.

"Stop," he managed with a laugh.

Emerson paused, his eyes implying the threat.

"So?"

"Just get the fucking keys."

Emerson rolled off in a casual blur. Long legs unfolding themselves, lifting him up. It was how he always moved. Smooth, natural as water. Neither loving nor cruel, perhaps equal parts both.

Amos yawned. "I take it your ankle's feeling better?"

"Actually," Emerson said, "I think the bouncing might've been a mistake."

They were laughing now, the two of them. Loud and loving. Content in themselves. It went out through the walls of the house. It was something that everyone could hear.

II

Mid-May. The city warmed, rediscovered itself. Restaurants opened their windows; the branches of trees vanished beneath leaves drinking sunlight. There was chatter in the evenings. Walking home, men carried their coats.

Past all this, Anna moved. Along the western edge now. To her right, the river shimmered like coins. She'd found the stride and the breath where she could believe that she might never stop. Eight months was enough—to form habits, to feel their grooves in one's life. Her lungs emptied and filled. She was unaware of each step, her legs turning over like rods on the wheel of a train.

Ahead, a man knelt, tying his shoe. For a moment she imagined herself as his laces, bending in his hands, coming together in the safety of a comforting knot. Then she passed him. He was no one. She ran on, obliterating herself. Whisps of hair clung to her neck.

THIS STATE OF bludgeoned apathy was one Anna had come to know well, and she craved it like an addict who thinks of the flask in their coat. The idea of it comforted her. That she could come back. That it would wait.

Her method was simple: she left and began, drifting from one street to another, crossing a bridge if she wanted, making her way to the next. She might go into the park or down past the piers, through neighborhoods of blight and neglect, and those, like her own, over which town houses loomed with their promise of comfort and peace. From afar it could seem all whimsy and chance, but every choice was a pure act of will.

Like this she went on until she was done. It wasn't fatigue that told her to stop, but the numbed, sedate vacuum inside her head. Then Anna would slow, sighing, skipping, tossing her arms like wet rope, until, finally, she'd look up to see where she was. In what borough. On which streets. Who was nearby. From there it was only a matter of finding the train. Any would do. One line or another always brought her back to the start.

Underground, she'd sink into herself. Her body shaking faintly as the cars shuddered, her eyes swimming with an opiate glaze. For so much of the day, thoughts felt like things she was working to hold underwater, constantly threatening to slip loose and hurl themselves into the air. But for those few moments she achieved, if not the right to stop thinking, at least an indifference to whether she did. Her life had been boiled away, reduced to only these clean, simple needs: she must get home, and she must eat.

TIME HAD BECOME STRANGE. Hours etched themselves with painful clarity, but months passed with anonymous calm. It had been October, then winter, now it no longer was. Everyone seemed to agree.

Perhaps as a result of this haze, Anna found herself returning to scenes from when she'd been younger. There was, for instance, the day she'd come from school and asked whether Santa was real. She'd been only five and it seemed obvious now that she'd simply wanted some reassurance. But, owing to a preternaturally frank, adult tone of voice, Claire had taken her seriously, saying simply, No, no he's not.

How Anna wept afterward. Her mother had apologized and tried to console her, but that, somehow, made it worse. So often tears came in frustration with something her parents wouldn't permit. But this time they agreed with each other—and yet that didn't matter. It had happened; she could never unhear or forget; there was no going back to before.

Anna could cry for such moments. And she had, more than once, in the months since their weekend upstate. For that five-year-old girl she had only kindness and understanding; from her, she could stand back, hover above. But when it came to things now—to herself now—everything grew quiet and clumped. Her thoughts were stopped up; nothing seemed to connect.

FARTHER ON, a crane bent toward the pier and wrenched a shipping container from the ground. For a moment she considered turning to watch as it climbed, swaying slightly, into the sky. But no. All the better to imagine, to keep running and give her thoughts somewhere to go.

Her mind tossed out scenes from the day. Cold eggs on her plate; school, always school; a pigeon's dumb, unthinking eye. Coming home, the sound of Claire somewhere in the house; the smell of paint and carpet and wood. And leaves, too. A window was open. In the kitchen, perhaps. Spring air had rushed in. And with it, a thought came to her about summer, a question she'd meant to ask.

It was this she'd gone running to escape. Because Anna knew she couldn't say it with a straight face, feared her features might confess why she needed to know. No matter how simple it was, how plain, there was no hope of delivering gracefully: So, do we have plans for August? Are we still planning to visit the Fords?

ONE MORE PART of the process remained, the thing she did before descending the steps to the train. She hated to put it like that; it embarrassed her to call it a process. But what other word was there for something you do every day?

First, she found a newspaper; one was always lying around. Then she'd choose where to go. Bookstores or groceries or museum gift shops, the kind of place that sells toasters and phones. Once inside, she'd walk the aisles, eyes combing the shelves. Perhaps she needed a thing, or could imagine some use. But that wasn't necessary. What mattered only was the moment an object called to her softly, said, Yes, it's me you came here to take.

Next, she'd find something nearly costless to buy. An apple, a postcard, a magnet of the bridge. In one hand went the newspaper, curled over whatever she meant to hide; in the other, this prop. Then she became charming, buoyant and light. I'll be thinking of you at breakfast, she'd called to a clerk yesterday after they'd agreed that poached eggs were best.

Outside she'd walk on, feeling a twist in her face. Taut wires, tight skin. Pretty, flustered girl, just come in from a run. Chatting brightly, laughing, never accepting her change. Who would suspect she'd come there to steal?

Sometimes she kept the things for herself, but not always. Just as often, she'd leave them on the sidewalk outside their house and then sit at the window, waiting for someone to come and carry them off. What she wanted to see was the kind of person who stopped. With that she could slip free of her own mind and enter the idea of theirs. If she were still painting this might have formed the basis for work, but of course she was not. The last thing in her pad was the toes in the grass; the brushes sat dry on the shelf.

It was a woman who took the vase—a wide hat shading her eyes, a small, imperious dog at her side. Instantly, Anna sketched out her life: the overlooked of two sisters with a fondness for china her husband couldn't afford. How sad, she thought, to labor under tastes one hasn't the means to enjoy. It was like sharpening a knife before turning it on yourself. And yet—the woman could hardly believe her luck!—here it was: a piece for which she would've longed, sitting unclaimed on the street. How nice to think of it on a shelf in her home, to imagine that, for a day or two, she might resent her husband a little bit less.

But then they were gone—the woman, the vase, and the dog. And the sidewalk was empty. And the world resumed its slow work of grinding Anna to dust.

It depressed her to think how transparent it was—the running and the stealing—how easily explained. Control, et cetera. She even said this to herself sometimes, letting it run through her head like a mantra, watching the words decay as it did. No matter what, if you repeated anything enough its meaning eventually dissolved in the mouth. She would know, after all. She had tried. Even with the phrase she hated most, the one whose cold weight she carried like a gun.

What he did. Both a statement and a question, or the answer to a question, the end of the logical tree. Had he done something? Yes. Well, then, what was it? This—this is what he did.

So, hoping it might be destroyed, Anna rinsed it, wrung it out and rinsed again. What he did. What hedid. Whateedyd. Whut eed id. On and on until the words broke apart and, for a blissful moment, slipped free of their bonds to slosh back and forth as inchoate sounds. Maybe he hadn't done anything? Who was "he" after all?

But it never worked for long. Because words were just words. And it wasn't an idea her thoughts hoped to shout down, it was an unchangeable fact. What he did. What he had done. What would always have to be true.

ANNA SLOWED TO a lilting walk. The streets had begun to narrow and fold. Here, the weight of age overtook them. The whole island sloped, tipped up; she felt herself slipping down.

Outside restaurants, people were gathering. They hugged, checked their watches, and went in. A woman ducked beneath the arm of someone holding the door. The light was leaving. The sidewalks were bathed in soft, velvet dark.

By a park on the corner, a man bent over a saxophone, his nails broken, his clothes ragged and stained. Behind him, a woman swept across a basketball court on roller skates. She moved with the music—like a bird, like a sheet in the wind. She wasn't graceful as much as certain: sounds happened and so she went with them. This body is mine, her gestures all said. I love it and I will put it to use.

Anna watched. She knew what she wished to think—that the city was beautiful, enduring, and grim. But that wasn't what filled her mind. Instead, she was seized with a jealous, hungry anger, an inkblot of rage. She wanted to shake the woman like a jar full of pennies. Give me that, she would say. Give it back. I had that and I want it again.

Her body, that was. Her own body. It had once belonged just to her, to use however she felt. She'd burped and then laughed, wiped sweat and snot from her lips; she'd tried a French braid, failed, and then pouted, stubbed her toe and let out a shriek. She'd run headlong across wet grass, jumped in the ocean, and rolled in the sand just to see how much would stick. And she'd thought of boys—their mouths, their rough hands; she'd closed her eyes and let them explore. Not actually, not yet. But in bed, in the private dark of her mind, having turned out the lights as she tried to see what she could feel, whether she could forget the fingers were hers.

Now she lived in an alien thing. A strange shell, a crudely made box all splinters and rust. When had she last danced? Or lifted her arms over her head and let them fall with the pleasure of their own easy weight? She had no idea. She could run, yes, but that wasn't the same. Exercise wasn't what anyone did who was free.

Anna looked down. She was already holding a newspaper. She'd not even noticed picking it up. It was dirty and slightly torn. The words were in Russian but it would do.

Farther up the street was a cramped, warmly lit shop. The letters on the window were fading, the Q in ANTIQUES nearly gone. Inside were mirrors, lamps, wrought iron tables on which door knockers sat with chess sets, ashtrays, and spoons. Crossing, Anna lingered for a moment. Then she fashioned a smile and went in.

The bell sounded faintly. The woman at the register looked up and considered her for a moment.

"You know, we're open till ten," she said.

"What?" Anna asked.

"There was no need to run."

Anna smiled. "Hold on." She gestured expansively. "You don't think all this deserves some hustle?"

The woman let out a pleasant, dry laugh.

"Give a shout if you need any help."

THE MORNING AFTER. What a phrase. Weighted, dense as a proper noun. Anna hated to think of it like that, to give it such credence. But whether she believed it should've or not, the night had passed, the next day begun.

On it, Anna had eaten breakfast. Or thought she had. The plate before her was empty—what else could explain it? But then her father had come to slide eggs from the pan and set a bagel beside them. Fresh, he smiled proudly. She nodded. Her stomach turned at the nearness of their heat.

Things continued to happen around her. Words rumbled like luggage dragged overhead. She was at the table, now in the car. Had she said goodbye to Sophie? To anyone? She felt like a traveler who'd been asked how she arrived. Such an obvious question and yet she had no idea.

A few years before, she'd slipped while climbing a tree. Her friend came rushing up. Oh my god, she said, are you OK? It's nothing, Anna replied. She shook her arms out and jumped just to show how fine she was. But your leg, the girl said. Only then did Anna see the torn flap of skin running from her knee to her hip, the blood leaking out. She felt herself sway, but no sensation came through. Her leg seemed distant and vague. The cut wasn't real; it might not even be hers.

That was how it felt as they drove home: like she was covered in gauze; nothing quite touched all the way. Whatever happened was gentle, almost calm. She watched her father's hands on the wheel. Both, then one, then both again. Her mother laughed. At something he'd said. She reached to stroke the back of his head. The city appeared. Tall, sleepy blocks. Red lights became green. Their car floated beneath them. Suddenly she was home—in her room, at last in the shower.

That's when it had come. When she'd remembered, or perhaps understood. At first, she watched her feverish scrubbing with a kind of bemused confusion. Hey, you, she wanted to say to her hands, what's the big deal? Maybe she'd even asked herself that very question. Because with the water spilling onto her shoulders and steam billowing up from her feet, Anna realized: she knew that she knew.

It came in splinters and flashes. His body, its smell of sunscreen and sweat. A hand at her throat. The way the washing machine crushed into her spine. She touched herself there. It was tender, her fingers described the inky stain of a bruise. Then his other—the worse, the more evil—crawling down to her shorts, wrenching her open like a door. The colonizing hunger of his grip, his uncaring eyes. Here they were, saying what she'd known, what she'd feared all along: you don't really exist, you're only a thing. It was true, she could tell. She did not doubt his contempt. Anna felt horror, she felt relief.

She was weeping, she realized. She had not been aware. Only the feeling of snot on her lips let her know. Her hands were still scrubbing. It made no difference. What she wanted to scald was inside, somewhere else.

ANNA TOUCHED a lampshade and shook her head vaguely as though noting a thought. She watched the woman's reflection in one of the large mirrors against the wall. Her face was pretty but tired, her teeth stained by tea. Anna imagined her bent over a desk, pen in hand, straining to see whether the store could survive. How odd to envision this at the same time as she looked nonchalantly for something to steal. It wasn't that Anna reconciled these ideas, so much as they seemed unrelated. She felt nothing. For all her smiling, she was hardly there.

She lifted a small bronze horse from a bookshelf, turning it over and feeling its weight. It reminded her of a glass swan she'd taken from a shop by the park. They were a similar size—dense, calming to hold. It was a pockmark-faced man with a mustache she'd charmed that time, leaving just as he laughed at whatever she'd said. Outside, she'd hurried to an alley, feeling suddenly that she wanted to hurl the bird against some indifferent brick wall. Like me, Anna had thought, looking at it curled in her hand. Beautiful, mean. She felt her arm begin to come up when something stopped her: the idea of a dog—brown, perhaps, a mess of white at the end of each ear—coming upon all those shards and getting one stuck in the innocent meat of his paw. She felt herself begin to cry. They were hot, frustrated tears. She was a good person; she didn't want to be bad or feel so far away from the world. Instead, she'd walked to the river and sent it sailing over the cracked, scaly water.

No, the horse wasn't right. She set it down.

"You don't have tasseled lampshades, do you?" Anna asked without turning.

The woman clicked her tongue and squinted at the ceiling.

"I don't think so. But you might like these."

She indicated across the room toward a set trimmed with lace ribbon.

Anna knew this moment well. "They're so beautiful," she said, "but my dad . . ."

Her tone was familiar, conspiratorial. The woman smiled and nodded.

Abruptly, Anna stopped. She'd found it. She knew as she always did—all at once. It was a cigarette lighter made of worn pewter. On one side was the dim outline of initials, nearly brushed away now by decades of pockets and palms. She could already see herself in her room, feel the way her thumbnail would fling the top closed—off on, off on—whenever she wanted, whenever she liked. She relaxed as it grew warm in her hand. It wasn't a matter of whether she'd be OK, she already was.

"How long have you had this store?" she asked, suddenly curious. She was lifting a bookend and pretending to inspect the felt at its base.

"Oh, I don't own it."

"Ah," Anna said, feeling a strange pang of disappointment. "Well, please tell whoever does that they have wonderful taste."

The woman smiled. "I will. That's kind of you to say."

A comfortable silence opened between them—Anna moving quietly about as the woman ticked things off with her pen. She liked these moments of being together, even with this person she'd never actually know. They were just living. They were both just spending their day.

"Well," Anna said, "have a good evening."

"Same to you."

She set the bookend down and made her way toward the door, pausing to look at a squat Chinese urn. Then she was up the steps and reaching for the handle with the small bell on its frayed yellow string.

"Hey," a man's voice said behind her.


ONCE, ANNA HAD BEEN out walking. It was January and nearly three months had passed. The afternoon was cold; snow whispered under her feet. She came upon a small park where children were playing, their limbs thick with clothes. Nearby, some women sat talking. They lifted the tops from their cups to blow at the steam.

"But *why*?" a girl's insistent voice moaned.

Anna could tell right away she'd been asking this over and over, refusing to accept each reply. Who knew what started it—something about the moon or a bird or the reason she wasn't allowed certain things.

"Just stop it," a woman hissed. The girl's brow furrowed before she broke into tears. Anna stood, watching from beyond the wrought iron fence.

"Oh, enough already," the woman said as she busied herself with her bag.

"But," the girl pleaded, "I just wanted to know."

It was strange, Anna would think later, that she had no memory of entering the playground. But there she suddenly was, standing over them both, feeling her weight in the balls of her feet.

"Why don't you just leave her alone?" Anna said. The

strength of her own voice surprised her. She felt her need for someone to defend.

The woman looked up.

"Leave her alone?" She laughed incredulously. "What are you talking about? I'm her mother."

For a moment no one spoke. Then the woman chuckled again in a private, disbelieving way. The girl regarded Anna with wary confusion before turning to give her mom an affectionate hug.

Anna left quickly, eyes down, feet moving over the snow. She felt ashamed and overeager. She couldn't make sense of herself. What had she been thinking? What had she been trying to do?

It was not until several days later that she understood. She'd been lying in bed, turning over the same tired questions. What was she looking for? What did she want? What could she ask of the future? Then, neat as the line in a song, it came to her. To know why. That was it, that was all. She must have an answer.

Why had he done it? Why had he done it to her? It was the only key to the door, the one thing that could save her. Why—just why. Why me? Why then and why that? Had she angered him? Done something wrong? Or was it—who knew? Who knew what she was trying to guess? Her imagination faltered and sputtered. She could not conceive of what the truth might possibly be.

No wonder her heart had rushed out to that girl. Hers was the only real question, the one it is our right to ask, and for which we're entitled to answers.

Anna stopped, aware how her rivers had met. Yes, we.

She and me also. All of us, anyone with a reason for needing the why.

ANNA LOOKED DOWN at her hands. Their skin seemed sickly in the bleached, halogen light. Her veins were like roads on an old map.

The room was functional and harsh. One wall was covered by shelves; on them lay vases, bowls in need of repair. There was no window and Anna felt suddenly that she was somewhere very deep within the city. The idea of the street and the sidewalk seemed a great distance away. Why hadn't she run, she wondered to herself. He'd never have gotten close.

"How old are you?"

It was the man who spoke—the one who, when she turned, was already striding toward her, his face angry with knowing. I think you have something of ours, he said as he reached her. He held the door shut while she shifted the paper from one hand to the other and offered him the small silver box. Follow me, he pointed to the back. The woman at the register let out a sad sigh as they passed. Oh, sweetie, she said.

"Sixteen."

The man grunted.

"Do you think our work doesn't matter?"

"No," she said softly.

"Do you think you're the only person in the world?"

"No."

"There's no point," the woman began. She had entered and stood against the desk with her arms crossed.

The man quieted her with a wave.

"Do you think other people don't matter?"

Anna looked up at him. Her eyes were wet. She shook her head.

Sighing, he stood. He opened his mouth as if to speak but changed his mind, looking at her instead with a complete, impersonal anger. After a moment, he reached to pick up the phone. As he did, his arm grazed her shoulder. Anna shuddered. He dismissed this with a look of bored irritation.

"Spare us," he said, setting it before her.

She could already see how things would go: there'd be no need for sirens or lights, just two tired officers laughing as they drove to the station. Perhaps one would give her advice. As they arrived, others would chuckle. Her? She's the one getting booked?

"OK," he said, lifting the receiver. "Now you're going to call your dad."


SHE HADN'T TOLD ANYONE. Did she want to? Of course. And of course not. How could it be anything other than both? She couldn't imagine living like this forever, but the only thing worse was the thought of what it would mean to confess.

In dreams, she'd sometimes come close, but even then she never got all the way there. She'd be about to speak—always to someone she couldn't quite place—when suddenly there arrived the sound of an approaching train, and Anna would realize they were standing just feet from the tracks. Not in a dangerous way, but near enough that as she actually said the words cars would be thundering by, devouring her voice like a thresher. Then it passed and they'd nod at each other, she and this person, in a polite, hopeful way. It was clear nothing had been heard and Anna felt sure she wouldn't say it again. That was when she woke up.

What did she fear? Everything, all at once. That telling will make it real, that it won't belong only to her. She feared both that her parents would be mad, and that they wouldn't; that they'd be too sad, or not enough. Maybe people will talk, maybe no one will care. And what will they think? What will they wonder? Will they believe her? Would it be worse if they do? Whomever she tells will hear and react, they will think things and do them; she will no longer have any say. She'll be changed in their eyes. Even though she's already different, the moment someone sees her this way the spell's cast for good. And whoever it is will tell people, too; eventually everyone does. The story will slip from her hands like something dropped through a drain on the street. And where will it go? What will it mean? How will things change?

Perhaps, Anna thought, if she simply managed, just gave it some time and got herself under control, then like a bad meal it might be digested—unpleasant at first, but eventually gone and forgotten. What a lovely idea. She could almost believe.

Plus, even if she were going to tell, what was it exactly she'd say? Hands were not weapons; people touched people all the time. What if the words she chose weren't right, or weren't true? What if they didn't convey what it had been to be her? Sometimes she almost wished he'd done more, that it had been worse; at least then it would be more obvious what she had to confess. If only she could just say, He raped me. Everyone knew what that meant. But then again no; no, of course not. How indulgent to think. What an affront to everyone for whom that was true.

And then there was the last question, the most thorny and hateful of all. Would anyone even want to know? It hadn't occurred to her to wonder, not at first. But when it came, the answer seemed as blunt and obvious as a wall.

It was December and warm. The week before Christmas. Storefronts glittered hopefully, but the streets were slicked with dark, dirty rain. Friday arrived. She knew what it meant, it came every year: tonight was dinner at the Fords'. Anna waited until early evening, lest she risk leaving time for it to be moved. Then she came down the stairs—hair wild and tangled, voice a conjured, dry whimper.

"I don't feel good," she said, sitting sadly on the last step.

"Oh, honey," said Claire. She crossed the room and lay a hand on her head.

"It's my stomach."

Her mother wrinkled her chin and sighed, stroking her cheek. Amos came in.

"Gritty," he said of her appearance.

"She's not feeling well."

"Shoot." Her father looked at his watch. "Are you sure?"

Anna nodded, curling her toes into the rug.

"Damn," he said with a twinge. "Damn. I was excited."

She knew it was true. He'd been bouncy all week, eager in his earnest way. It was Christmas in general he loved, but also this dinner. And in his disappointment Anna saw what she hadn't before: that no one would want her to tell. She'd not realized at first, but the logic was perfectly clear—how much they loved their own lives, how obsessed they all were. Every day, every meal. There was no end to what they found precious.

"And you're completely sure?" He grinned with a coy, pleading humor.

"Yes, Dad," she said. "Trust me, everyone will be happier if I'm not there."

"Not everyone."

She smiled, she thought she might cry. She wanted him gone.

"Fine, everyone but you."

He gave her a curt servant's nod, then vanished into the hall, leaving her with her thoughts, the silent kitchen, freckles of rain on the glass.

Anna knew it was because he loved their family that he was sad. Her mother did, too, but not in the same way. Her dad's was the boyish delight of a child who's been given the thing he wanted so much he'd not dared even ask. Perhaps Anna hadn't stopped to think that she loved him for this, but she did—she loved the idea of his being happy. Growing up so often felt painful and hard, but watching him gave her hope that it could also be fun. And Emerson was part of all that. They went back forever, the two of them; what they had was older than she.

At this thought Anna felt a sudden shiver of new feeling: anger, then more. Rage, announced like a brick through plate glass. How dare he? How dare her father make her feel bad? How dare he make her wonder what she should do? It was his friend, after all; it was *his* fucking friend. Didn't he know who Emerson was? How could he not have any idea?

"How could you *not know*?" Anna hissed.

She'd said it aloud. She was stunned by the sound of her voice. It was such an obvious question. Had she really not wondered until now? Or was it there all along—shifting, rotting, like the crack in a tooth that has finally split. But as fast as it came it was gone, and Anna felt bowled over by a swell of regret. Her dad hadn't done anything; he never would. It was just the idea of his happiness she hated—that it existed meant it was something to break. She hated that she hated it, too. What was worse than resenting your own father's joy? She could not think. Everything was poisoned; the floor of her mind was littered with shards. She had no idea how to get out.

ANNA LOOKED AT THE PHONE in the man's hand. She followed his arm to his shoulder and across to his impatient eyes. The light hummed overhead. Her shirt was stiff with dried sweat.

"Can I have a minute?"

"So you can decide how to lie?"

"Because my head hurts," she said.

Chastened, he set it down and recrossed his arms. The woman pressed herself away from where she'd been leaning. As she left, she put a hand on Anna's shoulder.

"It's not good, what you did, but it's not so big a deal."

Anna nodded. Not in agreement but to show that she'd

heard. What she could never have begun to explain, to them or to herself, was that her mind was filled with only one thing. His neck, the back of his neck. Emerson's neck was all she could see.

That morning—the morning after the night—Anna had decided: she wouldn't not leave her room; she wouldn't cower upstairs. So she'd swallowed, washed her face, and come down to the kitchen. His back was turned toward her; in his hand, a knife worked at the cold butter; and there, along the edge of his hair, a crescent of pale skin. A sliver, an eyelash of white. It confessed his haircut and summer of sun.

Into this she poured her fury. That he could get a haircut at all, that he might think to himself that he should. It was a thought she had sometimes, a thought everyone did. And if they shared that, what else was his, too? Everything. All of it. The relief of finding keys in a coat, the sigh one lets out when stooping to reach for a pen. Plus thirst, fear, even boredom. He must have hopes. He must have songs that he loved. As did she, as did she. All these things that made them the same.

Her anger was drenched in sadness she could not wring out. The thought of his neck made her heart break—for herself, perhaps even for him. Anna wanted to plead, to explain to the space between where he was tanned and where he was not, that they were the same, to ask why he'd done it when they were exactly the same. The faint rim of skin was the only true thing about him. No one could see it but her.

"OK," the man said. He tapped the phone with one finger, thick as a bolt. "Let's go."

HIS NAME HAD BECOME like a mine. Hidden under the stairs or in the garden, wired to blow when the piano was played. It would appear suddenly—Amos saying of a new restaurant, Oh, Emerson went and he didn't like it—to detonate its three crushing blows. Every time felt new. She was torn open again, her insides mangled and raw.

Though it sickened her to admit, it carried the same electric current one feels when a teacher calls out the name of a crush. It created an intimacy no one else saw. To the ignorant speaker they were just sounds, just shapes on a page. But she knew their history, the feelings and acts disguised in each letter's curve.

Did she hate him? She wanted to. She knew that she should and she had every right. And there were glimpses at first, like when she imagined him saying to Sophie, How's Anna? Have you talked to her lately? The thought made her want to wrench his jaws open, climb into his mouth and scrape her name off his tongue. That isn't yours, she'd say. Don't fucking touch what's not yours.

But that was anger, not hate. Righteous hate was just an idea, a theory of cause and effect. And when Anna tried it, it never felt true, never led anywhere but back to herself. No, she didn't hate him. Aspiring to do so was like falling for the trap in a maze whose designers know the key to despair lies in long, straight paths. Following them, one cannot help thinking they've solved it, that around the next bend they'll be free.

The hatred Anna craved was like a clean, bloodless incision, an unread letter tossed in the fire. But try as she might, it refused to come. Even when she smudged out his face, made him just arms and hands, it still didn't work. He was who she'd known—the same man who for so long had been good. All these years, her whole life. The best parts could not be erased.

Like the game he'd invented for making lunch. La Panini Bohème, Sophie named it. The kitchen's yours, he proclaimed, the whole thing, while the girls set about crafting sandwiches. He made one, too, peeking over their shoulders, then shielding his bread from view. Hey, no laughing, he said when they did. This is serious business. Finally, they presented them to be grilled. He accepted their plates with a nod, his gaze humorless, severe as a judge. At last, each was divided into four squares. They sat at high stools. Chewing slowly, forming their thoughts. Around them, jars and knives were scattered, sections of cheese deformed by crude, greedy cuts. OK, he would begin. So what do we think? What did we learn? Why does this one have three different mustards?

Once Anna had thought to try Brie with apples and figs. Had she seen it on a menu or in a window somewhere? Perhaps. But it felt daring, original. Exquisite, he'd said with a flourish. Then he smiled, his face sincere and collegial. For the first time, I think one of these might actually be good. This was how he could be. Just a word, even a glance. And she would feel like she mattered, that she was important and real.

She could go on. There were so many more. The movies, the forts, the puppets, the afternoon when she, then ten or eleven, helped him seal Christmas cards. Sophie had refused and left to go read a book. But Anna stayed, watching as he turned the wax over the flame and let it fall in thick, decadent drops. You're on ring duty, he'd said. It was gold, slightly burnished; for the seal, a sprig of ivy under a stag. Don't lift it up right away, he instructed. Let it dry until it tugs. And she did. He'd given her this task. He'd made her of use.

Of course kids want to be liked: in that sense it was nothing new. But he was different—what he meant to her dad made it matter. Like getting old enough to watch a show Amos loved, or read his first favorite book. Her father was being revealed, his life. She was joining him somewhere, she was arriving and being let in.

All this stood in the way of cold, unalloyed hate. What Emerson had done didn't discolor these memories; if anything, it seemed the opposite. Their lovely details shone brighter, glinted with the sadness of trophies. The thought of seeing him scared her, and yet she longed to as well. She didn't know why and was repulsed by the part of her for which this could be. But there it was: she felt it like illness at the back of the throat. Some days she even believed she'd like to hug him. If she could just squeeze his body, she might feel something true, might touch what his reasons had been.

Then, suddenly, it would all come apart. Her thoughts, her insights, the sense she had made. They were blown over, scattered like leaves in a gale. How needful and grotesque that she could think of him fondly. There must be some darkness in her, some irrevocable flaw. It was no wonder, then, no wonder at all. Of course this had happened to her.

And yet, and yet—in her weakness, she couldn't help but keep asking—how could the person who'd done what he'd done also take such delight in the way bread hissed on a pan? How could both things be true?

THE SHOP OWNER SAID call your father because he was a man, because in his mind that's who dealt with this sort of thing. But what he'd meant was call home, and that's what Anna had done.

As the phone rang, however, it occurred to her to wonder who she hoped would pick up. They'd both be nearby. It was Monday—she looked at the clock on the desk—and just after six. Perhaps they were standing in the kitchen together, one watching as the other chopped carrots.

A few weeks before, Anna had come into the library and found Claire napping on the couch. The room smelled of sleep and cozy bad breath. It was April. A rain had passed. In some places, the sun began to burn through. Claire's eyelids fluttered like paper. Her gaze grew serious and she shifted, revealing a bit of her stomach. The skin was pale, slightly loose, like a stocking bunched at the knee.

As Anna stood in the doorway, she felt something strange, something she wasn't quite able to name. She could slap her or kiss her or bring her some tea; she could go get a blanket and shake it out, as over a baby or a corpse. This helpless woman. Exposed and defenseless, stupid and vulnerable. She was a mother, yes, but also someone who slept down the hall. She had no special powers, no talents; she couldn't solve anything. But it wasn't her fault, wasn't anyone's really. It was just how we all had to be.

Anna looked down at her own feet. Her socks didn't match. She wanted to cry. She was a girl. She was flimsy. She couldn't even pay attention long enough to get dressed. She didn't want to grow up or need to be strong; she didn't want to have to be anything.

The phone was ringing now. Twice, three times. Amos's voice. Relief flooded through her. She'd wanted it to be him, she realized. Her mother was too frail, or too real, or too different. But not her dad. No, they were the same. It had to be him, there was no other way. She felt certain: he'd understand.

YEARS AGO, when Anna was first brave enough to ride her bike with only one hand, she'd loved veering toward a bush, sticking her arm out, and coming away with a fistful of leaves. Life could feel like that, too: as though time hurtled by and existence was formed from what you grabbed. Lately, however, it seemed she couldn't get hold of anything; at the end of each day, she had nothing to show, no way of proving she'd been alive.

She used to be funny. She used to be kind. She used to be mean, too. She used to be lots of things. She used to crave certain foods. Like dumplings on Sundays, or once, for no reason at all, French onion soup. Never mind that it was July and women at bus stops were fanning themselves; she had to have it. The joy was knowing—realizing that, of all the world had to offer, she wanted only this. How far away it seemed now. Not just the heat of the day, but the clarity with which she could say, There, that's the thing.

Before, she would watch, make connections, think thoughts about how it all was. Like the way seeing dogs' breath in the cold made them seem more alive and more like us, with their kindred set of functions and needs. But not anymore. Her mind no longer felt up to the task of new ideas; instead, it just searched its pockets, found only the same lint and change.

More than all this, however, it was showers that upset her the most. Once a source of such comfort, now the feckless water ran down her like words in a dead language: it conveyed no meaning; it did not concern her. When the idea of what he'd done seemed too big to hold, this could still break her heart. She used to be somebody. Not somebody special, but a person who belonged to the world. She'd had things that she loved. Card games, painting, jam on a scone. Now she was a husk. She just ran. She ran and she stole.

"I WOULD'VE DONE the same thing," the man said.

He was talking about the fact that she hadn't told Amos what was the matter. Dad, she'd pleaded. Can you just come? I'm safe, but I'm kind of in trouble. He'd agreed, his voice a mixture of anger and concern. He was leaving now; it would take thirty minutes, he thought.

"How long will he be?"

"Half an hour, he said."

There was a sink in one corner, a basin whose underbelly was rutted with plaster and paint. The man gestured toward it.

"If you want water."

She nodded gratefully.

"Can I ask your advice?"

He laughed thinly and set down his pen.

"Sure."

"For how to tell someone something."

"Don't worry, I'll handle that."

She smiled weakly. "No, about something else."

He looked down at his desk for a moment and seemed to accept that what work he'd been doing was mostly for show.

"OK," he said, sitting back. For an instant, Anna worried he might press her on what it was. But there was safety in his indifference; it was the reason she'd dared. "So why haven't you told anyone yet?"

"Because it might make a lot of things worse."

"Will it make anything better?"

This was the right question.

"I don't know," Anna said truthfully.

"Hm." The chair sighed as he looked at the ceiling. "Well," he said after a pause, "people don't need to know everything."

Anna considered this. "Do you have any kids?"

"No."

She nodded, then stood and went to the sink. Water thudded against the metal. The cup grew cold in her hands.

"I'm sorry," she said. "For stealing, I mean." She was embarrassed it had taken this long.

He said nothing and watched as she sat, then returned to his notes. It was true, Anna was sorry, though that's not why she'd said it. She'd hoped it might keep their conversation afloat. But now she could tell it was over. The illusion of intimacy had passed and with each moment the silence between them grew firmer, more set.

WHATEVER SHE'D ONCE believed her life would be like, it was different now. She had been changed and so she must reimagine the future. Everyone did this—tried to envision how things would be—but for her, Anna felt, it was an act of survival. She had to give herself somewhere to go.

So she laid the pieces together. Intricate, precise. She was building something—a doorway, a ladder. It became grander as she went. It was the only way out.

She would collect art. She would walk the streets alone, a great dog at her side. What a home she must live in, people would think, to own a creature that size. And they would be right. She could see the rooms. From the street one had no idea. But up the stairs and past the black door (of the two locks, she used only one) it threw itself open like the embrace of a friend. Large, vaulted windows. Radiators creaking like bones. There would be plants. Wide leaves, thick as books. In the afternoon, green light on the floor.

She would not smoke. No, that was too obvious. But she would befriend a healer, an old man on a stool at the back of a shop. He would sell her tea and gnarled mushrooms, given with instructions for how long they were to be boiled. Sometimes, in the still, quiet hours of the afternoon, she would make soup. Slowly, with the intensity of a seamstress or monk. And she would be firm; she would be strong. With strangers, with lovers. Everyone would be kept waiting, not one would complain. Men would long to steal glimpses of her. Even the sole of her foot as she dressed—they would promise themselves to remember it always.

As long as her mother and father were alive, she would visit them. If they moved, she might ride the train, borne out from Grand Central to the farm or wherever they were. But she would not stay the night. She would always come home, even when it grew very late.

People would seek her advice. She would not care if they listened, she would not even look at them as she spoke. She would grow old in the city, like one of those trees around which the sidewalk has split and deformed. She would watch restaurants fail. She would not mind as the faces on the street became younger. She would be made safe by how little they knew.

The clarity of all this gave Anna a dry, stony hope. With each detail she felt herself grow stronger somehow. They were like holds in the side of a mountain. They let her believe she wasn't simply stuck in this place.

There was only one thing that seemed never to change: no matter how opulent her vision became, it always felt bloodless and cold. The rooms, the air, even the stove at which she stood stirring broth. Its white metal so icy to the touch she would draw back as if burned.

Why was there no heat? Where had it gone? Perhaps, Anna thought, it was simply a matter of getting there. Yes, she decided, that was the key; one must wear the dress in order to warm it. And on certain days, she could almost believe this life might really save her. But then something would shift—a dog barked, the light changed—and she'd see it for what it was: drab, sad as a cheap set, all make-believe and false backing.

ANNA'S HANDS GREW WARM beneath her thighs. Their moisture clung to the chair. She'd not eaten since the morning, she realized. She felt dazed, almost tired. Her stomach was a cold, dried-out knot.

At first she'd tried to imagine what she would say when her father arrived, but there were any number of ways to explain and she trusted herself. Once, she might have worried, but that was gone. She had skills now. She'd learned how to lie; she could still her face or force it to laugh, could crush her feelings with a swallow. They were like scars, these talents, like things learned in war: even when they were of use, part of her wished not to know. And he was in them, of course. She knew what she knew because she was something Emerson had made.

It was this, the conniving part of her mind, Anna loathed most. Whatever its uses, it left her feeling distant and alone. Because nothing she said was the one thing, everything became a lie, every day an exercise in honing the craft. Hers was the lonely talent of a spy, one whose life becomes real only during those few hours spent alone in an apartment rented under a false name.

She felt it the afternoon when Sophie had arrived at their house without warning and rung the bell. Claire let her in, and Anna, knowing she could no longer be avoided, came down to the foyer, smiling, suggesting they go for lunch nearby. Outside, they walked quietly through the January cold.

"I know we aren't best friends," Sophie said as the waiter set down their plates, "but I still like you and it's nice when we hang out."

Anna felt a wave of sadness for how far she was from her old life. "You're right," she said. "I'm sorry. I just get like this sometimes when I've had a bad week."

Sophie nodded and picked up her fork. "Well, it's been more than a week." She smiled, taking a bite. "But I'm happy to see you, and I know my parents are glad."

Then they were off—talking, confiding, agreeing to ask for more fries when the waiter returned. The hot waiter, Sophie said. Anna gave her a look. Oh, stop, like you wouldn't?

As she'd walked home, what disturbed Anna most was her certainty that Sophie had no idea. She'd thought concealing oneself would be best achieved by moving to the edge of the frame, but the opposite seemed to be true. The key was existing in plain sight, that way people felt comfortable not stopping to wonder or care.

Only rarely did she feel the safety of her solitude threatened. What's up with you, Phoebe once asked after class—Phoebe who'd been tormented for her red cheeks and whose pitiable kindness smacked too much of need. It was no more than a flickering glance of concern, but Anna felt the ground move beneath her. She needed anger, she knew, otherwise it might all tumble down. What kind of question is that, she said, her words lunging like hands for a throat. What kind of dumb fucking question is that? And Phoebe, face wide with confusion and hurt, retreated to the hallway, leaving Anna alone, her eyes already swimming in tears.

EVEN FROM THE BACK ROOM Anna heard it. The bell on the door. A rush of sound from the street. She looked up. She already knew.

Her whole life she'd been feeling the weight of these steps. She'd absorbed them like music; her bones were their shape. They moved around her, moved toward her. Across rugs, onto trains; over bare floors and up stairs. They were like fingerprints at the scene of a passionate crime. On every-thing. The lamp, the knife.

Then the voice they carried spoke and she didn't hear it so much as feel it inside her. Like a shiver, like blood. Each word rose slightly because he was speaking and moving at the same time. This mattered so much—she could never have guessed, but it did. That he hadn't waited to get to the back of the store, that he began talking as soon as he entered. She could see his legs moving with assured, graceful urgency across the glittering room. Not a false step. He was coming, he was there.

"I'm looking for my daughter."

This one line crested like a gentle, confident wave.

She's in here, Anna wanted to say. She made a mistake and things are a mess. She can't really explain, but she's sorry. She won't ruin your life. She's trying as hard as she can to be

good. But she's sad—she's so sad—and she doesn't know
what to do. It's just that she's different now, she isn't the
same, she's having a really hard time. Please don't be mad,
though. Because she's not doing so well, and she's worried
she might not be OK.

III

# 1

Claire's father was visiting when Anna called, having come in for a matinee. The three of them sat like dignitaries: their words, their roles, all decided in advance. Between them, salad and bread, a bottle of Gavi. Claire had made mussels. There were bowls by their plates. John held his napkin in one hand, tapping a finger as he spoke.

"No one does anymore. It's not the end of the world, but you notice these things."

"Don't worry," Amos said, "they still run a pretty tight ship." He turned to Claire. "Remember the fuss when I only wore chaps?"

She allowed his remark a small, accommodating laugh.

"But you do know what I mean," John pressed.

Amos nodded. They were speaking about the fact that passengers no longer dressed well for flights. "Although," he added, "that kind of reverence for innovation does smack of a certain naivety. It's like people who were terrified by the first film of trains."

"I don't see it," John said.

Feeling suddenly tired, Amos shrugged. Claire was working her knife between the gap in a shell which had not fully split.

Her father went on, "Besides, what's to laugh at? There's no victim more defenseless than history. We can judge all we want."

Amos frowned. "I could probably think of one or two."

John was not listening. He had reached to help Claire. Then the phone rang and everyone understood Amos would get it.

SPRING AIR FLOODED the car's open windows. The light changed. He moved with the taxis, his fingers played in the breeze. She'd said she was safe. There was no need to worry.

John had scoffed when Amos asked Claire for the keys. Driving? he said. At this hour? And it was a bit strange, or at least unusual, Amos so often being the one to insist the subway would be best. At first he'd thought it was for Anna, but no, he realized now, it was so that he could feel like things were OK. Because in moments of quiet concern, he reached for the assurance objects could offer. Plus, he did like the car. Smooth and well made, it promised something, it gave him its word.

Ahead, brake lights filled the street. One lane was blocked by a cab. A woman bent by the window counting her change. Amos exhaled. Slow, wishful. He was calm, he wanted to be.

Coming back to the table, he'd said only that Anna had run too far and dropped her money along the way. Whatever the truth actually was could be explained to Claire later, when they were alone.

It annoyed him to be rankled by John. To think of him, even. The phrase alone—my father-in-law—felt obvious and stale. He pictured his face. It was pinched, competitive; despite his wealth, his eyes were like those of an inmate, his body spare and concave. He was cordial with Amos, but his was the warmth of a sweater offered to a guest who has forgotten to pack one. Thoughtful, courteous. It could not be kept or brought home.

Still, John's mere presence offered a kind of cold comfort as well. It was calming, the idea of a father who was just there; who, whatever his faults, could be counted upon to simply be as he was. Like a wall against which you could push, he remained, steady and unconcerned. He would answer the phone. He would fix his car. He would open bills when they came. He would pay them.

Taken by such generous melancholy, Amos would sometimes think to himself, Isn't that what family is? Imperfect people brought together by chance who nonetheless choose to wake up and try, who invest in making things work. And in this kind of mood he could feel himself wanting—craving in his inarticulate core—to call John his father. Just once, even. That would be enough. OK, he might say, flinging a coat over his shoulders, all feigned nonchalance. I'll be back in a bit, Dad. See you when I get home.

But then things would happen. Small, fleeting; impossible, he knew, to ever explain. Like the way it felt to ask where the coffee was kept, or how John ate from Claire's plate, the fact that he still called her Fig. And in these, Amos would glimpse the way for some people, family—the family they're apt to call blood—is like a religion. It has no logic other than faith. It cannot be reasoned with. Time spent together, acts of grace, clever words—all these crumble beneath the turn of its wheel. And when they did, Amos grasped how few assurances he'd really been given. It left him feeling foolish and naive, like the young actor who crosses paths with a man able to make his career and comes away certain he's been promised as much. Only as he tells the story to friends does he realize how little it was, how empty and thin.

AMOS CHANGED LANES. It was his daughter he should be thinking of, his daughter who—he turned at the light—sat waiting a few blocks away. Her body fragile and warm— and safe, he reminded himself; safe but caught in a bind. Whatever precisely that meant.

The city seemed to grow denser as he moved south. Squat buildings crowded the sidewalk; filthy windows, small plants on the sills. Night was falling, lamps were being turned on. The car came to a stop. Its engine exhaled. All at once, Amos felt weak and inept. Fear invaded him. Across the street, the name of the place she had said.

He was glad he hadn't called John his dad. That would've been wrong. A dad was a person whose caring was urgent, who struggled to open the door as he did now—fumbling, in a rush. It was someone who left the lights on, who didn't realize he'd forgotten the keys.

## 2

The air was lush, near, like that of a coat closet. Alleys cast in shadow, people coming home from the day. Ahead, a shout of laughter, women's voices, shoes clicking like the nails of a dog.

Anna was several steps behind him. Her unreadable face cast down, her small sullen mouth. She carried one arm like a wing and for an instant Amos was seized with the desire to yank her by the hand as if she were a dawdling child. It was pathetic, the way she was moving, or perhaps just for show.

He hadn't decided how to feel or what to think, but he was glad to be out of the shop. The presence of others had confused things. Now it was only them.

"Dad," she said. She pointed toward the car.

The lights were streaming into the dusk, the door hung open like a jaw.

He stopped. What went through him was mostly shock and relief, but within this was something sheepish as well. The whole image seemed to reveal him somehow. Like a glimpse of someone caught dressing or stumbling on the curb.

Amos sucked his teeth. "Good thing the thieves were all busy."

He regretted having said this. It was both too mean and too kind; it skipped necessary steps. He turned before he risked smiling and walked on, leaving his daughter to follow.

INSIDE, THEY SAT. The cobbled street like rumpled fabric. The deep, fragrant night. Anna turned. His face was mostly hidden. Only a bit of his cheek like a sliver of moon. She asked it before she could think.

"Will you tell Mom?"

At this, Amos discovered his anger.

"Anna, what the fuck?"

She looked at her lap.

"Of course I'll tell Mom."

He was right, she knew. The question demeaned them both. Amos turned off the car. They would sit here until she decided to speak.

"It's school . . . ," she began weakly, her voice betraying the fact that she had no idea how the sentence would end.

"Stop."

Silence.

He went on. "How long have you been doing this?"

His certainty shocked her. Anger she'd anticipated, but somehow—foolishly, perhaps—not this.

"What?" Anna said. It was all she could muster.

"How long?"

"Dad, I don't—"

"You don't give a shit about a cigarette lighter."

He'd been looking straight ahead. Now he turned to watch her face. The way he knew broke her heart. Someone else, her mother, would've berated her for starting to smoke. But he knew that she didn't, or that even if she'd begun, somehow that wasn't the point.

"I just—" she began. She swallowed, pausing until the weakness had passed. "I don't know how to explain. It just helps calm me down."

For a moment he said nothing.

"But why—"

She cut him off. "And sometimes things seem so big. I don't know. Like I can't figure out what I'm trying to do, or just—that life, I don't know. My thoughts get all tangled up."

He scratched at the back of his head. What do children deserve to know? How much truth is their right? Was it wrong not to tell her? Wrong to sit here and let her feel badly without knowing that he was the same? The same but worse. She was only sixteen. A child. How old had he been? Twenty, twenty-five, nearly thirty before he'd been forced to call Emerson from that makeshift cell at the back of the store and resolved to finally stop.

"You're lucky."

"I know."

"Do you?"

"Yes, Dad."

Amos let out a breath.

"Do you think you can stop?"

"I want to."

"What if you realize you can't?"

Here again: the thing no one else would've said. She longed to hug him. She could almost feel herself do it. The awkward way she'd twist to lean over the seat, how the buckle would dig into her hip. Then they'd drive home together and he would park, the trees whispering as they both shut their doors. Inside, her mother would greet them with glad, needing eyes. Let's all sit down, she would say. It would be a hard night, but things would go on.

He asked it again. "What if you can't?"

Anna knew what he wanted to hear.

"Then I'll tell you."

He nodded and put a hand on her head.

"What?" she asked.

Amos said nothing.

"Dad, I'm fine."

As he reached for the keys Anna felt a sad sort of relief, the melancholy of a successful disguise.

Amos looked at her. Knees pressed together, legs slung toward the door. Her weight, the way that she was. It wasn't all right. She wasn't. Suddenly he felt an angry lurch of disgust. It was for himself, he realized, that he'd been so willing to accept her reasons, in order not to have to explain. Because who knew better than him? He who spent years with his own habit of small theft; who, when asked the same question—why?—knew the challenge wasn't finding the answer but in giving words to something so impossibly big.

Amos rubbed his eyes with the heels of his palms. Anna

felt herself tense. Why had he stopped? Why wasn't he starting the car?

"There's no way, Anna. There's no way it's just that."

"It is." She paused, trying to make herself mad. "How
would you know?"

He accepted this as though fielding a toss. Calm, unhur-
ried.

"Because it never is."

She hadn't been ready. She was fraying; she felt herself
become threads.

"You don't know," she said. Her voice angry, insistent on
the partial truth it contained.

"I do."

"No."

"Anna, I do."

For an instant, she wondered: could he possibly? No, no;
there was simply no way.

"That's not true. You might think you do . . ." Her words
trembled like cups. "But you don't. You don't have any idea."

"I do," he said. His voice came louder now, with the resolve
of confession. "I did this, too. I did the same exact thing."

She turned. The soft skin of her ear, the bone beneath her
left eye. One by one her features moved into the light.

"What do you mean, the same thing?"

"I stole. I took things. Not for any good reason. Just because I was scared."

For a moment she sat quietly, considering this like a strange
coin.

"When you were my age?"

"No," he said, laughing disgustedly. "No, much older."

Again she paused.

"So what?"

It was a plea, almost a dare. Would he press her? Would he insist that she do the thing she most wanted but hadn't the strength to manage alone?

"So I know how it is. The way it can help, or seem like it helps. With something bigger you can't figure out."

"How can you tell?" She recognized her voice now. It was the one with which she'd ask what he thought of a painting or a paper she'd written for school; it was, Anna guessed, the same one she'd used when asking to be picked up and carried.

"Because I know you. Anna, I know you." He was smiling in his loose, easy way. He held out his hand. "Since this. Since you were like this. Like a cantaloupe. Or the world's biggest tomato."

Her laugh lived only a moment.

"It's—I don't—" She was crying now. Her words were all fragments. "I don't know, I don't know."

"Don't know what?"

"How to say it."

"Just . . ." He shrugged as if that alone might convince her.

She swallowed.

"A thing happened to me. When we were—when we were visiting. When we were upstate."

Anna turned. He'd grown quiet. His eyes were fearful and still. When he spoke it was slow, almost patient, like someone withdrawing their arm from a trap.

"Anna. Did someone . . ." He could not finish. He wasn't strong enough. His mind lacked the courage, the will.

She nodded. Or tried to. Her head felt heavy and thick; it was too much to move. Then she shivered, the air cool against her wet cheeks.

"Emerson," she said, turning to watch his face.

It was a strange, unexpected sound, curious and out of place. For an instant Amos felt relieved. That name was so plain and familiar: he'd misunderstood.

"Emerson what?"

Anna felt herself sink. She'd come so far, had thought she'd arrived. And yet. Would she really have to go on?

Amos started to speak again, his voice soft in the car's entombed quiet.

"Emerson . . ."

"He was the one. The one who—"

Every possible word was grotesque. The thought of them all made her ill.

"The one who what, Anna?"

The softness was gone. These words came stony and cold. Something was rising underneath, she felt it rush toward her. A moment of calm and then he was shouting. His voice crashed like a wave thrown up by a tremor below.

"Who what, Anna? What the fuck are you saying?"

"Dad," she wept.

A silence between them, holy and fleeting, like the moment between peals of a bell.

"I don't . . . ," he began. Softly once more, almost inaudible. "What do you mean, he was the one?"

She tried to find his eyes, but they were covered, or shut. He held his head in his hands.

"It was on the last night, when I went upstairs. It was just so fast, it was just—I was just there to do laundry."

"What was so fast?"

"He grabbed me and then . . ." She looked down at herself. At her small shorts. Her thin, angular legs. Could he just understand? Could she convey it like that? Could there be some way besides words?

The world swam. His thoughts slid, crashed into themselves like things on the deck of a ship. He was cold and then weak, hot and unwell. He turned to her; he reached out a hand. The feel of her skin brought him back. Edges returned to their shapes. She was there. Her face. Her impossible face. It was looking at him. It was needing him now. She had no idea—how weak he was, really; how unfit; how far from the person he needed to be.

"Dad," she said. He was touching her cheeks, he was hugging her. His lungs, she could feel them. Lurching and coughing as tears fell into her hair.

"Dad," she said, "Dad. Stop crying."

"No," Amos said, "I can't. I don't want to."

This terrible weight. She'd been holding it for so long. She was emptying her pockets, her drawers. She ripped books from the shelves, hurled them into the pile. Everything, every last piece. It had to come now.

"I don't know," she said. "I don't know. I don't know what to do—all the time, every minute—I don't know what to do. I wake up and look around and then—" The thought splintered and cracked. "I don't know what to do. I never—I feel like a window, like glass. And everything—it doesn't matter who it is—if it's you or it's Mom—it doesn't matter. Everything feels like a hammer is tapping. Or a rock. I don't know." She moved her arms helplessly. "I just feel hollow and thin."

He must speak, Amos knew. He was her father: he had to do something, at least find some sounds to make. But every time he tried, he felt himself stall and slip back. All these days, he thought, all these days since it happened. He'd been there the whole time—looking at her, talking to her. But not knowing. Not suspecting a thing.

"Anna," he said slowly. "I need to be sure. Is there any chance—"

"Dad," she sobbed. "Dad. I know, OK? I know what happened to me."

How awful it would be to remember that she'd understood without his needing to finish. His doubt announced itself from afar, his unloving mistrust.

"I'm sorry," he said. Feeble, pathetic, sincere most of all.

"I just want to think," she cried. "I just want to think about whatever I want."

Then, stillness. Everything was gone out of them. They could sit there for an hour without speaking, throats moving like frogs. Finally, Anna turned.

"Can we go home?"

He nodded. He did not speak. The headlights flung themselves down the street. In the dark, his hand reached for hers. It grew hot as they drove. The city poured by like rain. The air was still sweet. Her life had changed. He would not let go.

## 3

Would it have been different if John hadn't been there? Had Amos not, in a moment of inscrutable rudeness, lifted one hand when his father-in-law tried to insist that Anna couldn't possibly be too sick for the politeness of coming downstairs. It was a shocking gesture: his palm held out like that, as though to quiet a child, or a dog.

Right away he could feel the violation of terms. The room knew, the chairs. Claire let out a small breath. Honey, she said, as if offering a boy the chance to correct his mistake. That was enough. John waved it away, wielding his power as false magnanimity.

It wasn't just this minor clash which made Amos wonder, but John's having been there at all. His presence seemed to remind Claire of something—an ethic, a system of instinct as deep and invisible as the way a family behaves over breakfast. When he came to visit, she hardly resisted; her manner was both lazy and eager, like an exhausted child being tucked into bed.

Even so, Amos would never have guessed the evening might end as it did, with him lying beside her, eyes open to the dark, wondering whether she believed a word of what their daughter had said.

AFTER JOHN LEFT, Claire had gone in search of Amos. She found him in the kitchen. He was scrubbing intently; dishwater lapped faintly, clicking like tongues. It was the deathly moment after a guest has gone: particles of them still hang in solution, the house is not yet returned to itself.

She felt angry. Or rather, upset. More than was fair; enough that it seemed almost disloyal. But as was often the case, what struck her most was how easy it would've been for Amos to simply leave it be. Yes, her father could grate; his arrogance was acute. But so what? Who cared? Why pick fights when it cost so little to just get along?

Claire pursed her lips and ushered a few loose strands of hair behind each ear.

"What was that all about?"

He turned. His cheeks were stained, his eyes exhausted and weak.

"Whoa," she said gently. She went toward him. He received her; she felt his lungs empty. He looked up at the ceiling, the pots overhead. One breath. Another. Slow, fluttering, reluctant and afraid.

"Listen . . . ," he began before saying the rest.

Her hand found her face. A gesture from movies, from art. She looked at him, her mind turning over the words.

Later, Amos would accuse her of how calm she'd been, as though it were proof of some crime. And while Claire rejected the idea of what he thought it meant, the truth was that she did feel a staid sense of command. This had long been her way; it was, perhaps, why the work of doctoring suited her well. Medicine was the province of minds that didn't flee from risk or catastrophe, but imposed upon them the order of truth. Indeed, she'd always felt a visceral unease around people who lost their composure. When friends cried, she might be able to calm them, but beneath the show of concern was a condescending, almost hateful disdain.

So perhaps it had been the tortured look on Amos's face and the way it robbed him of handsomeness. Or maybe it was just that his obvious need for help made her want to withhold it. Not consciously, of course, but as one recoils instinctually from a festering sore. Whatever it was, she had taken the things he was saying and not simply absorbed them, but laid them out like garments across her bed. What fit and what didn't, how might some things work together. These were the questions worth asking, the ones he was too upset to see.

At last she spoke.

"Amos, it doesn't make any sense."

WHAT HAD HE THOUGHT she would say? He couldn't be sure, but never something so antiseptic as that. Stunned, he could think of only one question. It came in the meek voice of a needling child.

"Why does it have to make sense?"

This question enraged her, Amos could tell. He watched it spread beneath the skin of her face.

"He's your best friend. I've known him for fifty fucking years. Think, Amos."

"I know who he is."

"I just—Amos, it doesn't make sense. I don't mean she's lying, I just mean—sometimes girls—" She paused. "There are things you don't understand."

"What I don't understand is how this is the conversation we're having."

"Which one should we be having?"

"I don't know," he said. "I don't fucking know. But not this."

Her face betrayed the hint of an incredulous smile.

"Are you drinking milk?"

"Am I—" He looked down at the glass and the carton in his hand. When had he poured it? He had no idea. His hands were simply moving, his body in search of something to do.

"What the fuck, Claire?"

She turned toward the living room, then stopped. He watched her precise mind form the question like an engineer testing the strength of a joint.

"Wait," she said. "Where was she? She called you to get her so that she could tell you all this?"

It had gone wrong, he realized. It was a mistake that might matter. Having not realized the need to present certain things in a particular order, he was left to describe what Anna had done as though it were his confession to make.

With one hand on the counter, Claire touched her forehead.

"Amos . . . ," she began.

"It's a fucking cigarette lighter."

"And?"

"She wouldn't just do this."

"Plainly she would."

"I mean for no reason."

Claire laughed acidly.

"You mean it's because of him?"

"Not literally."

She let out a breath.

"Something happened to her, I believe that. She's upset and that breaks my heart." Claire pressed her hands together as she might when offering instruction to a patient's family. "Tomorrow I'm going to hug her and sit on her bed and let her explain why she would've done this."

Amos felt himself weaken slightly, his tone more plaintive than mad.

"Why would she lie?"

"Because she fucking stole, Amos. That's what kids do when they steal. Because kids lie—girls especially—at this age most of all."


THEY'D SPOKEN SOME MORE, though the substance was lost to him now. Eventually Claire stood and smoothed her pants. Nothing's made better by getting no sleep, she said with a sigh. He nodded, following her up the stairs.

As he did, Amos found himself overcome with exhausted relief. That anything could be normal, that even after a night such as this they could still stand at the sink—brushing, rinsing, waiting to spit—was a source of deep comfort. Known rhythms; the habits of their dense, dependable life.

Plus, he'd extracted from her at least one promise: that she would not contact Emerson. Not yet. Not before he did. Not until they both felt more in command of themselves, until Claire had spoken with Anna, until they had a shared sense of what they intended to do. And this mattered. That he had asked it of her and she'd said yes allowed Amos to feel that what took place wasn't an erosion of his convictions, but a discussion between equals, partners who cared most of all about what was best for their child.

Once in bed, he discovered with more than a little chagrin that he could barely keep his eyes open. Shouldn't a father be unable to sleep? Shouldn't he spend the night pacing, planning, setting things right? He'd not even checked whether she was awake, or gone in to say something kind. Like that he loved her and it was all right, that he believed her, that of course he knew she was telling the truth. And he did, didn't he? He was sure, almost certain. It was just that—wasn't the best world the one in which she was lying? Asked what he wanted most of all, wouldn't he have said it was for Claire to be right?

His thoughts had begun to mist over. He felt his fingers

loosen, the jerk of one leg. He reached weakly for Claire. The shape of her. She was so warm, her breath hot and close. She did have a point, didn't she? Never mind, never mind. There was no need to decide. He would just—he would wake up and see. Things would be clearer when he wasn't so heavy, so drenched with sleep.

A last thought, as if spoken: Hey, muskrat. Hey. Don't worry. Don't worry, I'm coming.

# 4

How quickly a mind could be filled. To walk or take a cab, whether to deal with the pebble in one's shoe. The matter of lunch. Was bitter the right word to describe how arugula tastes? The way the woman under the awning, a run in her stocking, shielded her cigarette from the wind. And what had Sophie meant about not being the one in need of perspective? Lately his teeth had begun to feel old; he was sometimes afraid of an apple. His nails needed cutting. He should organize the photos of his father; there might come a day when someone was glad to have them all in one spot. A phone ringing. Questions to answer. These papers there, those papers here. And then home. Chewing, talking, dishes, and bed. His hand reaching up to the lamp. The day winking out. Darkness at last. All of which was simply to say: Emerson thought of it far less than he would've guessed.

Days would pass with not even a flicker, and for the

briefest of instants it could feel almost as though he'd forgotten. The mere fact things appeared normal seemed to confirm his sense that it might not really have happened—or, if it had, that it was mostly accidental, taking place during a strange schism, a period capable of being left behind.

Of course that wasn't true. It was still there, like a lump in the skin. And when something brushed past, he would realize he'd been feeling it all along, had never once stopped.

That's how it had been when Claire called. She'd said she wanted to talk about Amos and there was no reason to think this wasn't true. Emerson's face showed nothing, no more than the briefest of shadows. But inside was a feeling of readiness. Not fear so much as anticipation, the spring-loaded way one waits for a knock at the door. Yes, he said, absolutely. She should come by whenever.

Then there were other times—a moment before sleep, or with his eyes shut in the shower—when it would return, fully formed and alive. A spasm of color and light, the feeling of moisture and skin. Cramped air in the small, fragrant room; the hot smell of her fear. It was total, subsuming, almost distorted by clarity. And when it came, his mind flailed to keep any one thing in focus, like turning a gem and trying to follow a particular glint.

It was not, however, something he could summon at will. Such attempts always proved lifeless and flat. It had to simply burst forth, plunging up through the dark of his thoughts. And in a sense, he preferred it like this. The uncertain thrill, the potential of each passing moment to pluck at this hidden, electric chord.

Exhilarating as it could sometimes be, this was the excep-

tion to the way he generally felt, which was normal and un-
fazed, calm, even bored. For most hours of most days his
life simply went on. It was why it had been so easy—amazing
to say, but yes, easy was the right word—to spend time with
Amos. Most shocking of all, their friendship seemed better
these last few months. It was like the tender, sedate peace
after a cleansing fight and the fuck that follows: the air had
been cleared; the traffic was gone. They were closer for having weathered the storm.

In addition to calling each other throughout the day, they'd
returned to their habit of dinner without children or wives.
Not deliberately, but with an unspoken ease that made it
all the more pleasant, graceful, familiar. Even when Amos
brought Anna up, Emerson felt himself listening closely,
thinking hard about what advice he could give.

"Girls," he said with a sad sigh after hearing how she'd
taken to running and lost visible weight. "Girls and their
bodies."

He went on. "The key, I think, is to listen. Don't talk
about the exercise itself, just see how she is."

It was the right thing to say. And more than a little bit
brave. Because what if Amos did ask? What if she gave the
one answer? That was a risk he'd been willing to take to
help his friend, to give him the tools to be a good father.
And how bad could someone who did that really be? What
did a word like bad even mean?


THEN THERE WAS the question of regret and whether he
felt it. Surely he must, Emerson thought. After all, it wasn't

just bad but wrong. To make sure, he turned on himself like a finger-wagging schoolmarm. Are you sorry, he asked. Yes, he answered. How sorry? Very. I won't ever do it again.

The last part he meant. Of that he felt certain.

Perhaps it had something to do with the risk, or that what first compelled him was wrapped up in the unforeseen shock. But whatever the reason, this certainty mattered—his promise that no, there would not be a next time. For what moves us more than a tale of redemption? How much lovelier when the man teaching violin once served a sentence for aggravated manslaughter? The lesson was clear: we must be allowed to move past what we've done. Bread must be made; trains must continue to come.

He'd hoped such poetic logic might settle things, yet sometimes a feeling would arrive to blot out his thoughts. Not often—perhaps once every few weeks—but when it happened he'd find himself, glass in hand, staring into the sink without any idea what he was trying to do. Or he'd cough awake in the night, gasping as though having been pulled ashore from a wreck. He rarely fell back asleep. Instead he lay, breathing slowly, alert to a choked feeling of amorphous and paralyzed dread. As the hours wore on, this was replaced by an acute loneliness, a sense of something that could not be outrun. Like checking one's account and finding all the money's been spent, not knowing why or when or on what.

It would be easy enough to label such moments the symptoms of a troubled unconscious. And some days he did. But in a more hopeful mood, Emerson could get by on a belief that it was merely life in all its rich tapestry. Because people coughed, lost track of their thoughts, misplaced keys, and felt sad, all without it meaning one goddamn thing. So what made him special? What really mattered? Perhaps the idea of mattering itself was the problem, a wrong turn based on an illegible map. Maybe nothing was anything. And if he was right, maybe that was the cause for these bouts: they were merely symptoms of his having freed himself for a journey which must be made alone.

This kind of thinking offered some comfort, but not without feeling like a desperate sort of dance. Ducking and twirling as if to avoid the stabs of a tireless foe. And when it did, fear crept in, intimations of forces unseen. Then, trapped, he would come to, like the student awoken by a hand crashing down on his desk. Ah, right, sorry, yes, where was he? The living room. Retsy. Her face. Her mouth and its question. Yes, no—the garbage—no, he hadn't yet but he would.

FINALLY, ANNA. What about her? When it came to his friend's daughter, the first few weeks left him vacillating between vivid extremes. Some days he felt an intense closeness, as though they'd been melded together. Crazy as it was, moments would pass when he'd be certain he could describe exactly her feelings at that very second. Never mind that he had no idea where she was, what linked them was delicate and invisible, a gossamer strand that stretched across the city and along which traveled the vibrations of their innermost truths. Did she think of him, too? Could she feel what he felt? In those instants he was sure that she must. Then, with a flash, this would be replaced by the cold and deathly fear that he might turn the corner to find her waiting, arms crossed, feet planted like ballasts. What would she want? What would he do? He knew he couldn't approach her. Her eyes were fixed on a point beyond reason: no charming words might bring them back.

With time, however, this began to dim. The intimacy faded; it became a struggle to imagine where she might be, and the sense of her emotions grew vague as distant, inaudible shouts. The fear, too, seemed to have gone. If she planned to tell, surely she would've already? Though he couldn't say what they were, she must have her reasons. Perhaps one day he might even ask. He imagined the two of them talking like old men, soldiers in the same army who've not seen each other since the end of the war.

And though lately he thought of her less, when Anna did cross his mind Emerson soothed himself with the idea of particulars. She must have read articles, ordered a root beer with lunch, bought a shirt or a new pair of shoes. Surely she'd been given a test at some point, had studied and received her grade. And he hoped she'd done well. He was rooting for her with what could only be described as fatherly pride.

Her future, too, was real to him. He saw how it would be. She'd meet boys. The first would be weak, the next cruel. But eventually her eye would mature and she'd begin to cut through like a scythe. He could picture them all, even the one she might nearly marry.

Peter. He would cover sports for a magazine. He would be kind. He would tell bland, inoffensive jokes and villainless stories, his voice soft as an old coat. One in particular Anna would hate. It was about his grandmother having eaten chocolates so quickly she'd forgotten they ever arrived. You know, that's not funny, Anna would say as they drove home from a dinner at which he'd told it again. OK, he'd reply. Well, I think it is. He'd be speaking in the tone he used to disagree, all doubt and poor posture. He was twigs. She could crush him. She would.

What explained the clarity with which Emerson saw this? Why bother at all? It was a dream he was building, one that had to come true. He knew she could go on and be great, make herself into whatever she wanted. What mattered was that she wasn't still up in that room, that her life hadn't stopped like one of those clocks found frozen in the rubble of an earthquake. In this, his need to believe, Emerson felt most exposed. Because if some part of her was, if the image he'd conjured weren't true, then—

Here: a catch in his throat.

# 5

Amos sat in his office. Across from him, legs tucked beneath her, a woman was speaking. She described her day, how it had gone wrong from the start. To begin with, her boyfriend hadn't called until nearly lunch, and when he did, it was only to ask whether she might be free that night.

"I don't know," she said. She held out her hands, palms toward the ceiling. "I just want something more—fulsome?"

A moment later he would be crushed, but first, Amos smirked. Dumb, doglike. The woman hadn't noticed, but he was already off, his thoughts whisked away. He saw Emerson's face, its self-serious, quizzical tilt.

So, are we going Full Sam?

JULY IN AMAGANSETT. It's for Sam Hackett's wedding they've come. Beyond the tent, the house looms like an ocean liner. Grass—soft, black—runs to the edge of the lawn. The sea sleeps.

Emerson sits, his arm draped across Retsy's chair. She turned thirty last month; Sophie will not be born for another four years. Amos looks toward the bar where Claire waits for a drink. The speeches are over, the band has come on.

It begins in his hands, the toe of the foot of the leg slung over his knee. They move with the sounds, bouncing like string. He's a little drunk, he thinks to himself, but not really. He's had, what? Three?

"Let's dance," Amos says.

Without a word, Emerson empties his glass. There wasn't much left; the gesture was the point. Retsy sighs.

The floor is thinly occupied. A few couples, cousins, friends of the bride. They're dancing the way people do at weddings: bobbing slightly, feigning an exuberant move. But these twists and dips are a kind of joke; they're meant to say, Ha ha, imagine if I was like that.

Amos enters in smooth, gliding steps. Hands behind his back, legs leading him forward. Emerson follows, clapping. His movements begin, as they always do, in his shoulders.

"Oh, hello," an older woman says as they pass. Her dress is red, her teeth an unnatural white.

They arrive in front of the band. Amos can feel himself begin to warm. They're both good dancers, but it's not about that. How they're dancing doesn't shout, Look at us. It's just fun. It's easy. It's bodies moving because they can.

Now Sam has joined them. He opens his collar with a garish sweep of one arm. His wife kicks off her shoes. Her smile is grateful: this is what she imagined.

Sam is from college. A few years older, they know him mostly from New York. That's part of it, too, what makes this so fun. That they aren't that close, that this isn't a performance for a good friend. It's just that sometimes, on nights like tonight, they decide to turn the volume all the way up.

Others are dancing now, too. They rise from their seats, leave their cake, and come out. Wives pull husbands by their hands, the husbands relent, and not unwillingly either. They want to, they realize, maybe for the first time in a very long while. Because the love of friends is a gravity—debris is drawn toward it without knowing why. Romantic love seals itself off, it pairs and withdraws. But friendship is a ladder: it's something you climb; it's two hands knit together to let you see over the fence. Sometimes one person feels it, sometimes the other. But then there are times like this, when it's both together, when each of you knows that you've gone somewhere you can't get on your own.

Shirttails, arms, Emerson's hair. Cymbals and saxophones. Wine flies from glasses; no one cares where it lands.

How fit they both are. These are years when people have begun to let themselves go. But they haven't. You can see it: Emerson's back, Amos's legs. They move like children. They are not diminished. Emerson's shoes are black flashes. He twirls. His arms snap like ribbons; his fingers are loose. The air becomes young, the thought of the morning far away.

The dance floor has filled. The two of them still pulse at its center. People feel like they're inside, like they're close. They can't say to what, just that they love it, that it feels like something they've been wanting to feel and hadn't known how to describe. But they're not—close, that is. Because it isn't a question of nearer or farther. They are only tourists; they have to go home.

Emerson holds Amos by the shoulders, tightly, almost as if he is mad. But of course he's not mad, he just wants some way to show how he feels. And it isn't because they don't know how to use words, it's because sometimes a squeeze does more than words ever could. Amos reaches out, grabs him in the same way. Now they're jumping together, straight up and down. Laughing, singing. Their voices have gone but they don't stop.

More people join; everything is hot breath. Amos is whirling. He sees as flashes of color. White shirts flecked with ties, the dash of a dress. Claire—they embrace; she's smiling, kissing his neck—then she's gone, spinning off like a top. He will find her again. He will find everything again. He will find whatever he wants.

Some older men stand by the edge of the tent. Too proud, too rusted to join. Uncles, men who own stocks. Their faces are swollen and pink. They are the ones who, tomorrow at breakfast, will say things like, Wow, let me know where I could've got some of that. And Amos, looking up from his plate, will reply, You mean coffee with dessert? Sure, they'll nod, grumbling slightly, not wanting to allow that this might be true.

For a moment, Amos breaks away from the crush. He watches it—this thing they have made. He thinks how it must appear to everyone else.

It's small, what they're seeing. Some dancing, no more

than that. But of course it's only the tip of a very large thing. It's small right now because it can be small when it wants: excess allows modesty and below is a well that will never run dry.

Emerson stumbles toward him, his shoes slap the parquet like stones. Look, he says. He holds up the end of his tie, then squeezes it in a fist. Liquid runs out between his knuckles and drips onto the floor. Amos stares for a moment, then they are laughing, shrieking. Noiseless, pure laughter. How can it be? Do you have any idea how much sweat it would take to soak all the way to the *end* of a tie? Not just enough to make it wet, but so much that you could actually *wring it out*?

Amos swallows. There are still tears on his cheeks.

"I need water."

They sit at the edge, in chairs with other people's jackets hung over the back. Emerson stretches his legs out and groans. Around them, plates are being cleared. Waiters pour the remnants of glasses into the lawn.

Amos sighs. The breeze has come in. It brushes his neck and plays with the ends of his hair. He feels the ocean nearby. It's behind him, out of sight, but the thought of the inky black swells comforts like the idea of one's bed.

They keep sitting, their shirts beginning to dry. Nothing needs to be said. The night is alive, it is healthy. It can manage on its own.

Amos runs his hands through his hair and imagines how tomorrow will be. The town bleached by sun, the sea returned to a glittering blue. Will people remember how much fun they had? Will they know why? He doesn't care, he realizes. He doesn't need credit. What matters is that they have this way about them, and that they put it to use.

WHO SAID IT FIRST? Amos had no idea. He couldn't even be sure it was in regard to a wedding. But at some point one of them had wondered aloud, in order to ask what kind of effort an outing would be given, whether it was going to get a Full Sam. And like that it was born. Coherent, entire, needing no explanation.

Full Sam? Not after a week like this.

There's a nontrivial chance of Full Sam.

I know it sounds crazy, but I might be in a Full Sam kind of mood.

It'll be fun, but not even close to Full Sam.

Are we talking FS, or . . . ?

Of course Amos had heard people say fulsome before. Likely in this room as often as anywhere else. But isn't that how collisions work? Everything matters: the angles, the wind, the depth of the tread in the heel of one's shoe. And it did feel like a collision. As though he'd been doing his best to get through a day—here he was, after all, seeing patients, attending to others and what must be done—when it careened into him.

Fulsome. Full Sam. His friend. That tent. Hands on shoulders. Music, light. Amos could feel himself begin to break up. His face would betray him; his chest might heave with small sobs. Because how—how could there have been such a night and—

"Does that make sense?" the woman asked.

Amos started, then continued to nod. He studied a spot on the rug.

"I think so," he said, finding his voice with a swallow, "but—can you try putting it another way?"

# 6

Claire had said only that it was about Amos, knowing this would ensure Emerson didn't mention it. It was also because she wanted to be looking at him when she asked, because she needed to see his face when she did. She would know. She was certain. One way or another, she would know.

Her steely self-confidence showed in such moments. Whatever was needed—instinct, intellect, the clarity detachment affords—she believed was already inside. Her life was the proof: things had gone as she wanted; the world behaved as it should.

It had rained earlier. A drenching, insistent rain that swept over the city. Warm air followed, thick as smoke. Now the streets were littered with puddles. At curbs people paused to jump.

She stood at the corner, looking south to where the buildings became short. It was there, thirty blocks or so more, and a bit farther west, that Amos would be. And it was, she thought, where he belonged. With his books and his art, in his space for sweeping debate, principles unencumbered by the health chart at the foot of a real patient's real bed.

That was putting it harshly, and she didn't quite mean it. Not all the way. The world needed people like him—people who helped, who tried to see only the good. But it could not survive on them alone. Eventually things must happen. Roads built or torn up, borders drawn and enforced. And he held his ideals like myths in a primitive village. She understood why, of course. After a childhood such as his, what were more reasonable wants than clarity and order? She didn't begrudge him for these, at least not most of the time. But what part she did was bound up in the fact that, despite having given her word, Claire was on her way to see Emerson, to ask him directly whether what Anna had said was true.

CROSSING THE STREET, she pictured her daughter. It was two o'clock, or just nearly, which meant she'd be in class— head cocked slightly, pen twirling over her knuckles. She'd spent a whole weekend teaching herself how to do it.

And here was the thing about Anna. She was sly, composed as weather, as trains. It was how she had always been. One felt her arrogance in the way she might rearrange flowers or look up from a book: utterly within herself, not a thought for the world. Claire sensed it especially when Anna's eyes moved over her, through her, as though she were not even there. They picked her apart like birds, they left and were gone.

True, Claire had noticed certain things lately. The hours away from the house, the running, the tight skin by her cheeks. And her eating. The slow, narrow way that she chewed. But what of it? Mothers watched daughters' plates and the size of their bites, that's just how it was. And more to the point, the way Anna had been wasn't unusual, it was simply life for a girl her age—one discovering her body, the strengths it possessed, the risks of living within such a lovely thing.

But what came under threat was not without power. A certain kind in particular. The world understood victims; it ran to them with splints and gauze. Not always, of course. Not all the time. But weren't they vaunted in some sense? Wasn't there glory in wounds? Ask veterans, climbers who've fallen and lived. And accusations were violence—thrilling, seductive. Like setting your finger across a live wire: the prickling sense that you can—if you want—just do it. All it took was some words and the world began turning. It sat up and listened; it formed a new shape because of what you had said.

It wasn't that no one should be believed; men did all kinds of terrible things. But it was important to remember how it was to be a young girl, to discover this power before you quite knew what it meant. It was why she could see how Anna, cornered and in trouble, might simply have grabbed for something close by. Like the knife one remembers, forgotten until it was needed. She didn't know that she knew it would work. The knowledge was already inside her. Just say this thing—a man did this to me—and the rest would take care of itself.

GLEAMING BUILDINGS CROWDED the streets, buildings of windows reflecting the sky.

Within them, drawers, the smell of ink, whirring systems, and outcomes being ordained. People came and went through the doors. They moved briskly. They went toward places they knew.

Funny to think she'd been Anna's age when Claire first walked these blocks—sent, on Sundays mostly, to retrieve her father from the morass of some deal. Afterward, the two of them would ride home in a taxi while he explained the particulars and asked her opinion. Am I giving too much away? Am I driving too hard a bargain? Then he'd listen to whatever she said.

Anna's age. Yes, sixteen was a hard one to be. Confusing and sad, joyful and forlorn. But also, it must be said, intoxicating. And thorny. And not without guile. Claire understood, she remembered. It wasn't so long ago.

It was the age when you could feel a man's gaze on the subway and know precisely what went through his head. And you could hate it and you could love it, but more important, you'd realize that you could take his thoughts and wrap them around his neck and let him keep thinking whatever he wanted because he had no idea that you were in charge, that the power was in your hands. Because you had this thing—this thing which felt both ancient and new; this thing he could only ever guess at, because he was nothing and no one and that's why he looked.

Claire knew because she'd done it herself. Certainly by sixteen and perhaps even younger. Talking to her father's friends she'd learned to touch her neck while describing a book, or not laugh when they told their joke, knowing all the while what she was doing—which was to cause that little rupture of desire inside them, the one they couldn't stop from rippling over their face. Then she'd leave and go upstairs, stopping by the mirror in the hall to regard this new person, the one who'd made herself richer and stronger, realer and more alive.

None of which was to say Anna had done this. Or that if she had it should make any difference. It was just a fact, a thing that was true of girls her age. And because it was true, Claire knew she must take it into account.

Likewise was the way Anna reacted to the questions she'd asked. Soft at first, calm, like a wounded animal who is afraid but too injured to run. But then, abruptly, she'd turned bitter and intelligent; her face flexed like a muscle. I told Dad, she shouted. I told Dad all that. Baby, Claire tried. I just want to hear it from you. She laid a hand on the mound of her foot. But it was no use. Get out, her daughter screamed. Get the fuck out.

What to make of that? Nothing one way or the other. It was just something to consider, a detail worth giving its due.

Worthy of emphasis was also the fact that what Claire was doing—moving slowly, making sure—wasn't some sort of betrayal; it was an act of love. Because believing was easy, even when it came to something like this. It was always simpler, giving yourself permission not to think. That way you were free to feel whatever you liked, convinced it was right and proper and true.

She'd once spoken to a woman whose son was an alcoholic. For fifteen years, the woman said, I tried to help. You know when things changed? She laughed to herself. When he got arrested and I didn't pick up.

This was different, of course, but the point was the same. Love was hard. Love was work. Love was taking time to make sure the foundation would last. And she loved her daughter. More than anything else. More than anything else she could ever imagine. That was the reason she had to go see.

THE LOBBY WAS QUIET and damp. The crowds had already streamed in. The doorman smiled flatly, then returned his eyes to the desk.

Had she smoked, Claire thought, this would be the time. She wasn't nervous, or hadn't believed that she was; but, having arrived, she found herself wanting some small extra thing to do first. The toes of her socks had grown wet. Her feet were beginning to wrinkle and itch.

Something else had occurred to her, too. And while there were obviously considerations of far more importance, and while it was not, by itself, a meaningful fact, it must still be said: Emerson had never tried anything with her. Not once. Not ever. Not even when Claire had been at the height of her powers—powers which, though sometimes outshined, weren't so meager as to be entirely written off.

She'd been between calls when this thought first occurred, standing, both hands on her desk. It was a day or two after Amos told her, and the delay was important; it meant logic, not jealousy, was at work.

Yes, everyone knew about the bitterness of mothers, their fear of being replaced and so on. But that was shopworn, beneath her; Anna's beauty gave Claire no trouble to admit. This was something else: it was a reasonable question asked by a woman who wanted nothing more than to get to the bottom of things. And wouldn't he have? If he were that kind of person. Wouldn't there have been a glance or a gift or a pause that felt like an inquisitive, too-forward hand?

Of course she'd not wanted him to, and Claire resented how pointing this out could make it seem otherwise. But when you'd known someone that long—someone good-looking and decent who, for a time, wasn't exactly discerning about where he slept—questions were bound to come. No, she had always replied. Truly. I don't see him that way. She didn't go so far as to feign disgust, it was just something that could've happened but hadn't. Which was fine. Things would've been fine either way. Then there was Amos— which she loved Emerson for; which she'd said many times was the great gift of her life—and neither since then nor before had so much as a hug suggested there was more he wanted to know.

She entered the elevator first, followed by two men talking in boisterous, jocular tones. Their pale necks gathered like wax at the tops of their shirts. One was holding a newspaper. He tapped it against the other's arm as he spoke.

"I'm serious," he said. "You could sleep in them."

"I already told you I'd go."

The first turned to Claire. "Suits," he said. "I bet your husband could use better suits."

She smiled and said nothing.

What if he truly had done it? In that case, it went without saying. She would stand with her daughter. She would cast him out. She would apologize to Amos. She would tend to her child and make the world safe again. But try as she might, she couldn't seem to keep this idea in her mind. It wasn't so much slippery as too big to hold. Or too central. What it would mean was too much. Like trying to strip a painting of only one pigment, or imagine a house without the load-bearing wall. Each configuration failed because something essential was gone. The scope was too vast; the canvas had already dried.

Instead, she returned to the comforting logic: it didn't make any sense. No matter what direction she came from, this remained unassailably true. Yes, people did things; friendly neighbors were found with freezers full of human remains. But those were strangers, not people she'd known her whole life. Even their parents were close, for god's sake. They sent Christmas cards, asked after each other, went to the same parties and agreed it was a shame when new buildings went up by the park. All of them, these families, were braided together, bound up in something that couldn't simply be broken apart. It was older than them, bigger. And Emerson knew; more than anyone else, he understood the way their world was.

The doors released her into the office's aseptic hum. The sounds of shoes and pens, low voices bent over desks.

"Is he expecting you?" the receptionist asked.

Claire nodded as she walked by.

"I know the way."

SHE COULD SEE HIS FACE through the door. It was all there: his eyes and their inevitable brown; the fine nose, the lips. But as she looked, they seemed, for a moment, to be only pieces; they sat on him like props for a show. He'd not seen her yet. The carpet hid the sounds of her steps.

It was true that he could have a cruelty, an edge. Though in practice this was something for which Claire felt mostly respect. He was harsh with Retsy, and Sophie sometimes, but that was to be expected of someone like him. Amos might have been smarter, more clever, but Emerson possessed a ruthless wisdom: he grasped the nature of things.

Through the window seeped a clammy gray light. On his desk were papers—spread, Claire thought for a moment, the exact right amount.

Sensing a presence, he turned to look. His features leapt into place. First a smile, then something like it but less. Friendly concern. Affection. Familiar gladness. His arms came out to hug her, his eyes invoking their past.

"I need Amos," he said. "You know that, right? So unless he's fine I don't want to hear whatever this is."

## 7

Watching Claire lower herself into the chair, Emerson realized he'd lived through this before. Without knowing when, he'd imagined it all—not consciously, but by instinct. He'd readied himself; he knew what was to come.

Everything confessed it. The thumb along her lip, the small frown before she spoke. His hands were folded in his lap. He leaned back. Patient, alert.

"It's about Anna."

Emerson inclined his head slightly. Claire took a deep breath. It was harder for her than he would've guessed.

"What happened?"

"Well, for one thing, she was caught shoplifting."

It was a shocking betrayal, this choice. There was no reason it should've come first, no need to have mentioned it whatsoever. He could hardly believe his luck. All that remained now was to wait.

"Shit," he said. "Claire, I'm sorry. Kids can be . . ."

He gestured vaguely.

She nodded.

"But, Emerson, it's not just that."

Immediately the two of them felt how strange it was, her having used his name. He allowed it to pass without comment. He was her friend, he was listening to whatever she had to say.

A knock at the door.

"No," he called without looking.

The sharpness signaled an intimacy between them. Claire closed her lips in a show of gratitude for his understanding that the matter had weight.

"Please," he said, urging her on.

"She said something happened."

She was watching him now. He could tell. This was the moment in which she'd decide. He felt her eyes crawling over his body like hands. A doctor's eyes. Careful, informed. He looked back at her with dutiful, almost tolerant expectancy. There was no rush, his gaze seemed to say, he'd be here whenever she was ready.

"I'm sorry to put this so bluntly, but she said that you touched her—that you," she searched for a moment, "groped her."

"Jesus Christ, Claire."

"Did you?"

He leaned forward and laid his hands on the desk. He could feel his shoulder blades move under his shirt.

"No," he said. "No."

The room smelled of paper, of agreements and deals.

"Claire, I haven't even seen her in—"

"October," she said. "When we came upstate."

Emerson stood, affecting a restless agitation.

"I need to call Amos. Does Amos know what you're saying?"

"Look at me."

He did as he was told.

"Emerson."

"No—Claire, no. For fuck's sake. My best friend? You? Jesus Christ."

She was weakening. He could see it. She'd begun to bend like a match which has nearly burnt itself out. The key was this: she wanted to believe. She'd come to him in fear and desire, a child needing only to be assured the nightmare isn't real. He stood and went to her.

"Can I?"

She nodded. He was behind her. He laid his hands on her shoulders. They rose and fell like something bobbing in water.

"Why would she?" she cried quietly. "Why would she just make it up?"

He didn't reply. It was not for him to answer, it was something she needed to say. He came around, knelt, and took both her hands, pressing them together as though in a prayer.

"Claire," he said. "Whatever this is, she'll be OK."

She wiped her nose. Her hair had come loose from behind both ears. "I'm sorry," she said.

He shook it away.

"But Amos . . . ," he said.

Claire nodded. "She told him first."

"Jesus." He stood and moved toward the phone.

"Stop."

"Why?"

"Because we were supposed to ask you together."

To this, too, he said nothing. It was delicate, the place they were in. He must not assume too much or press his advantage. Why, then, had he said the thing he did next? What need was there? What had he been after? Emerson would wonder this for a long time to come.

But that was far away now. Not just the moment, but also the man. What he was doing wasn't to Amos himself, but rather to some idea of him—an abstraction, a particle caught in the light. Plus, it was so they could go on being friends. He knew how that might sound, but still, it was true. They would have to get through this, and so he was bringing Claire along first, making sure she stood in the right place. It was unseemly but necessary, and history was an abstract painting: it forgot this or that brushstroke; it wasn't concerned with the shadow under an orange.

Or perhaps it was simpler, not so different from the impulse that had led him to this place. Perhaps he did what he did because he could, because the exercise of power was its own pleasure.

Whatever the reason, it was with an air of ghostly calm that Emerson sat on the edge of his desk and crossed his arms with a neat, professorial air. It should've felt worse. He could still picture his friend on the sidewalk, could still

see the relief in his face. For someone to tell, for the joy that
was to confess and not be cast out. But even so, it didn't feel
bad. It felt easy, even right.

"Maybe Amos can talk to her," he said. "About the stealing, I mean."

8

Claire walked north. The day had changed. Outside restaurants, tables were being reset. Busboys unstacked
the chairs. The sun had come through—a hot, prickling
sun—and the light seemed almost blinding. Cars swept down
the avenue. A man shouted in vain for a taxi to stop.

She felt a vague sense of disquiet, as of one boarding a
plane who fears the house may have been left unlocked. But
this was distant and fleeting, overwhelmed by a turmoil of
questions that forked toward competing answers and the
feelings flooding their streets.

The main thing was that he'd denied it. Perhaps such was
to be expected, but it would be wrong to simply breeze past
this fact. What, then, to make *of* his denial? She'd thought
he might get angry and that this would smack of guilt. But
he hadn't—he'd been upset and confused, fixated on the

need to call Amos. And wasn't that right? Wasn't that how it should look?

Claire tried to recall the precise moment she'd asked, but for all her effort it seemed dim and out of reach, as though her focus had interfered with paying attention. What she remembered was what she'd felt: relief, of a running, delirious nature; the kind she imagined her patients might when scans came back clear. Importantly, however, she'd not let that show. Instead, she pressed him—demanding he look at her, making him repeat himself into the stark, unambiguous room.

At the park, she stopped to sit on a bench. An explosion of green lay before her. Trees, languorous grass. Nearby, the shapeless chatter of tourists, the soft clap of hooves. She was immune to all this. She paced the halls of her mind, slowly, like a detective stalking the scene.

There had been a moment when the conversation turned, when it ceased being the one she'd gone there to have and became something else.

"What do you mean, 'stole'?" she'd asked impotently, clearly not knowing whatever she should. "Like when you were in college?"

"No," Emerson said, shaking his head. "After. Well, maybe—but we were late twenties when I found out."

She looked at the ceiling and let out an incredulous puff of air.

"As an adult? What kinds of things?"

She was no longer watching him closely; her thoughts were messier now, the beam of her attention tumbled like a flashlight dropped in the dark.

He shrugged. "Everything, kind of. Everyday stuff. I think it was deodorant when he got caught and called me."

She held one hand out, its palm turned up as though the questions were too many to list. The tears of a few moments before were gone, replaced by curt disbelief.

"Claire, this was forever ago," he said, shaking an arm to straighten its sleeve. "All I meant was that he might know how to talk to her."

She moved her head slightly to show that she'd heard.

"And you know how he is. He didn't—"

"I was with him then," she cut in. "We'd been together for at least two years."

Emerson sighed, and for an instant Claire was overcome by the acute sense that her life had not happened, that no time had passed since the moment, now nearly three decades gone, when he tossed his hair back from his face and said he had a friend she should meet—someone he thought was the right amount smart and the right amount mean that she might actually give him a chance.

"We all need secrets," he said, breaking the spell. His voice had grown expansive and generous. "You know that. Of course there's stuff Retsy doesn't—"

"It's not the secret," she insisted, realizing this was true. "It's just fucking weird." She paused. "He was an adult. Anna's *sixteen*."

At this Claire had felt a touch of misgiving. To discuss

her daughter like that was too much, too regular; it implied a certainty he did not yet deserve. Emerson seemed to sense this as well and returned to the chair.

"The thing about Amos, is that he isn't . . ." He paused, considering his words. "He had a hard time. You know that. You and I, we don't know. We can't know what that was like."

These few clean, simple lines. They contained something real. The two of them were different—they were like priests in the same ancient sect, bound together by doctrine, by time. It was neither good nor bad; it was merely true. And yes, Amos was owed understanding, empathy when it was due. But those were given *because* of this difference, because he was outside and it was not within their power—not within anyone's, really—to let him all the way in.

Claire wasn't realizing so much as remembering. Something she'd known all along. Something Amos knew, too. What was she talking about? Money, plainly, though it was crass to say so and not quite complete. What Claire meant was that it was she who made their life possible, she who'd ensured how it had been for the daughter they both wanted to have. A life sturdy as beams. The comfort of not fearing that years would continue to come.

A sense for money was a singular kind of knowledge. Not how it should be managed and maintained, but the ability to hold it in one's mind, to see the world through its prism. Could it be taught? Perhaps. Claire didn't know. But what was certain was that it was most often absorbed. Not passed down like lessons, but taken in through the air, the surface of one's skin. It was a country to which you could not immi-

grate; the only citizens were naturalized at birth. It was ele-
mental. An authority which doesn't think to assert itself—
not because it is timid but because it is total. Like the man
who knows in all of life there are only three stories, it understood that nuance would always burn off.

They'd talked about it, she and Amos. Once in particular.
They weren't yet married, but she could no longer imagine it
wouldn't be him. Sometimes it feels bad, he had said, that
it's always your family, that it will always be them. I know,
she replied. She held his face with both hands. But they don't
care. And neither do I. It's why my dad worked; it makes
him happy to do. Then he had taken her clothes—slowly, as
though unwrapping a gift. And she had looked up at the
shadows around his lithe arms, the appetite smile he allowed
on his face. She loved him for how little had to be said. He
simply assumed the right role, like a bellhop who understands
the discreet manner with which to accept his tip.

And now this. To call it a revelation felt dramatic; after
all, it was decades ago. Still, Claire was convinced: it did
matter; somehow and in some way. But what did that *mean*?
Was it important to the question at hand? Did it have anything to do with their daughter? The obvious answer was
no, and yet that didn't feel right. But if it wasn't, then what
stitched them together? She had nothing to answer this with
but instinct and faith. A dense knot at her core reason couldn't
undo.


THE PARK WAS BEHIND HER to the west, the museums,
rooms of art, marble halls cool as spoons. It had been a day

of too much, and Claire felt the pleasant, annihilating blur of an exhausted mind. Familiar streets welcomed her home, stores she knew. From that one came bread; from there, milk and eggs, sometimes figs or a cheese.

The world arrived differently now. She saw the thick certainty that was a kind of New York. The dignity of its streets, the great rivers streaming down. She had welcomed Amos into this place. A world of waiters, coats white as teeth, rooms filled with the sound of glasses being taken from the rack. And their smiling, untroubled child who slept on the third floor. And their blazing, immortal days. All this, all this she had given to him.

As for the other parts, the ones made together, Claire wouldn't deny they were real. But walking now, muffled by the lush fatigue that attends overthought, those seemed incidental, decorative even.

She felt released, freed finally to understand what she'd been feeling since leaving Emerson's office. It wasn't anger or sadness—either at Amos's having kept this from her, or the idea of what made him do it—it was revulsion. Not overstated, not even righteous. It was the kind of disgust one feels toward someone found cheating at cards, whose very life seems at risk of infecting one's own.

With each step she sensed her convictions beginning to set. Things were being decided. Claire knew it was unfair. She should go to her husband, explain what she'd done, ask how he felt and let him be present while the clay was still soft. But rather than hurry, she slowed, even stopped for a moment, to fill her lungs with the sweet, rotting air.

## 9

The sounds of the market received them. Voices, jars, weights being discussed. Retsy smiled her thanks to Sophie, the door flashing closed.

"What should I get?" her daughter asked.

Retsy consulted the list.

"Grapefruit. And capers and endive."

A nod.

"And anise, if they have it."

The cookbook still sat on the kitchen counter, a stout candle holding open its page. After choosing what to prepare, Retsy had written the ingredients out in tight, careful script. She could feel herself making a ceremony of the process, but she didn't stop. Because the truth was that she felt buoyant—she was in the mood to try something new, to feel like she was living her life. She knew why, too. It had been building for weeks.

There was no other way to say it: Emerson had been good lately. He seemed enlivened, more present. Retsy would catch him at odd moments looking into the middle distance, his face lit as though by a sun she couldn't see. Her first thought had been that he was cheating. It seemed an obvious enough explanation and she'd tried to comfort herself with how routine such things were; how, with the right attitude, they could be survived. But as the days continued to pass, this explanation rang less and less true.

Whatever it was showed itself in the way he stirred rice and how he'd taken to sitting at the table with Sophie long after dinner was over. Retsy glimpsed it as he poured wine, or asked, and then listened to, what she'd done with the day. It was also in how he fucked her.

She'd said something once. On a night when his body seemed especially real. She could tell he hadn't gone somewhere else in his mind; it was still her neck he was holding. And though she worried that to speak might break the spell, it came out anyway: Your hand feels new. He'd looked at her strangely. It was a strange thing to say. What did it mean? She had no idea.

From its inception, theirs had been a clear-eyed, intellectual love. The life they built together wasn't without affection, but that came second, almost incidentally, to the feeling of a prudent arrangement. What they admired in each other was a shared idea of the world and a steely conviction about the forces behind it. She'd said on their second date that she suspected her first marriage would end in divorce. At this, Emerson let out a quick explosion of laughter. She could tell it had stirred something in him. Not merely competitive, but kindred. He harbored the same brutal sense of how things could be.

Still, there was a part of her, nearly forgotten but lately emerged, which nursed a small hope that with age this might eventually change; that he would soften, tire of meanness; that a child would overwhelm the nihilism at his core; and that, were all this to pass, they might slip into something more earnest. A grateful hunger. Clutching, actual love.

So what to make of things lately? Had it finally happened? She could hardly bear it, such a trite and whimsical thought. How far it would mean they had come. Just think of that night now ten, fifteen years ago. The two of them in a car, her thoughts swimming with wine. They were on their way home from a party at which he'd left her alone. Not a thought, hardly a word.

"Everyone can tell you don't give a shit about them," she said. She was curled against the door like a cat.

"What?" he replied.

"When they talk. You can't even feign interest."

Emerson looked at the buildings going by. Banks, hotels, a jewelry store behind two panes of glass.

"Your whole life is breadcrumbs," he said without turning. He opened the window, moving his hand as though along the surface of water. "People chew, and you eat the crumbs."

The car slowed to stop for a light.

"That's the meanest thing you've ever said." Her voice was flat, impassive.

"I know." A small gesture with his chin. "I know."

Retsy hadn't forgotten moments like this. Who would? But that didn't mean things hadn't changed. And what a relief it would be, what a joy, to no longer feel like the goal of each day was moving soundlessly through her own life.

Despite herself, she began to feel the pull of a fledgling hope, a giddiness even. Having spent so many years nursing a contempt for the idea of who she was—years when she'd surveyed the many medications in the vanity and thought, Well, yes, of course someone like me would have a cupboard like that—the thought of letting this go offered the delicious pleasure of sleep after too much sun. The fullness of her relief surprised her, the thought of being so tired without having had any idea.

It was no mystery where that debased self-regard had come from. How old had she been? Sophie's age? Slightly younger? Yes, maybe thirteen. The details of the fight were lost to her now, but she could still remember where they'd been standing. Retsy at the bottom of the wide, wooden stairs; her mother at the top, one hand on the banister. They were shouting, their voices battering each other like slaps.

Retsy could tell that her words weren't working. They seemed barely to reach. So finally, she said it. Was it for the first time? Certainly the first time like this—to her, *at* her. But she wasn't afraid. It felt right, severe and mature.

"You're such a *bitch*."

Silence. Her mother knit her fingers together and held them under her chin. It was as though she'd been waiting for this, as though what she were about to convey was important and Retsy must be sure to listen. She looked down. On her face, a smile like the edge of a blade.

"Rets." A small shake of her head. "You're too boring to ever be mean."

Outside, they walked south. The streets had begun to fill with commuters hoping to catch early trains. They streamed by, touching their pockets, thinking a last few professional thoughts.

"Can I see?" Sophie asked.

Retsy handed her the list.

"What's ouzo?" she said after a moment.

"Ouzo. It's a thick wine."

"Can I try it?"

A look passed between them.

"Maybe."

At the corner, Sophie flung an arm toward the space between her shoulders.

"Ah," she said, squirming, "bug."

Instinctively, she turned so her mother could inspect. Retsy did, plucking and smoothing her shirt. All at once, her hands felt full of yearning tenderness. These tools, she thought. Meant to stroke and to calm.

The light changed and Sophie skipped ahead. But that was OK. She'd let herself be touched and fussed over; she hadn't minded being her daughter. Suddenly, it seemed, there was cause for hope wherever Retsy looked. Even dinner last night, when she found herself expecting humiliated chagrin and instead felt nothing at all.

Robert Eden had come over for drinks and was nodding at what she said, adding that he'd thought the very same thing. Emerson was tipped back in his chair.

"Right," she smiled. "It's evocative of Kandinsky, I think."

Immediately, Retsy realized she'd already used this word twice. It was a feeling she hated—tied up, of course, in the need to ensure that she was a woman of extremes, one who had thoughts and ideas of her own. But now here it was, evocative for the third time, and yet where she'd anticipated shame, Retsy found indifference, ease, even comfort. There had flashed across Eden's face the briefest shadow of recognition, but by this, too, she was undaunted. The conversation went on. Retsy smiled, or felt that she had. Perhaps it was just the feeling of lightness that comes from a burden being set down.

From one angle, it could seem such a small thing. But wasn't life small? If someone were to ask what her marriage was like wouldn't whatever she said amount to some version of how it felt to say something dumb over dinner, whether she gave any thought to reusing words?

AT HOME, she put a record on in the kitchen. It was such a simple, obvious act. She couldn't remember when she last had. The first notes seemed to settle the room; it became calm in their wake.

She worked slowly, her rings set aside. The knife sparkled occasionally in the soft light; gleaming vegetables dripped in the sink.

Retsy thought of how often she'd claimed to have no respect for couples who remained friends after divorce. They seem proud, she said. Of what? More than any others, she declared, such people had never been in love. But did she even really believe this? Or was it the sort of conviction she thought the person she wanted to be might hold? Retsy no longer cared. What she'd realized, what this change in Emerson let her discover, was how exhausting a fetish originality was. To be a caricature was safe, almost cozy; it was honorable in its way.

For instance, here she was, preparing a meal for her husband away at work, her child now back from school. And what of it? Why should she apologize or feel regret? She shouldn't; she didn't. Instead, she looked forward to the click of the latch on the door, Emerson's greeting as he stepped out of his shoes. Would he lean over the pot? Feign stealing a taste? Maybe she'd knock him away with her hip when he did.

This was the life she'd forgotten she wanted. Regal, domestic. Days like shelves full of books. And at last she had it. The time they'd lost to meanness no longer mattered. It had gone. What she wanted had come; it seemed to have come.

There it was, the lock turning over. Now came the sound of her name in his voice. Retsy looked up as he entered. She made a small gesture with both hands, as if to say, Can you believe it? All around lay evidence of her hope.

Emerson nodded dimly, then took off his glasses and rubbed his eyes with the heels of both hands. She strained to read his face. It was not how she'd thought it would be.

"Claire came by the office today," he said.

# 10

The room was quiet. His last patient, a young man, had canceled that morning. The chair across from him sat empty. Its leather was a clotted red, almost brown.

"I understand if you have to charge me," he'd said when he called.

"It's fine," Amos assured him. "Don't worry about it."

Soon he would stand and go home, but for now he continued to sit.

Outside, trees caught the last of the light. The tables at restaurants were beginning to fill. It felt good to be motionless, and Amos was glad for the bit of unforeseen space. It allowed his thoughts time to drift, settle down.

There were two things he wanted to discuss with Claire, his plan and his dream. He'd start with the dream, describing it as they sat on the couch and she sorted the mail. He could see the way she'd sigh at first, her antipathy to dreams already well known. He'd insist, though, burrowing the toes of one foot in her thigh, until eventually she conceded a smile, turning to listen. It wasn't that the two were related, but, Amos thought, might together create a certain atmosphere. One of braiding and union, a history of affection in the form of their minds taking up the same thing.

In the dream, he and his father had been sitting at a café in France. Which of course made no sense. Arthur never went and Amos not until long after his death. It was late afternoon. Waiters stood by the bar. His father mumbled inaudibly, until Amos hissed for him to speak up. At this, Arthur had opened his mouth and from it poured not words but the burnt, devouring roar of a car—a spent muffler, a dying machine. Then, suddenly, they were wrestling, flailing, graceless as drunks. The waiter appeared. *Messieurs*, he said, all politeness gone from his voice. Amos looked up from where he lay. His clothes were twisted, the floor hard on his back. Faces in the window. People had stopped to watch. An old woman, a cat, an arrogant boy on a bike. He wanted to wave. He felt himself trying. He knew he could not.

So, anyway, he'd say to Claire, a real doozy—adding with a smile, though not that inscrutable either. By then he hoped she'd be chuckling, agreeing his brain could really string one together. That way things would be feeling good when the pitch of his voice changed and he said, Hey, I have some ideas on how we should approach this whole Anna thing.

The truth was that in the days since, Amos had grown uneasy in Claire's presence. What he sensed wasn't the calculated chill between lovers, but something fainter and worse. Dressing beside her in the gray morning, Amos felt as he imagined one might in a shelter—among people who owe you nothing, who already seem miles away. Why, he wanted to ask, had she grown so cold, so out of reach?

What had been most unbearable about watching his own parents career toward the wreck of their lives was the fact that they did so alone. Maybe, he thought, if they'd each managed to choose someone better, the rest could've been survived with some grace. It was from this conviction that Amos fashioned his hope. The person you marry, he often said, is the one you want nearby during the worst moments of your life. The togetherness was all, the promise to work through it together.

Yet here they were, he and Claire, faced with what Anna had said—this awful, unthinkable thing—and somehow a space seemed to have grown up between them. It was why he needed this little dream story and the way she'd interject to say, A muffler for a voice? What do you think, Sigmund? What does the literature have to say about that? It would be a moment of regular softness, a reminder of how they could be. Then she would be ready to hear about his plan.

It was simple: it had to be over a meal. Amos was certain. On their own, either might approach Emerson any number of ways. But since they'd decided to do it together, it must be over a meal. And it had to be quick, the question asked in one stroke. Without preamble, without the slightest change in tone. The key was to create a moment in which the floor dropped out beneath him, that way they'd get a glimpse of his face. Everything else—his words, their delivery, would be a pale abstraction compared to what happened on his face.

Asked what he was looking for, Amos couldn't have said. Only that he knew the answer would appear. Whatever was true would be in there somewhere. However well or poorly disguised, it would be there because it couldn't not be.

He felt, in some strange way, proud of his plan. It struck him as something of which Claire would approve. Having heard it, she might even say, Yes, perfect, we should do it exactly like that. And then she'd remember that it was them, the two of them, who were what mattered. And Anna. And Anna needed their help.

Amos stood. He was resolved, even clear. He considered the desk and its mess of notes but decided to leave them for tomorrow. He thought of their house—its colors, its several floors. Ceramic pots, rugs of burgundy, pine. Bowls of fruit in the kitchen, pastries, French rolls in white paper bags cracking like twigs.

He sighed. He would be glad to return. He was always glad to return. In the innermost rooms the city could be forgotten entirely. The windows shut with delicious precision; the temperature was always correct. For noise, only a low hum, as of air outside a plane.

With a gesture of utter habitualness, the kind one barely feels, barely even performs, he lifted his bag from the chair and went out. The light was already off; there was no need to reach for the switch.

## 11

What shocked Retsy more than the idea itself was the immediacy with which she felt certain: he'd done it—she knew that he had. Hers was an understanding beyond sense; she felt it as one feels the needs of an infant. And as she did, Retsy understood, too, that it explained the new, good way things had been. What joined them she couldn't explain. It was simply the truth.

There passed an instant in which she saw him anew. Like the moment one loses track of the face in a cliff and it returns to being angles of rock. He was just skin—cheeks, chin, the shape of a nose. Just objects, just parts. Anonymous pieces which had conspired to do an inconceivable thing.

Then it was him again. Her husband, her daughter's father. The one who put his hand on the counter this way, whose pants gathered like that at the tops of his shoes. His gaze searched her. Retsy looked back. Her essential brilliance conjured it all; she was like a butcher who can tell the cut's weight with only a glance.

What would she do? Leave him? Take her daughter, her lotions, a suitcase stuffed with her favorite tops? And then what? How long does the truth keep you warm? What about on Tuesday three months from now? Or the Thursday in August that will come in five years? What about then? Will there be butter for toast? Plates on the shelf? Will anything still work or make sense?

She could see the apartment in which they would live. Bitter, confined, like those expelled from a church. How well she'd come to know its wainscoting and thick plaster walls. There would be a mirror by her dresser. Tall, in the corner, along its edge a faint misting of dust. She saw Sophie, in college by then, coming home for Thanksgiving. Her bedroom at the end of the hall. Years pass. Retsy opens the door, now it's she and her husband who've come to visit. Yes, he will say, of course he can help get something down from the shelf.

Speaking of Sophie, will she explain it to her? Would that be worse? Is it something she should have to know? Perhaps she'll be made angry. Not for an hour or a week, but in a fundamental, ongoing way. Hers will become a life steeped in brine. She'll cease being herself; she will have been made the daughter of a father who once did this thing. It will change what she eats, who she dates, her thoughts as she drifts off to sleep. And why should she have to be changed? What sense was there in making it her burden to bear?

This came to Retsy not so much as a vision but a feeling: she won't leave, she can't go. The idea of doing so faded like a drunken plan—lofty, foolish, untethered. No, no. Of course not, of course not, of course not. It won't work. It wouldn't solve anything.

But then what? What would it mean to doubt him and stay? Wasn't that more unthinkable still? To know he'd done such a thing and yet continue to undress for bed, keep asking whether she should put on enough water for two cups of tea?

All this went through her at once. Not as a sequence of logic, but a kind of total, pure knowledge. Like light, like the way a dropped bottle shatters outward in every direction. It's not one shard at a time: there's the moment when something is whole and the next when it's not; when it isn't just broken, but everywhere. All these ideas. Life if she left, life if she stayed. Her daughter, she must think of her daughter. As quickly as this unspooled, Retsy decided—though it hardly felt like deciding; more like the mechanics of a simple machine, the obvious way one's leg swings forward to take the next step—that he hadn't done it. No, definitely not; to believe anything else would be absurd. Had she ever thought otherwise? Already she couldn't be sure. And it wouldn't make sense if she had. So she hadn't, she mustn't have. What had been there was fading, was gone.

Her throat rose and fell, then closed like a fist.

"Em," she began. "My god, I'm so sorry. Are you OK? Anna said what? She must not be all right."

# 12

A thin, threadbare rain was falling. Rain like the memory of rain, rain that lands on awnings without a sound. Beneath it, Amos walked. It was less than a week since Anna told him, but his life had become something new. He moved to get space; he needed distance to see what it was.

To his right, the river lay like a sheet of hammered tin. He stopped for a moment and looked out. A tugboat urged a freighter under the bridge, its motionless cargo regal, pathetic as a drunk.

Here's what he knew: Emerson had done it; he would never admit it, but he had. And Claire believed him. Not only that but they'd spoken—she'd broken the one promise, the only thing for which he'd asked.

It was too much to hold. Every time Amos tried to follow a thought it crumpled, or cracked, or wrapped itself in a knot of angry despair. His mind felt like someone rushing from room to room after they've been robbed. What's broken? What's gone? What might be lost forever?

THE NIGHT BEFORE he'd been reading when Claire returned from work. Having not always shed the concerns and language of medicine, she sometimes arrived hard in a particular way, encased in haughty distraction which caused questions of hunger or movies or upcoming plans to be received with vague, hostile confusion, as if she were still listening to a patient's heart. And though Amos knew this, eagerness had not let him wait. He stood at the sound of the door, one finger still pinned in his book.

"Hey," he began as he kissed her. "Want to hear a strange dream?"

That's when she'd put a hand on his shoulder and looked at him, her face sealed in blunt dispassion.

"I went to see Emerson."

He stepped backward, not so much in shock but a visceral need for more room.

"Claire."

"Leave it."

"*Leave it?*"

She sat and gestured faintly. He shook his head.

"You talked to him about her?"

She nodded.

Amos turned toward the window. His hands rose to his neck. His fingers worked small circles against the skin by his jaw.

"I don't even know where to begin."

"He says he didn't——"

"Obviously he says he didn't."

"He said she needed help with the laundry and he moved her out of the way. He was clumsy, I'm sure. You know how he is."

What she was saying was strange, out of place. They were words for another conversation, the kind about why someone hadn't said thanks or properly cleaned the stove.

"Amos," Claire said, her voice rounder now, "all he cared about was you."

"Not our daughter?"

She looked at him.

"Yes her. But mostly you—he kept wanting to call."

Amos looked down at his feet, his shoes of fine, burnished leather. Had he really tried? What if she'd let him? What would he have said? The words Amos couldn't imagine, but he heard his friend's voice—deformed somewhat by urgency and nerves, but still the same underneath. A voice of uncountable hours, thick and heavy with years.

"But he didn't."

"I wouldn't let him."

Amos made a sharp, derisive sound. "Naturally. Because we talked about this. Because why would you want me to know you were there?"

"We did." She reached out a hand. "I'm sorry. But Amos, you're too—you're not the right one to see if he's telling the truth."

"Why?"

"Because you used to steal."

How obscene that for an instant he'd felt the cold chill of

discovery; how much less far he'd come than he thought, if he could be so quickly, so easily wrenched back. But then that feeling was gone, and Amos knew—knew in a way he couldn't possibly have before—Emerson really had done it.

He turned. His mouth opened slightly. His mind was a scorched whiteness, like losing one's vision after stepping into the sun. My best friend. My daughter. It hung there, his jaw, in something like a half smile, as though he'd been shot and still thought it might all be a joke. He'd done it. He had. Nothing else could explain why he would've told Claire this ancient, irrelevant fact; a thing so old it seemed no longer even a secret.

His words came quiet now, cool as acid.

"What on earth does that have to do with anything?"

"Why didn't you tell me?"

"Claire."

She looked at him, the thin line of her mouth. He went on.

"You mean then? You mean twenty years ago? Twenty-five fucking years ago? Who gives a shit? It has nothing to do with this—it has nothing to do with our daughter."

"It does, though."

"How?"

"Because of what you'll believe, the way you'll excuse this kind of thing."

"Claire." He turned to her. "He did it."

"You're wrong."

"Why would she lie?"

"Because she got caught. And when kids are in trouble that's what they do." She paused. "Adults, too."

Amos turned away from the water, the bridges looming behind him, gaunt, pinning each shore in place. He touched his hair. A faint wetness like dust. His skin was cool, alert to the wind. At the entrance to restaurants, men in suits met and shook hands. It was early for lunch. When the food came, they would eat in large, thoughtless bites.

He could picture so clearly how she and Emerson must have discussed him, even the tone his friend would've used. Not vindictive but sad, soft with the concern of a nurse explaining that someone was a terminal patient and the only thing left was to put them at ease.

Amos clapped his hands and let out a small, furious cry. It was so obvious that the conversation should never have become about him, about whatever he'd done all those years before. How had it happened? When had he let it slip away?

"But *why*?" Claire demanded. "Why didn't you tell me when that was going on?"

Her voice was gentle but firm, motherly even.

"Because," he'd said, "I was ashamed. Because it was embarrassing and pathetic and I knew what you'd think."

"Which was what?"

They were both sitting now.

"Which was that I wasn't worth it. That I wasn't good, or right. Or not a fit." He waved his hands. "You know what I mean."

"I don't think I do."

"Fuck you, Claire."

She took his hand. He let her keep it.

"Baby."

Silence.

"Amos."

"What?"

"You do see though, right? You understand where I'm coming from?"

"No, actually," he said. "I don't understand how this could possibly be what you're worried about."

She sighed. "That you never told me makes it—I don't know. It makes it realer, somehow. It makes it truer, or more true *about* you."

This was bullshit, he knew. A convenient place to hide her disdain, a technicality on which the sentence could be hung. Just imagine if he'd tried to tell her when things were still so uncertain and new. How would he even have put it? Hey, girl of my dreams, it's me, the guy with the fucked-up dead parents; the one with no family, with these stories of want and neglect. Anyway, I thought you should know that on top of all that, I'm a thief, too. Not a serious one—no, nothing that brave, just a flailing child trapped by compulsion and fear.

"It *was* true about me," he said slowly. "It was true about me more than two decades ago. But now it's tonight and you think our daughter's lying because I used to steal toothpaste."

She gave him a disappointed look.

"Amos."

"Think, Claire. Think why he told you. Why now? Why then in that moment?"

"Because," she said with brusque disbelief, "he thought you might be able to help."

Amos laughed bitterly. He could feel her next to him. The windows were clean. The books sat on their shelves. His words didn't matter, he realized, but still, he couldn't not say them.

"No," he scoffed, "no, that's not why."


WHAT LITTLE RAIN there had been was gone; the day hung damp on the line. Lunch was over, work resumed, and the few people he passed seemed intent, annoyed not to already be where they were going. Among them, Amos felt dispossessed, almost criminal. Had he been stopped, he might simply have run.

He saw now how elegant it was. He couldn't bring Claire back to the sidewalk outside that store, or explain how it felt to hear Emerson say they should've worried about him. And because this was lost to her—because no one could ever be all the way inside what they'd had at that moment—she could not comprehend what it meant that Emerson picked this of all times to betray it.

One thing of which Amos felt certain was that he hadn't been waiting for such a chance. Emerson's genius was one of intuition, a lethal intelligence like what exists in a wolf. He sensed more than he thought, he lunged without wondering why. That's how Amos knew what it meant: a mind like his would only do something so vicious if it feared being trapped. This had simply been within reach.

Once he was sure, it seemed as though he'd known forever. Not that his friend would do this, but that he could. It was like a disease carried from birth—a break in the code meaning nothing until the doctor points to a scan and explains they can't help. Could something be both shocking and obvious? Could hatred look like friendship? Even for decades, even for one's whole life.

It was wicked, what Emerson had done, brutal, abhorrent and foul. But was it unbelievable? No, the signs had been there, the clues. They came back to Amos like pieces from a wreck.

There was the swooping ease of his arms, or the obscene immunity of his smile; the decadent way he flung the door shut after parking a car and how, when they'd been young, he opened beers on the train. Let the ticket come if it will, his gestures all said. I'll be here if someone wants a word.

Now Amos could see it in Emerson's hands—hands that hardly knew what it was to hold things that weren't theirs. He saw it, too, in the way Emerson turned from those serving coffee—with something beyond rudeness, something total. His back obliterated them; to slip from his gaze was to no longer exist. He inhabited the world as though it were a restaurant: a place to order, eat, and then leave. What happened beyond that—questions of tablecloths and silverware polish—wasn't simply someone else's concern, it was barely even real.

And yet, hadn't Amos loved him for this, too? Not simply

envied but adored. Because to be close to Emerson was to edge toward the source of some greatness—a currency, a kind of raw power the world understood. And whatever his faults, he'd never hoarded what he had: he'd brought Amos in, taken pains to keep him around.

At this thought, his anger gave way to a sprawling chasm of sadness. To know his friend was capable of such a thing was not to know why. Why at all, yes, but more so why her? Why had he done it to *her*? Anna—her name stuck in his throat like a pill; it lived as a pain in each breath.

Amos had stopped. Across the street stood a key shop. Dirty windows, faded displays. A man was leaving, stooped slightly, engaged in adding one freshly cut to a ring of faded others. Envy came for Amos, enclosed him—the pure ordinariness of this chore. It was like the garden in a provincial town, concealed beyond a high wall. One felt its presence, the impossibility of approach. Something so small, so necessary and routine: Amos couldn't imagine needing anything more. Errands were a kind of religion, or could be, as long as you believed in your life.

He watched the man go, carried by steps, this man for whom something would open when it needed to. Amos wanted to be home. He wanted not to be home. He wanted some idea of where to go next.


"WHAT NOW?" CLAIRE had said as they continued to sit in the dense, tired silence.

Amos thought for a moment as though it were really a question to which there might be an answer.

"I don't know," he said, having found his mind a bare and windowless room.

"I won't try to stop you from talking to him."

"How magnanimous."

As soon as he said it he wished that he hadn't. To be mad at her was to be all alone.

Claire reached out a hand to straighten the edge of his sock.

"Don't," she said. "Don't go so far away."

He nodded, afraid he might cry.

"I love you," she said.

He nodded again.

"Amos, I love you."

# 13

Anna's suggesting lunch had surprised her. Even when they'd been close, it was always Sophie who made efforts like that. And lately, her friend had been entirely absent. There was the time at the diner, but since then nothing—not a word, not a question about whether she was happy or not, whether she was doing OK. Still, Sophie was glad to hear from her, and as she stood considering which of two shirts to wear, realized that seeing Anna might serve a small, useful purpose as well.

A month or so earlier, her father's friend had come for dinner. His name was Patrick. He was in from London and staying at a hotel on the park. Sophie had encountered such accents before, but for some reason found his newly thrilling and was left with an aching desire for one of her own. Not a complete overhaul; no one would buy that. But a handful of sounds and a few proper phrases might do. Small flourishes were, after all, what turned plain, blocky letters into rarefied type.

How had Patrick said it exactly? Something about keeping a flat in an arrondissement. From the moment she heard it, Sophie loved the word. Apartment seemed cheap and American; it filled one's mouth like too much food. But flat was altogether different: it was trim and precise and elegantly spare; it evoked a life of rugs and scarves.

The trouble with becoming someone new—even just swapping one word for another—was that people you saw every day were too close, too attuned; they'd notice the effort. The key, Sophie knew, was never to appear having tried.

She'd first discovered this when, nine or ten, she sat listening as her mother and her mother's friend discussed an actor.

"They're grotesque," the woman said of his films. "Basically smut."

"Oh, maybe," Retsy allowed. "But *he's* talented."

"Yes," the woman said dryly, "a real up-and-*coming* star."

At this her mother let out a sharp, open-mouthed cackle and Sophie felt a jealous longing to be part of the moment. She chuckled, too, a noise she hoped would sound like knowing. The women turned toward her with quizzical intensity.

"Did you get that?"

Sophie shrugged, her gesture meant to say something like, Of course, what'd you think?

For a moment, she met her mother's eyes. A look passed between them and she knew she'd been caught. Sophie felt her face working. Please, she tried to express, please just play along.

Retsy dispatched a single cruel snort and, like an official refusing one's papers, turned back to her friend.

"She has no idea."

Sophie looked down at her book, her cheeks hot and embarrassed. The lesson was clear: she must guard her desires; elegance meant having without deigning to want.

AT FIRST, they'd sat strangely in Anna's room, both of them on the bed. They spoke in quick, splashing bursts. Did she want to go see a movie, Sophie asked. No, Anna said, it was too nice for that. Maybe they could walk somewhere for lunch?

They had ordered. Their menus were gone. The plates sat empty and cold. Anna was unfolding her napkin. She'd lost weight and grown prettier for it. Watching her, Sophie felt accused by the lines of her face.

"He's an asshole," Anna said. She was talking about the teacher of a photography class.

Sophie nodded. She sat forward and smiled. When they'd met Anna had seemed distracted—hugging her oddly, words tripping out in a rush. It was unlike her and, in a way, made Sophie feel good. How delicious to wonder whether her friend was all right. It left her in an excitable, generous mood, and she clapped her hands at a thought.

"Do you remember when we opened all those rolls of film?"

Anna narrowed her eyes.

"Maybe?" She said the word slowly.

"We were playing dress-up in your parents' bedroom and, I think you—it must have been you—pulled the film out for something to wear."

"Oh," Anna cried. Her eyes shone brightly. "Oh, god. And then we wrapped—"

"Yes, yes—all up our arms—like a boa."

"We did it with at least four or five?"

"We were covered," Sophie said.

"Just the way real princesses would be."

"Why was there so much? I don't even think we used it all."

Anna rubbed her eyes. "It's my dad's thing."

She was smiling now. Sincerely, for the first time. The others had been something else.

"But it wasn't a secret. The whole point was to show off."

"Right, right. We paraded around like we were proud."

Anna was gesturing with her hands. "It does wrap well."

"Truly."

"Like it was made to."

They nursed their drinks, a close, convivial silence between them. Dishes clattered softly nearby. After a moment, Anna spoke.

"We've known each other for so long."

This sounded different, Sophie thought. Something had changed in her voice. Her eyes, too, had lost the tenderness of memory. She tensed. How familiar it was—Anna coming and going from one instant to the next, leaving you to wonder what you'd done to no longer deserve her attention. Or was she mistaken? Seen from another angle, Anna's face could appear tentative, hesitating, like someone unsure whether to cross the street. Should she ask what it was, Sophie wondered. Would that be weird? Were they the sort of friends who did such things? Were they even friends at all?

An arm interrupted her thoughts. Their food had arrived. Anna had ordered a sandwich and it seemed, sitting there, the obvious, self-assured choice. Sophie's omelet embarrassed her. She took a small bite, smiling as she withdrew the fork.

"How are your parents?"

Anna shrugged. "My dad is my dad, and my mom—"

"My mom's been the worst," Sophie said breezily. Here was her chance; she'd not even been looking. "I swear, I need my own flat."

Anna's face, which had been soft with distraction, regained its shape. She raised her eyebrows and lifted her glass, extending one pinkie for a small, dainty sip.

Sophie felt a bolt of anger go through her. Just leave it, she thought. She might as well have been staring at her mother again. Please just let it go.

"What?" she said.

"Flat?"

"Apartment, whatever. You know what I mean."

Anna set her elbows on the table and lifted her sandwich with both hands.

"So, what's Retsy's problem? What's so bad you might need your own *flat*?"

"Don't be a cunt."

"It's great, thank you," Anna said. She was talking to the waiter who'd come to ask how things were.

She turned back to Sophie, seeming to have forgotten entirely what had just happened. Her tone was wistful again.

"It's funny," she said. "How you never really decide to stop doing things. It just kind of . . . happens." She paused, one fingernail working against the edge of her napkin. "Like dress-up, I mean."

"Right . . . ," Sophie said. She chewed slowly and drank from her water.

Something was going on she couldn't quite parse. There were currents, there was noise, things she could feel whose source was unknown. What was Anna after? What was the correct thing to say?

Maybe, Sophie thought, she should just ask, say simply, Hey, are you OK? And she should press—not too much, but a little—when at first Anna insisted she was. Because hadn't she had such days herself? Days of hoping someone might not believe her when she said things were fine and that nothing was new. What if she did that now? The weird thing. The one that felt strange and wrong but might also be perfect.

The scene flashed through her mind: their lunches forgotten, the two of them on the same side of the booth; and both crying—not sadly, but with the happy relief of discovery—indifferent to the scene they were making. The day would be good. Years later, they'd remember it with a smile, the world a kind and worthwhile place.

For a moment, the thought hung in suspension; it felt possible and close. But then, in a breath, it was gone and Sophie's skin crawled at the idea. How desperate it would seem, how sentimental. And who knew what Anna would say. Maybe she'd turn on her, make her feel silly and dumb. Am I *OK?* she might repeat. What are you, my therapist? We're not even friends. I don't even know why I asked you to meet.

With this, Sophie felt herself descend into a new, chillier conviction. No, it was time to go, to leave Anna behind. Because fuck her. Fuck her and her judgments and the way she could be mean one moment and needing the next. It didn't work like that—not anymore. Who were they after all? Just people whose parents liked to hang out. And that wasn't anything. It wasn't her job to care about someone she'd not even picked—someone who sensed immediately what she was up to when she said flat and refused to just let her have it; who sprang—not only now, but for so many years—at every chance to make her feel small.

No, things had changed. Were changing. Sophie was teaching Anna a lesson. She felt herself turning away, withdrawing like a hand pulled into the sleeve of a coat. They would see each other again. But something was happening now, something that would last.

Perhaps Anna had begun to feel it already. Looking at her, Sophie sensed an unease she hadn't before.

Anna lifted her sandwich then set it down without taking a bite. Her teeth pulled faintly at the edge of her lip, her cheeks hollowed as though she were about to speak. Something was coming, Sophie could tell. She watched it begin to form.

In another world she might have been eager—too eager—to hear what it was. But not anymore.

The waiter crossed nearby, his hands full of stacked plates.

"Excuse me," Sophie called. He stopped, his face a strained smile. "The check, please. When you have a chance."

She turned back to Anna. "I'm sorry, I don't mean to rush off, but—" She moved her hands. "You know."

# 14

The elevator was out, the doorman said. He apologized. A service had been called and would be there in an hour or two. He held open the entrance to the stairwell. A thin strip of arm showed between his cuff and his glove.

"I don't mind," Retsy said. "Five floors." She shrugged. "Give my best to the people on ten."

He smiled and thanked her. He was young. Twenty-six, no more than that. As she began to climb, Retsy pictured his bedroom. Its few posters, its books, the window looking out at smokestacks.

Suddenly, a voice from below.

"Mom?"

Retsy stopped. The sound of an approach—quick steps, slapping like applause. Her daughter appeared. She was smiling. She seemed to be in a good mood. Was it a boy, Retsy

wondered. Had she undressed? Was there blood? No, she decided. Soon, perhaps, but not yet.

"Well, this is an adventure."

"I believe in us," Sophie replied.

They stood for a moment. Above, several flights up, a door
opened and closed. The noise confirmed their solitude. Retsy
felt it at once: meeting like this—in a place both familiar
and yet also apart—leveled things. They weren't equals, not
quite; nor were they colleagues. But a change was underway.
One could imagine them in a few years, discussing the handsome host of a party and his second wife.

"Here," Sophie said. She took the bag from her mother
and began climbing the stairs.

Retsy watched her go with a bemused smile. Inside was
stationery, lotion, a box of candles for the dining room table.
It was light—so light as to make help unnecessary, so light
that it was little more than a gesture. And yet, didn't that
make it bigger, too? That it *was* a gesture, that her daughter
understood the value of such things.

Perhaps she was getting carried away. Wasn't it really
rather little, taking a parent's bag? Wasn't it the least one
could hope for a polite child to do? Maybe, Retsy allowed.
But then again—no, never mind. That was unfair; it was
selling both of them short. Because it wasn't just the bag. It
was the idea of consideration. It was poised and natural ci-
vility.

She began climbing now, too. She felt her legs working,
lifting her up.

So often she doubted herself, so often she wondered. But
she was a good mother, wasn't she? Just look at this girl.

Her legs, her gait, still a bit boyish; the knees too visible, the arms too far away from her sides. But that was passing. One morning—tomorrow, even—it would fall from her like scales. She would grow. Her face would appear—her true face, the one she was waiting to achieve.

She would be brilliant, subtle, shrewd, the woman one longs to charm. After college, she might live briefly in Lisbon, in Rome. She would send letters about the mushrooms that grew in the street. Museums, wine, luggage bound with buckles and straps. She would go to the Tate, to the cathedrals of Viollet-le-Duc. And not only that, she would be good. She was already and would remain so.

"That's a nice skirt," Retsy said. "It suits your hips."

A faint aroma was trailing her daughter. It wasn't perfume or odor, it was just heat and hair and skin. It was the way a person smells who is alive, who has chosen clothes and put them on.

Some days it might seem like Sophie had gone. Like maybe Retsy had infected her—made her too small, too calculating. Or perhaps that she'd failed to protect her from the petty cruelties of her father. His withholding of laughter, for instance, or the way, by merely touching his chin, he could make clear how unwanted you were. These were small, quiet acts; they sloughed off him like dander. Had his daughter inhaled too much? What were the signs? How could a mother prevent something so subtle, so everywhere?

And yet, here they were, seeming to have reached the far shore. She felt a great outflow of generous warmth. Her family, whatever its stumbles, was precious and worthy and rare. It meant everything, this fact. It meant that Retsy had managed, that she was decent, that she had not failed. It meant Sophie would not forget her, that in the end she would come back.

"Where've you been?" Retsy asked. Her ring tapped lightly against the railing.

"Getting lunch with Anna," Sophie said without turning. "It was OK."

Visibly, Retsy showed nothing. Her steps were assured, her face pleasant, composed. Beneath, however, a bloom of concern.

What a lunatic thing that had been that Emerson told her. And yet—four days later now—it was already fading from view. The thought of him was all but normal; only the faintest, the most passing sensation, accompanied the idea. It was like a watch dropped in the ocean. The last glimmer is impossible to perceive. Was it the band or just water catching the light?

"What did you get?" Retsy asked.

"An omelet," Sophie said. Her voice was easy, uncaring. It concealed nothing.

"Yum."

"Without potatoes," her daughter added.

"That's smart," Retsy said. "It's so much easier, you know, forming good habits at your age."

Sophie nodded. They had reached their floor. The landing was dusty. A mop stood among pipes, its ends dry as grass.

As she looked at her daughter, Retsy found herself thinking of Anna. Anna—the name itself had become faintly astringent; it made her feel uneasy, almost afraid. Still, she hoped the girl was all right. Amos, too. He must be upset. How could he not when his daughter was acting this way? It would be a shock, certainly, given what a lovely, kind child she'd been. One of the good ones. You weren't supposed to say so, but you really could tell—which were worthwhile and which didn't have any juice.

Retsy smiled, restrained but sincere. Whatever this was, this final touch of affectionate heat, was like some ritual performed by the last of a tribe. After this, it would be remembered no more.

"It's nice, to get lunch with her. But you know," she said, "it's OK to grow apart, too."

Beneath them, several flights down, men were laughing.

"I know," Sophie said. She seemed to understand that something was being imparted. More lesson than command, a kind of instruction for how to live. Her eyes watched her mother; they longed to be brutal and wise.

"And Anna is . . ." Retsy waved her hand. "She's wonderful, of course. But you can choose your friends, too. It's just that you're so smart, and I don't ever want to see you held back by old things."

Sophie nodded. Retsy touched her by the ear. Below, the doorman was greeting the mechanic. His mouth was stained at the corners. His belt was sagging with tools.

## 15

Dusk. Pale, depleted. The sky an old shirt, the room surrounding them with a terminal calm. Amos stood. He ached with confusion. Somewhere below, trains shrieked in tunnels. The walls swallowed their sounds like the sea.

"No?"

He said the word back to her as though it were a strange object he'd been handed.

"No," Claire repeated. "There's no way."

He massaged the bridge of his nose.

"*We* asked what she wanted."

"Amos." She said his name like it were the answer to a question. "We can't. We can't. That would be—that would make everything worse."

"How?"

"You know what she means. She wants to confront him, to accuse him, to make a whole scene."

She turned as she said this and stood framed by the drapes. Along the street, lights had begun to come on.

Was it the same her who looked away from him now? Her eyes were her eyes—calm, assured brown—but the rest was harder, more ossified. Twenty years had gone by. Their life was no longer pretend.

"Make a scene?" he said weakly. "Did you see her?"

"Yes—to give herself a stage, so this feels exciting and real."

She looked toward the dresser. One drawer was slightly ajar. Her shirts lay on the floor, the bed. She knelt to gather them, folding each as she spoke.

"Because what will he think? What will he think, Amos? If we insist on staging this," she looked up, searching the ceiling, "this *trial*?"

"He might think we believe her."

"Yes."

"And that will make everything worse?"

"Stop."

How, he wondered, could she say it so bluntly. They'd left Anna's room only moments before, had hugged her—both at the same time—while Claire said they would talk, that things would get better and someday be OK.

"Have you not even considered it? Have you never wondered for even a second?"

Claire spun sharply.

"Of course I've *thought* about it," she hissed. Her voice angry and close. "I'm her mother, you think I've not thought about it?"

She turned away. She was remembering something; it came

as she spoke. Picnic tables by the water, a tent overhead. Paper plates. On them, lobsters red as sunburns. Her father was holding one up. The legs, he was saying. That's how you know a man's worth his salt—check to see if he eats the legs. Next to him, Amos sat nodding, brow furrowed in mock fascination. He risked only a glance at Claire. She looked down so as not to laugh. Then something else came, a new feeling. Couldn't he not? Couldn't he just let her dad have his moment without needing to remind her that he was smarter, or better? Because who cared if John's wisdoms were pompous and trite? Hadn't he been generous enough? Don't smirk, she thought. Don't look at me. Don't tell me my dad's a big joke.

That's what Claire felt now, an indignant rage at the sneer of his question. Had she never wondered? What a thing to ask. To suggest she might not care. It was possible to do both, to suffer for Anna's sadness and to mistrust its cause. This was what Amos refused to see: that what she did was the hardest of all. Her heart broke to see her daughter upset, but she was caring at the same time as she was saving their family. Because someone had to think of life after the storm. To make sure there was water, that the savings hadn't been spent. So how dare he stand there like that, drunk on easy conviction?

Her words came quickly now, self-assured.

"You think only you love her. You think I'm just some partial person. But I'm not. And I do."

"Claire—"

"You aren't the only one who cares about things," she said, blowing past him. "The rest of us give a shit, too."

She pressed her hands together and held them to her lips.

"So what if? What if it happened? What would she need? To relive it over and over? To see him again? To make her whole life about a couple of minutes?"

"Claire," he said, "I see people. The people I see, they were kids . . ."

"No." She was bitter, emphatic. "No, you don't get to do that. I don't want to hear you make this into some fucking idea."

Her voice slowed, slipped around him.

"She has to go on, she has to move forward."

She crossed the room now and knit her fingers behind his neck. "Just like you. Like you, with your parents. You had to leave, so you did."

"It's not the same." He shook his head. "It's different. You have to see how it's different."

"You only think that because you're so hard on yourself, because you never believe that anything you do ever counts."

The line hung like the last, right note of a song. He was stunned by her crass intuition. Wasn't it true? Not the part about Anna, but that he so rarely gave himself credit. For a moment he shivered at an emerging new thought. Did she have a point, after all? Was there something to what she said? He was so tired—of thinking, of being mean to himself, of always feeling on guard.

"So, yes," she went on, quietly still. "Even if. Even *if*, it needs to be over."

Silence engulfed the room like smoke. Shadows washed the floor.

"It has to be," she said again. "You see what I mean? It can't be a whole thing. Because once there's a question . . ."

Claire stepped back and looked at him. She sensed something give in his face like the soft spot on a peach.

"What if I told?" he asked. "What if I just told people the truth?"

He'd thought this might shock her but she merely shrugged, went to the table and turned on a lamp. The light climbed her neck.

"I know them, anyone you would call."

"You think they won't believe me?"

"It's not a question of that; they may or may not. It won't matter. They don't want to. It would cost them too much."

His mouth opened slightly.

"Not like that. It's—you don't understand. It's like fine china. You don't know. And they don't know either, they just sense it. There can't be cracks. There can't be anything."

"But Claire, I can't just—we can't not . . ."

"Amos, you can."

He looked up. He seemed to become newly aware of the room.

"No," he said. His voice gathered speed. "No. Because how does she live like that? If we act like everything's fine?" He stood. "And if that means—if his life gets fucked up, if Retsy is mad—I don't care. It isn't our job to care."

Claire felt things at risk of slipping away. He wasn't speaking to her so much as himself, and what patience she'd managed to summon abruptly burned off. She wanted to reach out and slap him. Not like a man but a child. A boy who isn't paying attention, who won't stop crying and just sit up straight. It was the same incensed lurch she'd felt toward Michael Roman. Both of them clumsy, ignorant to the fact that she'd already decided how things should be.

"Just fucking stop," she snapped. Her words like something flicked from the sleeve of a coat. Her hands ached to clench him, to rattle his face. Of course people shake babies to death. Because they won't listen, because there's no way to just make them see.

Amos flinched. Weakness rippled under his features like fish in the shallows. Claire took a long breath. It wouldn't work, her anger. She saw now that it would drive him away.

"Please," she said. "I don't want to fight."

She held him by the button of his shirt.

"Just come back. I'm not the enemy and you don't have to fight. There's no war, Amos. Not against him, or my dad, or any of us. We can all just be OK."

"But," he said again, "we can't do nothing."

Yes, there. She'd regained her grip. He settled like a horse beneath her sure, steady hand.

"I'm not saying that. We can take time. We should; we should've already. We can go somewhere. I'll take a month. France, maybe. Not Paris, a small town. Let's just go and be there—all three of us—we'll just be there." She paused. Her fingers swam through his hair. "Together."

Together. The word beckoned. The whole image like a beautifully laid table. He could see it. Quiet mornings, leaves underfoot. Bicycles left against fountains in the square. Cats—dark, impassive—curled in the window of the *boulangerie*. Anna rising late. The sole of her foot appearing like a sprout from beneath white sheets. Juice, coffee, the soft clink of a knife in the jam. In the afternoon, they would drive. All of them, Claire in the back, would explode around turns like birds flushed from the reeds. To Amboise, Dinan, Cassis—places they'd picked over lunch.

He reached toward her. Her shoulders went limp in his arms.

"I just don't understand." She was weeping now. It began suddenly, without warning. "I love you so much. I love our life."

"What are you saying?" His voice was weak, searching. His questions floated up from the deep. "What are you saying will happen?"

"I don't know. I'm just—I'm trying to explain so you'll see." Her words came in almost a whisper, each thin as eggshells. "Why we might not survive it."

Amos felt his anger go slack. Had it come like a threat it might have been different. Then it would've been an attack, an act of aggression to which he'd respond. But this wasn't that. She was forlorn, almost bereft. They were words she did not want to say.

And what was it he'd felt since Anna first told him? Wasn't lonely the only true word? His daughter was sealed in her story, his wife inside hers, and somewhere beyond the walls of their house was the best friend he'd not spoken to, whose thoughts he could hardly stand to imagine, thoughts he longed more than anything else to know. And Amos had been alone, adrift, tumbling like a climber through the thin air of his life.

He couldn't bear it, the idea that things might simply be like this now. Not again, not when he'd done it for so long already. As a child he'd had no choice but to turn inward, it was the only way to inure himself to the chaos of his mother's screaming about unpaid bills and a father who died having lost half his teeth. Plus all that fear—fear like a ground that never stopped shaking, a floor always about to cave in. It might have worked for a while, sealing himself off, but where had it left him if not alone?

Yes, along the way there'd been friends. Even good friends to whom he felt close. But that wasn't the same. Just think how well he knew when to step aside as a photo was taken, how rarely anyone would protest. Not because they were mean, but because it was right. Everyone understood he was only a guest.

There, the phrase of his life. Only a guest. How much it explained. The gratitude, of course, the teary-eyed sense that he'd been given more than he could ever repay. But also how delicate everything seemed, the way nothing had roots. Because what if one day someone needed a new, better friend? What if they simply got bored?

Then, at last, he had found it: the thing he'd wanted for so long, whose shape he could describe only by the hole its absence had left. It was a family, it was people he cared for, upon whom he could rely, and who said of him, Yes, we'd like you around.

What an unspeakable relief it had been. Not so much a feeling of coming home as discovering it for the first time. All his life, Amos's mind had been a turbulent froth, and yet with this came, finally, some quiet. A life of some quiet. Some rest. A sense that things might be all right.

His hand reached toward Claire's face. Her cheek was cool and wet. She climbed into his lap. The bed creaked like snow.

"I get it now," she said. "I get how it must've been to see Anna like that—to see her . . . I don't know, like you."

She kissed his neck. Softly, once on each side. Then his lips. They were dry. He ran his tongue slowly across them. Her hot breath in his ear.

"I'm not mad," she said. "I'm not mad."

He nodded. He did not speak. The warmth of her was pulling him down. He was flooded with images, scraps of their life.

Sunday, July, afternoon in his apartment. The cool, simple shade. They'd been lying in the limpid glow of half sentences, fingers on a bare back. Looking down, Claire saw a last teardrop of moisture remained. She took him, still heavy with lingering blood, and drew a small heart on his thigh. The light from the window caught the sheen. There, she said. All done. It was like the last hour of the day which is salvaged, made of some use. Amos felt awed by her power. She was the sort of woman to whom he might give everything.

What if? What if she were right? He didn't mean that she was, but what if she were? Might his friend not be lost forever? Was there a world in which they could still sit by the fire upstate? Yes, perhaps—he could almost believe. Not right away, of course. It would take work. First, a lunch; some weeks later, dinner; then a long walk in the park, at the end, sheepish, teenage smiles, a tentative hug. Maybe it would take years. But if they cared enough to try, it could be done. Wasn't that the one thing Amos believed? That love looked like the effort you were willing to make.

"I wish you didn't hate me."

She spoke past him, to a spot on a wall.

"Claire."

Her arms squeezed to keep him from pulling away.

"I don't mean you don't love me, I just mean—when you hate me, why do you?"

Amos felt suddenly that it was a simple question, that he had known the answer forever, that he'd been hoping someday to be asked.

"Because you don't want me to be who I am."

Claire sat back. She looked at him for a moment, holding his head like a vase. Then she went to the window, opening it as though to let his words slip into the night. She turned and sighed. Her face soft with pity, contempt, the faint glow of anger which has recently left.

"Neither do you," she said. "Neither do you."

# 16

E merson had nearly been through the door when a voice called out.

"Ford," it shouted. He turned to see Nick Cutler coming up the block. His cheeks were boyish and fat and shook slightly. He had small teeth and thin hair.

They embraced lightly, then stood, like chairs missing a table. Without explanation, Emerson felt seized by an exhausted disdain; something like hatred welled up in his chest. The strength of it surprised him: Nick was irritating and dull, but even so, this was more than his presence deserved.

He was getting remarried, he announced. He'd chosen the ring.

"From the most scrupulous mine, I'm sure," Emerson replied. It was a joke that made vague reference to Nick's having been expelled for cheating.

Nick waved this away.

"There's no such thing as a diamond someone didn't bleed for, the only question is where on the ledger it happens."

In response, Emerson made a small sound. A laugh, or something meant to suggest it. Nick accepted it without question, grinning his satisfaction. Would Emerson be there, he wanted to know. It was to be small, no more than two hundred people, and his presence would mean a great deal— not just to him but his parents as well.

Emerson smiled.

"Without a doubt."


UPSTAIRS, HE SHUT THE DOOR to his office and sat. He was relieved to be alone. His mind was moving; things were coming back. One moment he was at his desk, the next in the shade of his grandfather's garage, thoughts blurring with the gasoline's sweet, mechanical smell.

Sandy, a man whose austerity showed itself in the blunt violence with which he cracked nuts, collected cars, keeping them like statues under rumpled brown tarps. It was something of which Emerson had retained only a dim awareness, until one visit when his grandfather insisted the two of them go for a drive. The way he said it seemed to imply some importance; there'd even been a kind of ceremony with which he led Emerson to the carriage house—by the long, lunging strides reserved for when he was excited, or mad. That one, Sandy said, pointing. Deep, green paint; its grille gleaming like teeth. Find me a girl who'll say no to that. Emerson nodded to show he agreed. He was seven years old.

Then they were off, he and his grandfather, sailing past

branches that shimmered with leaves, the roads carving the
fields, rail fences, cows. Sandy worked the clutch in cruel,
abrupt jerks; the car jumped to respond. Emerson sensed
there was a way he should feel, and what was more, that it
had something to do with his being a man. But no matter
how hard he tried, he just didn't care. Toward their speed
and the rumble in the soles of his shoes and the curious
heads turning when they stopped, he felt only indifference.

Suddenly and without thinking, he reached to take his
grandfather's hand. The touch shocked them both; instantly
he knew it was wrong. Sandy wrenched away as if stung,
staring down with a boil of anger and fear. It was bad, what
he'd done; he'd made an important mistake. Emerson looked
at his feet. Sorry, he said softly. But it was to no one that he
spoke: the wind's roaring crumple swallowed his words.

They drove on. Sandy stiff and alert; Emerson hunched,
hands under his thighs, where they grew hot and clung to
the leather.

The drive left him with a feeling he'd had before, that he
wasn't the right kind of boy. Emerson sensed already that
there was a way he should be—not just as one in general,
but as one like him. By then tall for his class, he had intimations that certain things would come easily. His face looked
the right way; in summer, he browned the proper amount.
Though he didn't have words to describe it, from the fathers
of friends he sensed a vague, threatened disquiet—the idea
of him meant something, reminded them of what they didn't
have. Friends of his mother stroked his hair. My god, Mary,
they said. Children aren't supposed to be handsome.

That's how it had gone: at each stage of his life, things

had made sense. There seemed, for instance, something inevitable about the fact that people called him by his last
name. Ford, they all said. Ford, get over here. Even teachers,
even girls. It was cool and right; it was as it should be.

Then Amos had come and insisted on calling him Emerson. He'd never said why, he just did. Even when no one else
would, even as he met friend after friend who knew him as
Ford. None of that mattered; he continued on just the same.
And the most remarkable thing was how much it meant.
Emerson had never been aware of such a desire, but when
Amos arrived with his choice, the sensation was like being
caught off guard by music. It left him sad in a happy kind of
way—blindsided by poignant gratitude.

What an odd thing to love someone for—just calling
you by your real name—but he did. Because in sensing that
it was truer and more right, Amos showed he understood
who Emerson was. Such an obvious thing to say of one's clos-
est friend, but still it seemed a big deal. Ford was simply a
sound to which he'd respond, an idea of someone like him—
handsome and rich; arrogant, charming, and tall. Emerson
was the name of the person he felt like inside; Emerson was
the part of him that didn't care about cars or sports all that
much, the part that sometimes wanted nothing more than to
talk about a line in a book, or the particular sadness when a
girl lost interest. It's kind of like dying, he'd said to Amos
one night. And as his friend laughed with recognition, it had
seemed to Emerson that his thought wasn't just true, but perhaps even smart.

This, too, was the gift Amos had given: to make him feel
like he had some substance, some core. Didn't it vouch for

him, being friends with someone possessed of such brutal intellect, whose life had been formed amid a turmoil of poverty and neglect? Because why would a person like that choose a friend like him if he weren't worth being around?

What a relief it had been to find someone who seemed to believe that he was. Perhaps, Emerson thought, it might be the antidote to his long-held fear that he was flawed in some terminal way. What he meant by this was more than not living up to the promise of his teeth and his hair: it was a darkness, a break, a space at the center where something should be. Was it possible that in a real and unfixable sense, he might not be a good person? No, Amos's friendship seemed to insist. It was the proof, the evidence the jury cannot dismiss.

EMERSON LOOKED DOWN at his desk. The stapler sat in its place. Through the window, the light fell in shards. The papers waited for what few notes he might make.

He understood now why he'd been so upset at hearing himself called to and seeing Nick's smooth, unthinking face. Fumbling and accidental as always, he had stepped into Emerson's life with no purpose other than to remind him of the person he'd be if not for Amos.

The thing he said to Claire about needing his friend, perhaps it came so easily because it was true. It had been intended as a show of affection, but was it really just that? No. What he felt now was less regret than a wavering fear; to say he needed Amos was a statement more structural, more literal, than he'd realized at first.

Lately Emerson had begun to understand certain things. Not as ideas, but as truths that could not be outrun. He felt the chill of a narrowing tunnel. A process was beginning, one he wouldn't survive. His breath would grow sour, his hands would shake in the cold. And who would come with him? Who would make sure that he was all right? Because he was a good man. Not always, of course. But he wasn't all bad. People thought he didn't care about things, but he did—they needed to see that he did. And he wanted to be OK in the end, to be fine, to shut his eyes and not feel as if something were slowly tearing him away from the center, stretching him like a skin left to dry in the sun.

Yes, there was Sophie. She loved him, didn't she? Retsy, too, on certain days. Plus all the others. How many had come to his birthday? Fifty, one hundred, perhaps. Oh, but who cared? He knew they didn't add up. They were like objects on the shelves of his house: Amos was the walls. He calmed him, he made things work. How had Emerson not understood? How had he not grasped this until now?

Wait, Claire had said. Let him come to you. And he had. For more than a week now he had. But things couldn't keep going like that. His first instinct was right: he should've called Amos while she still stood there in his office. The realization came as a cold twist in his gut. To cower like this seemed, if not guilty, at least not quite innocent. Just imagine, he thought, what he would've done if it really hadn't been true. Wouldn't he have brushed Claire aside the moment she'd asked and gone to find Amos wherever he was? Wouldn't he have taken his hands—yes, he could tell, touching like that would not have felt strange—and squeezed into them the need for him to believe, to know he would never, of course he would never.

He'd fucked up—he saw that now, and with this came a vision of the world not only in which he wasn't believed, but where he really had done it. It flashed like a frame on the news, silent footage taken during a war. And as it did, he saw it almost for the first time. Or newly again. Or newly from the right angle. This act, this thing he had done.

For a moment of forlorn amazement, Emerson felt only wonder. How could he? What had he been thinking?

The room sat silent around him. It gave no reply.

It was, he began. It was just . . .

His thoughts were breaking, coming apart. He searched for phrases. Everything crumbled like clods of dirt.

It was nothing. Yes, nothing, that was the word. It was nothing at all. That was the problem, the tragedy. It was what he must go now to Amos and explain.

## 17

A new man sat at the desk. He was short, only a sliver of his head showed. As Amos approached, his smile searched him for signs of belonging.

"I work upstairs."

A slight pause of unease.

"On six." Amos pointed to his name on the board. "I promise."

The man nodded gratefully and Amos walked on, his legs feeling gangly and new. It was only a moment, but in it he'd glimpsed himself as a stranger; he saw how it would feel to arrive and be unknown.

His office was downtown, overlooking streets whose names gave him a faintly arrogant pleasure to say. The lobby was small, but pleasant. Toward the back were elevators like those from a dream: they rose slowly, clanking at each floor. He shared his with an architecture firm, a law office, a magazine that published explicit stories and poems. Inside, shelves climbed the wall behind his desk, the spines of their books dark as wood. The furniture was simple, expensive. To one side was a narrow kitchen where Amos made tea.

He came four days a week, though Wednesdays were reserved for paperwork, calls. It was exactly the right amount, leaving him taxed but not tired. It gave him purpose without grandeur, demanded effort without toil. That way he had everything to give—he could listen entirely, help people make sense of their lives.

And what a refuge that was. If the world of his past were one in which people could die in the living room, their gangrenous leg leaking pus, then his office stood as a monument to the world he'd built for himself—one of steady, dependable days, work that mattered, walks home past wine stores whose owners he knew, walks beneath clean, October light.

Lately, though, it had begun to appear different. In the week since Anna told them what happened, he'd walked the halls as if beneath the gaze of a judgmental crowd. The doorman's gloved wave, the matting around his diplomas. Everything pointed, everything knew.

It was no secret what made all this possible. Could he have had it without Claire and her family? Of course not— not in the same way. In such a world it would matter how many patients he saw and whether they filled out the right forms. In it, he'd live far from his work, he'd change trains; the stairs to his apartment would be trimmed with rubber. And Amos knew he hadn't the strength for that. Perhaps he'd have tried for a year, maybe two. But eventually he would've succumbed—gone to law school, pressed his friends for jobs at a bank. He would've joined the incurious crowds shuddering slightly aboard trains bearing them to the desks at which they would sit until it was time to go home. All so he could read menus from left to right, so he might not feel ashamed of the address on his letters.

Yes, he loved Claire. But how to untangle love from the promise of a life in which certain things would be so much easier? Was theirs a transaction? Was anything not? It went without saying that when they had met certain thoughts crossed his mind: the house they would own, their children's inevitable schools, the way he could work as he wanted without paying the cost. Plus, just imagine how much more present and loving and open he'd be. All because his days weren't filled with deadening hours, because his mind was no longer so clenched with dread.

AMOS LET HIS COAT slip down his arms. The lamp clicked softly; light fell on the rug. In the courtyard below, a man stood smoking. After a moment, he crushed the end with his heel. Birds fled from his feet.

Claire's one line had changed everything. We might not survive it. Had she realized what it would mean for him to hear? She must have. But also, how could she? It was as though she'd stood at the crest of a hill and swept her arm across the horizon. All this, all this is mine. What she'd said wasn't nearly so strong as a promise, not even something more likely than not. It was simply the chance—the assurance that a door would be opened. How wide was not within her power to say.

The man outside was gone. The garden, the benches, sat empty.

If she left, she would go totally. That part Amos knew. The machinery of such things worked with cool assurance. He would be crushed by her wake, left like a gambler who's lost everything but his last suit. And then what? How would the days come?

His mind flailed as it tried to picture them. He would move through the rooms of his apartment, pausing for a sip of cold coffee. His thoughts would grow old in his head. His feet would ache, his teeth by then yellow and thin. And the world would withdraw—not in horror but quiet disgust. He'd be revealed as a guest after all; one who'd charmed the hosts for far longer than anyone expected, but whose time to leave had now come.

It made him weak to imagine. He knew he wouldn't survive. Because somewhere inside him were the parts of his father that let himself wither and die; his mother, too, and the fear which devoured her mind. They sat like explosives left by an army in retreat. No matter how many years passed, he must always tread lightly. When he was young, doing so took all that he had; now, Amos feared, there was nothing left.

The vision Claire had painted of France whispered like a breeze in his thoughts. Even if she were wrong, she might still have a point. Wasn't everyone tired? Didn't it make sense to reset, take a rest? They could just slip out of their lives for a bit until things were all sorted out.

Amos wheeled on himself. How dare he think in such abstract terms? What was he saying if not that he might abandon his daughter, leave her to be ground down by the doubt of the world? She had asked for only one thing. Just to see him, she said. She just wanted to see him. Of course Amos knew why. If they let her, she'd know they believed.

Yet here he was like a widow whose fortune is lost. All these lovely things, he thought, touching them one by one. Gleaming wood floors, wide-paneled and rich. Nights in Capri, Gstaad, the ring of forks on their plates. The way Les Clos looked as he poured it, how Claire's face opened when he set a glass by her side. Or mornings with patients, notes written on thick, heavy paper, his pen scratching like ice. But not just stuff—no, it was so much more than that. What he had was a place that didn't shake under his feet. It was beautiful, wasn't it? His weakness, his complicity, were etched in each detail.

The phone on his desk shook slightly as it rang. There was a pause, then the new man's uncertain voice.

"Would you like me to send up your guest?" he asked.

Another pause, a murmur beyond his cupped hand, then the line became clear.

"Mr. Ford?" he said. "Would you like Mr. Ford to come up?"

# 18

They stood apart, bodies timid, concave. Like parentheses clutching dates, their history was between them.

Amos had refused Emerson's hug. That mattered. He must continue to feel the room was still his. Emerson smiled. Weak, reaching, a smile for an old lover seen at a party. Amos felt himself long to receive it. He turned toward the window.

Behind him, Emerson's voice.

"I would never."

The words landed softly in the still, quiet room. Amos showed no sign of having heard. Emerson took a step forward. The rug accepted him without a sound. Clever mind, it had given him words that might be true. He wouldn't ever—not again. Saying made him believe.

"Don't," Amos said.

Emerson watched his friend's shoulders, the ends of his

hair. He couldn't help sensing his weakness. He hadn't been looking, it was plain.

"What can I say?"

Now Amos turned. It was all there on his face—a turmoil of confusion and conflicted desire, the searching eyes of a boy who's lost hold of his mother's hand.

"Don't sit," he said.

These words undermined him somehow. They were too bold, self-aware. He looked back to the window. "Why would she say it?"

Emerson's voice was gentle, almost faint. "How can I know?"

"Because you were there."

Amos moved toward him without thinking, an awkward, instinctual lunge.

"Because you were the only one there. And you've known her her whole fucking life."

These words, the truth of them, sharpened his mind.

"She's my *daughter*," he cried out. It was the only right thing he could say. His face looked windblown and raw.

Emerson knew he should wait. His movements must be graceful, assured. Amos wanted to be led without feeling the reins. It must be like nothing, like air.

"Why would I?" He let his arms fall to his sides as though it were a truth too obvious to explain. "We have the best life. I love all our days."

Amos was scratching his head with both hands. They were the thoughts he'd already had.

"Amos," Emerson pressed. Gently, barely.

"I know."

"People don't have friendships like ours."

"I know."

"No one knows anyone."

Amos felt the set of his face limpen. It was fragile now, delicate as damp paper. Outside, strangers were calling to taxis. On the radio, voices discussed traffic, the prices of shares.

Emerson spread his arms. "Amos," he said again. He was gesturing toward everything, all of it. It was too much to describe.

Amos crossed to his desk where he sat for an instant before leaping up. He wanted to shatter the peace.

"Why the fuck would she say it if it weren't true?" He stared at him. "Why the fuck would she?"

The words battered the walls. Emerson said nothing. He let them settle, fall away. A sweet, vulnerable silence formed in their wake. Finally, Amos spoke again.

"Then you tell me—you tell me what happened."

Emerson shrugged helplessly.

"I moved her. That's all. Roughly, maybe. I don't know. Maybe it was a shove. Kids, girls—they imagine too much."

Amos shook his head. The answers piled on him like stones. One question remained. He was ashamed that he hadn't asked yet. Because he was afraid, of course. Even now, even still. His throat opened, closed, opened again. He looked up.

"Then why did you tell Claire?"

"Tell her what?"

"Don't," Amos said. His voice cool as a blade.

Emerson knew it had been a mistake.

"I just assumed," he tried again. "I thought by now it must have come up."

"No," Amos shook his head. "No. I don't believe you—I don't believe that. You knew how that was for me; you knew what it meant."

"Jesus."

"You wanted a wedge."

"I wanted to help."

"You wanted her to remember that I'm not like you."

Emerson snorted but said nothing. Amos looked at him. His face like one's childhood home. The brown eyes—their lightness, the sparkling belief in themselves. Plus the rest. The same skin, the nose. It was eighteen, it was thirty, it was now; it was smiling as it sat down to lunch; it was laughing at a joke Amos had made; it was confiding in him; it was being nearby.

Amos rubbed his eyes.

"Do you remember what you said when you set us up?"

"That you were the best person I knew."

"To me, I mean. Before I left to go meet her."

Emerson waited.

"You said don't take the bus."

"Why are we talking about this?"

"Because you wouldn't have said that if you understood— if you had any idea who I am."

"I was *twenty-five*."

"It doesn't matter."

"Why not?" Emerson said, suddenly, authentically, mad. "*You* want to be forgiven for everything. When you're aloof, or you're sad, or you're in a bad mood, or when you don't return someone's call for a month and they have to ask me if things are OK."

He'd found a rhythm; he rode it like a runner in the calm middle miles of a race. "Then we all need to just understand." He held up his hands. "'It's how Amos is. It's his mind, his parents, et cetera. Don't take it personally, just let it go.'"

He paused and exhaled, reached an unthinking hand toward his head.

"Don't touch your fucking hair," Amos said.

This strange, unexpected line caught them both by surprise. Heat prickled under Emerson's skin.

"Fuck you," he said. "Don't throw this at me." He was pointing. He felt his hand shake at the end of his arm. "Don't throw all this at me like it matters. Because some things don't. Some things are just nothing."

"It's only nothing to the person who doesn't care," Amos said calmly.

Inside Emerson, a small, sudden rupture. How certain Amos seemed of himself. It was the one idea of his life, the thing on which he'd tried to build everything else.

Emerson crossed the room. He felt himself looming over the desk.

"You aren't better." His voice was quiet, savage. His features quivered. "You aren't better than us."

Amos sat still. What had he just seen? Something new? Or old, but familiar? Once, maybe. Yes—that night in college. The two of them passing in a party's dark basement; Emerson was drunk and moved in lurching, inelegant steps. But that wasn't what Amos saw then or what came back to him now. It was Emerson's eyes. They were distant, predatory—

more than those of a stranger, they confessed a removed sort of hatred, the contempt one feels toward an object of no possible use. They looked past Amos, through him; they went toward something that did not exist—a coldness, a place desolate, remote as a forest at night.

Amos swallowed. He understood something he hadn't before. If Emerson had done it, that's where he had been, that was the place in his mind he'd have needed to go. It was like understanding the logic with which a crime has unfolded. Ah, yes, and if they fell like that, the vase would've been within reach.

"What am I to you?" he asked finally.

"What?"

"What *am I* to you?" Amos drew the words out, laying them down slowly, like banknotes. "What's my point? Why did you ever want me around?"

Emerson's anger vanished. This question pushed itself slowly into him like the end of a pin. He winced. It was his friend he was seeing, the one who really did wonder; who, despite himself, longed to be reassured. What had he done to him? What had he done? The air was rushing out, the room constricted like a dry throat. He let his voice crumble slightly, as though it were almost a laugh.

"I can't do it," he shrugged. "I can't. Without you, life would only ever be partway."

Amos seemed not to hear. "Why would she?" he asked again. He was speaking to no one.

Emerson waved his hands loosely.

"You know that I can't. You know that I need you around."

His voice came differently now, differently than Amos

had ever heard it before. The strength was gone out of it, the heat. Now it seemed desperate, like a man at the gallows still pleading his case.

"Amos, please," Emerson said. "Think. All these things. All these days. You want to give this all up?"

Amos felt himself falter. Sadness choked him like smoke. What was he doing? What was he losing? How could it not be a mistake? The summer was coming, it was already here. Soon restaurants would open their windows, voices drifting onto the street. But then, just as fast, frost on the grass, dead leaves in the gutter, the packing of snow underfoot. And who would he call tomorrow? Or in ten years? What about when he was dying? His family was gone, they were clouds from a storm that has cleared. It was only last fall he'd gone to the dentist nursing fears of the worst. And whom had he told first? Not Claire—no, it was Emerson who'd let him be scared, who knew how to take things seriously and still convince him they would all be OK.

The room waited. It seemed suddenly that they'd been there for a very long time. The plaster was setting, the exits were being blocked off. This room in which he had given so much advice, in which people had sought him out. It would crush him. All his measured words, his careful opinions: the years had left them worthless, so precious as to be without value. And at the center of it, skillfully hidden, his need to be wanted, like a rash concealed beneath a fine suit.

He looked at Emerson. He imagined how it would feel, forcing his body against him. One arm pinned to his neck, books tumbling as their limbs moved in rough, ugly jerks. What would it do? What would it mean?

Then, a vision of Anna, a memory. Clear, unflinching. They stood at the dock in Maine, Claire's brother taking people's hands as they stepped onto his boat. Anna turned to Amos. This, she said, tugging her life jacket. No one else has to. And he knew what she meant. She'd stood willingly while he spread sunscreen over the sharp hills of her shoulders, had accepted without complaint his need to double up on the bridge of her nose. But she wanted to be regular, too, not to feel like some dragged-along thing. Don't be crazy, he said. I just haven't put mine on yet. And then he called to Eric who, with a shrug of indifferent confusion, tossed another one over. Anna grinned. He grinned back. And together they rode—laughing, screeching—as the boat hurled itself over the waves and spray thickened their hair.

Amos studied his friend. He seemed suddenly dull, tired, like the sadness of a bar in the morning. Hadn't it felt so much bigger? Were the surfaces really this worn? Did the floors always cling to one's feet?

He let out a small breath and shook his head. A little echo: You want to give this all up? Amos hadn't replied. A space remained where his words were meant to be.

"No," he said. "No. But if I can't, none of it was ever mine to begin with."

A minute passed. Their eyes were drinking each other, the last sips. Within the walls of the building, elevators rose. People were being carried to where they would go.

"I'm so fucking lonely," Emerson said. The words shocked him. They seemed not to be his. Amos exhaled in disbelief. Emerson went on.

"What do you want to happen to me?"

"I don't care what happens to you."

He nodded.

"What do you care about?"

"Her."

Emerson received this without expression.

"I have a question," he said. For the first time he believed they really might not speak again.

"Why didn't you call me by my last name?"

"What?"

"Why didn't you call me by my last name?" he said again. "Everyone else did."

Amos looked at him, his eyes incredulous, filled with a stranger's rage.

"Because I didn't want to."

Emerson sighed. He rocked himself away from the wall and began to move toward the door. He looked like a vagrant shooed off by police. His body was aimless; he didn't know where he was expected to go.

"Well," he said, "I was glad."

"I know."

"Did you really?"

Amos said nothing.

"Someday we'll get dinner."

His voice was absent, thin; it did not quite believe in itself.

"When you're ready," he added. "When you want to."

IV

VI

A mos sits. His eyes are closed, breath lifts his chest. He's shut them for only a moment. Just to linger on the idea of what could be nearby. His fingers lie folded, arranged in his lap like a corpse.

June. A month has passed. The trees are a heedless, drooping green. In the morning, men rinse the sidewalks, crates of cabbage grow warm in the sun. People spill from Grand Central, the backs of their necks already damp. Heat arrives. The streets hold it like kilns; from them rise little quavers of air.

Evening now. Claire's in the kitchen; he can hear the sound of her taking down plates. The sun is slipping away, the western faces of buildings are brilliantly lit. She has not spoken to him in nearly two weeks and they haven't fucked since he told her. They exchange only short, essential sounds, like workers building a fence.

I hope you'll understand why I had no choice. That's what he said before explaining everything else. Then he went on— about the way he'd called, and how Emerson's voice sounded when he picked up the phone. Tomorrow? Of course. I'd need to move something, but yeah, yes, lunch tomorrow is great. Then a pause. Hey, I'm so glad to hear your voice.

Amos arrived first. It was busy already. The tables nearby were filled with men. They unbuttoned their suits as they sat, their laughter greedy and loud. He inspected the menu. Shallots, Roquefort, *poisson entier*. He wouldn't be eating; in a moment or two, he would stand up and leave.

He'd had no choice, he told Claire. If she'd been there, she would've understood. Not just then, at the table, but a few days before, when Anna approached while he knelt, undoing his shoes.

"Dad," she said. Her voice like the downed limb of a tree. "Why won't you talk to me?"

He bent his head. He'd been running. His forearms were slicked with sweat.

"Anna . . . ," he began.

He'd been trying so hard to do it Claire's way, to help without going too far. Just let it be over, she said. Just let it be something we can move past. And he'd done his best. He kept his words vague. He circled the thing as if it were ground which might collapse into a cave.

"I'm right here," he said. "You know that."

"But you aren't," she cried, her eyes suddenly wet. "And you were laughing—the next morning you were laughing together."

Somehow he'd known right away what she meant. This wasn't a plea to be believed. It was something beyond that. She was simply describing her life, truths without need of proof.

"Anna," he said. He was holding her. "Anna. I didn't know. I didn't—"

"How could you not *know*?"

Her body released the question like a gasp. Relief rushed out as she said it.

That's when he'd seen something big. Not just about her, but about himself, too. About his parents and their parents and everything else.

As he'd been telling Claire this, Amos opened his arms; he needed to express how expansive it was. Jesus Christ, he said, just think of it. Think of her in her room, reeling from that. And then what does she hear but her dad laughing, her own dad and this guy—this man she's known all her life. It's . . . , he tried, it's too much. It's too much to even imagine.

Maybe that's why it had been at this moment that things became clear. As Amos stood in the hall, he saw finally what she deserved: a faith so total she never stopped to realize that's what it was; the faith that someone was there, that if she were tired or sad or just emptied out, she had people against whom she could lean. That's what he hadn't had, what he'd spent so long trying to find.

But, he told Claire, here was the thing, the essence he'd grasped: what was the point of transcending one's past if the cost were giving those same hurts to his child? And wasn't that what he'd be doing? Because how could she live? How could she breathe? What healing was possible if her own parents refused to acknowledge the truth? And what was life, after all, if not the question of whether we'd spot the real moments of meaning? Could we, through force of habit and will, know when to shed our selfish, small skins? And, if we did, would we act?

Claire had been wrong: it wasn't enough just to be gentle and nice, to bring her tea or go for long walks. One needed to do something—*he* had to do something—to behave like someone who believed what she said. Maybe his whole life had been about this, Amos thought. It might be the one choice that would count in the end. He knew how she would feel, he told Claire as she paced. But he had to, he just *had* to, and he hoped she would see.

Emerson came through the door. Amos saw him at once. The maître d' listened, then nodded and gestured. Amos lifted his hand. Not a wave, merely a sign.

"Sit," he said when he arrived, his tone stony and clipped.

Emerson did. He offered an ungainly smile.

"OK." Amos nodded. "OK."

He set his hands on the table as though he were about to press himself up.

"I have no idea what's inside you. But I hope you know why I'm doing this, and I hope you understand what it means."

Then he stood. He searched Emerson's face. It was clear: he really had never guessed.

His eyes are still shut, his hands still in his lap. But it's as though it's real, happening right at this moment, the scene is so vivid it glows.

Amos sees himself turn toward the bar, beckoning with one hand. Together he and Emerson watch as she moves through the tables—slow, unceasing, like the hull of a ship. Her steps do not falter. She's afraid, but she's not going to stop. Waiters dart like sparrows around her. The sounds of the crowd have dulled to a roar; distant, faint as the sea.

For only a moment, Amos looks away from his daughter to see what's happened to Emerson's expression. At first there's a look of amazement, a stunned kind of respect. Then this is gone, displaced by muted, wrathful calm.

"That's one way to do things," he says.

But Amos barely hears this, he's already walking away. He'd asked her before, Do you want me to stay? No, she said. Not right there. But can you be close? They pass each other. He touches her shoulder. She seems not to notice at all.

Two minutes, maybe three: she's there for no more than that. Her head is mostly bent, once or twice she looks up. She sits on her hands like a child. Their mouths are both moving, but the words don't reach him. The room devours them before they even get close.

Then she's up, coming toward him, and he has to stop himself from rushing to gather her in his arms. Behind her, somewhere, is Emerson. But Amos can't see him anymore. He's already dissolved—into the high-backed leather booth, the eddy of faces, the amiable, meaningless sounds.

You did what, Claire had said. You should've seen her, he said. Claire, you should've seen how she was. For the first time, he said. She was her again. She was herself again for the first time. We talked about this, Claire said. She was pacing. Her fingers rose to her neck. And now what, Amos? And now what?

He'd known she'd say something like this. It was true to her nature. Clinical, grounded, ennobled by the presumption of farsighted reason. As she looked at him, Amos understood what she saw: a man of reckless whimsy, like the farmer in a story, convinced to sell everything for a few magic seeds.

And perhaps she was right, maybe it wasn't solved; it might not be enough. But she hadn't been there. She didn't realize that it was something, that it was a start.

They burst through the door and into the heat. Anna walked quickly away. Amos hurried to follow. They were like thieves, like people fleeing a wreck.

"Dad," she said. She turned. She was crying, but her face wasn't sad. "Dad."

Then she screamed. Only once. Her knees bent slightly,

her hands clenched in knots at the ends of her arms. People moved around them, only some turned. When he reached her, she began talking, or trying to. He hugged her, but she shook herself free.

"Did you see?" she asked.

"Anna."

"Did you?"

"See what?"

Their words were punchy and breathless.

"Are you OK?" he said.

"His face."

She tried to explain. She began thoughts then tossed them aside, like someone rooting through a chest full of tools. He listened. He'd told himself that was all he would do. No questions, no details, not unless she wanted to share. She was piling them up—little phrases, gestures—asking after each, Do you know what I mean?

Bit by bit, he understood. There'd been a moment, just one, when she thought Emerson was afraid. It sounded crazy, she knew. But that's what it was. No, Amos said, it didn't sound crazy; he believed everything she said. And though he was listening, what she expressed came to him now as more than just words. Her fingers, her arms, their electrified movements. He got it. She'd made him see what she saw.

A quick twist on Emerson's face, a tiny spasm of panic. But not for fear of being caught or in trouble, it had only to do with the fact that Anna was sitting right there, that she'd wanted to see him, that she had willed it to happen. It was something about her, something *inside* her; it was whatever he hadn't been able to break. And when she saw in his eyes that he knew that he hadn't, she'd been run through with a current of power.

Amos held her shoulders like a colt. Her breath was beginning to slow. The sun roared down on them. The sidewalk shimmered like glass.

"I'm so thirsty," she said.

A pretzel cart sat on the corner, taped to the side a small sign: COLDEST WATER ON THE BLOCK. Anna laughed. A real, true laugh. She took a bottle, held it to the back of her neck. Her eyes shut as if by instinct. A few strands of hair clung to the plastic like vines.

Amos watched her. What was he seeing? Not something new, but something returned. It seemed so obvious now, but only after the painting's rehung do we realize how bare the wall felt. And here it was again, at last. He saw it. She was within herself. Her body was a place she wanted to be.

Claire's making pasta. He hears it rush through the strainer and imagines her leaning back from the steam. Outside, shops are beginning to close. Birds huddle in the eaves of a church.

Anna comes in and sits. Amos has just called to her through the floor. The table is small; the leaf is in the closet under the stairs. If he wanted, he could reach out and touch the back of her hand.

Claire arrives. She makes a move to stand again, but Anna has already noticed.

"I'll get them," she says, and comes back with the napkins.

That they're eating together doesn't mean things are OK.

Claire's too practical, too considered, for that. Indeed, it's obvious things are not fine. Every movement reminds him. The way, between bites, she touches her bracelets; how she set down his plate, not letting it make a sound.

Things like this are what scare Amos, and some nights he feels the fatal grip of a chill in his groin. Is this how it ends, he wonders. Have things already begun? The fear is all there, it hasn't left, but what's strange is that it has not destroyed him.

The obvious answer to why is the fact of Anna—that she's real and right here, that if he squints and looks closely, there are even signs she's starting to heal. And while surely this is part of the story, there's also more to it. He's not a good enough man for it just to be that.

Amos runs his knife along the butter; a small curl grows at its edge. The windows are open. Evening air blesses everything. His hands, the back of his neck.

Sometimes he'll be in a room and Claire will come in, not having realized he's there. And when she does, something happens: he watches it play on her face like wind in a sail. Beneath her contempt and her anger is something else—it's discomfort, even fear. And what he could not have foreseen is the relief, the pleasure, the very real joy that is to glimpse this inside her. Her fear is like a cool, cleansing rain. It means she's aware of him. His presence impacts her. He takes up space.

"It needs pepper," Claire says. "Anything while I'm up?"

Amos swallows the last of a bite.

"Maybe more wine?"

She nods, setting the bottle beside him. Spaghetti climbs

Anna's fork as it turns in her hand. Watching, Amos tries to think of something to say. Then he stops himself: the silence is fine, it is more than enough. Instead he looks out at them both, and feels, for the first time, that this house is his, too.

Yes, that's one way it could've gone. Perhaps. But who knows?

Amos blinks and things return. Edges, sounds. The plane begins to move. Claire's eyes are closed, a book rests in her lap. She's breathing calmly, indifferent to the groan of machinery under their feet.

Beyond the window, a tower slips past. Two men, arms folded, stand talking. They step closer, shouting over the roar of the jets. The edge of the sun has just touched the horizon. Shadows lunge from their boots.

Anna's across the aisle. To her left, an old woman works at a crossword; to her right, another, younger, leans forward and whispers to boys—brothers? friends?—in the row ahead. Twice already she's had to stop them from hitting each other.

Under the dim cabin light, Anna's face lies in shadow. Its skin is tight, like a curtain drawn in by the wind. Her eyes are weary but alert. She sits back and sighs. Her foot's not in a cast anymore, though she'll need crutches for another two weeks. Stress fractures are no joke, the doctor said. So take it easy, roadrunner.

Now she looks up as though a thought has occurred. She fumbles in the bag at her feet. Amos can tell she needs a pen. A feeling of terror invades him: he must get one to her.

He doesn't know why. Otherwise something awful might happen.

He searches his pockets. There, in the back. His fingers close around it with desperate relief. He reaches, but she doesn't see. Her face is turned and he can't catch her eye. Anna, he tries. But the cabin's too loud. His arm is stretched across the aisle, the buckle digs into his hip. Then, a tap on his shoulder. Sir, the stewardess says, her face calm as rules.

He wants to explain, he feels the words coming like vomit. But the moment is gone; she has already retaken her seat. Claire sighs and shifts. Her hand finds his thigh.

Now the plane shudders, gathers speed. Cups shake softly in the rear. A woman crosses herself and exhales. They rush forward, tip back, the nose lifts as though receiving a rite. Light pours through the window. The wheels slip from the runway. Like fingers, they leave it behind.

There's a town by the sea, south of Nantes. Small, but real—the realest place you've ever been. That's how Retsy had put it when Claire told her about their trip. There was a vineyard, too, though she couldn't remember the name. Emerson would know. When he got home she would tell him to call. That would be perfect, Claire said; and Amos, nearby, had nodded. They would go there first, settle in. After that, Anna could choose.